DE-173

Book 2

J G Bell

Chapter One

The military members present saluted as the civilians applauded, Tannis too stood her hands together as she watched her team, Major Charles, Admiral Hennessey and Dr O'Brian receiving their medals of commendation for their actions against Phoenix when the Joint Chiefs had been compromised.

The recipients had voiced their opinions when Tannis and Ned had declined to receive their honours. But as Ned had explained Elea would kill him if she found out what he'd been up to and as for Tannis, she shared the same train of thought as the other recipients she hated all the fuss and besides she was only doing her job. She had laughed at the time because she and Ned had the choice to decline, the others, however, had not.

As she stood and watched them now returning their salutes, she felt genuinely proud of them all.

The ceremony over the men left the stand and began to make their way through the crowd of well-wishers. Tannis stood alone for the moment away from the melee admiring the surroundings; they were in the grounds of a beautiful period house in New England. Security was tight but as discreet as possible, to her trained eye she could spot them a mile off, but she felt reassured, she didn't have any bad feelings so assumed Phoenix were either none the wiser to the occasion or they were busy plotting something to piss them off with later. She longed to take her sandals off and walk barefoot through the soft green grass she stood on, but that really wouldn't do would it she smiled to herself.

Ben was tactfully trying to make his way to his wife without offending the many high-ranking officials that lined his path. He could see her standing patiently, a little way from the crowd, she was beautiful in the floaty chiffon dress she wore so elegant yet unassuming; he smiled inwardly as he remembered Dr O'Brian's comment that Tannis could make a bin liner look good, it was true he thought.

Finally, he made it to her and heaved a sigh of relief as she smiled up at him and kissed him on the cheek, 'I'm so proud of you,' she beamed. 'You too,' she said as Jack joined them now and gave him a peck, 'shame Caroline couldn't be here,' she made a moue, 'don't see why she couldn't, they all know what we do.'

'But they don't all know what you did Babe,' Ben lowered his voice. It had been decided that Tannis' little trip back to *The Wind Dancer* should be kept under wraps. As they had now passed a ruling, that time travel unless an authorised mission was against regulations. Although at the time both Jack and Ben and if he was honest Hennessey could see by the look on Tannis and Ned's faces that they were going to have trouble making that one stick.

'Kids would've only got bored,' Jack shrugged, he knew he was already and began to wonder what the required time was to stay at one of these things before it was not deemed disrespectful to leave. The Admiral and the doctor joined them now bringing a glass of champagne for everyone, they toasted one another and then took a drink, as he did so Dr O'Brian looked around at the other guests. His eyes came to rest on Major Charles who was looking awkward in the company of two female Lieutenants from the US Navy, 'Oh dear man down,' O'Brian grinned as he directed his companion's gaze in the Major's direction.

'Looks like he needs backup,' Jack turned to Tannis who just rolled her eyes and handed her glass to her husband, 'Surrounded by decorated heroes, and they send me in,' she teased as she headed over to the Major.

'She's a rare one that,' O'Brian raised his glass once more, and they all drank to Tannis.

'The only tribute she's going to get today, unfortunately,' Hennessey grumbled.

'She wouldn't have it any other way sir,' Ben said, proud of her and much the same as Jack, wishing he'd had the choice too.

'Sam,' Tannis chastised gently when she reached her target, 'you promised me a tour of the grounds,' she turned to the two women. 'He can be so forgetful sometimes, excuse us.' And with that, she linked arms with him, and he led her away.

'Thank you, ma'am,' he whispered as they made their way across the lawn.

'You call me ma'am again, and I'll take you straight back over there,' she frowned.

They laughed together as they walked on and once out of sight Tannis gratefully removed her sandals and felt the cool grass beneath her feet, 'Oh I'm not cut out for all of this pomp and circumstance,' she confided as Sam offered her his arm again and they took refuge in the walled garden.

'Congratulations sir's,' a woman's voice broke into Ben's conversation with Dr O'Brian, she was a US Marine Captain flanked either side by another of the same rank but male. Ben turned, and a look of recognition dawned, 'Captain Makin.'

'You remembered me sir,' she smiled at him.

This instantly grabbed the attention of Ben's companions, 'Aren't you going to introduce us?' Jack raised an eyebrow at his subordinate.

Firstly, Ben introduced his coalition companions then turned to the three newcomers, 'Captain's Karla Makin, Ross Tyler and Paul Ronson, we were stationed together when we first went to Iraq.' He turned back to the three newcomers, 'So; I guess you're part of the coalition now?' He could talk freely as only screened personnel and cleared guests had been invited to the ceremony.

Karla didn't give her two companions a chance to speak, 'Yes sir, we've just completed basic training and will be leaving for our posting next week,' she was referring to Atlantis. 'I can't wait and you,' she gestured toward both Jack and Ben, 'I can't believe I'm talking to the legendary Alpha Team,' she gushed.

'I wouldn't say legendary,' Jack felt uncomfortable enough as it was today without all of this. Hennessey too was not in the mood for such blather, so he excused himself and made toward the Joint Chiefs.

'I'm looking forward to meeting Tannis,' Karla carried on regardless, 'It's a pity she's not here today to accept her award too,' she looked around the grounds; 'although I've never met her, she's become a sort of role model for me, I've read all of her mission statements she must be a strong-minded woman.'

'Oh, she can be that alright,' Jack took a swig of his drink not correcting her about the fact that Tannis was present, she could do without this young enthusiast hassling her all afternoon.

It was around then that Tannis and Sam walked back into view, she had reluctantly put her sandals back on before they came out of the discretion of the walled garden. They re-joined their friends, and Tannis took her drink from Ben and waited to greet the newcomers, it was Jack that did the honours, firstly introducing Sam but he wasn't given a chance to get around to Tannis as Karla jumped in feet first apparently dismissing her as not worth the acknowledgement.

'Major Charles, you have led some outstanding missions,' then realising Tannis was still present, she looked down her nose at her and sniffed 'and what exactly do you do for the coalition?' she took in Tannis' civilian clothing, 'clearly you hold no rank,' she pursed her lips, 'did you volunteer?'

Instantly ticked off by Karla's tone of voice she gave her CO a curious look, Jack just shrugged, *let her run with it* he thought to himself, *could be interesting.*

'More like press ganged,' she muttered in reply.

'How can you say that it's a privilege to be allowed to volunteer?' Karla snapped.

'I would imagine it would be to have that option, but like Jack and Ben, I wasn't given a choice,' Tannis frowned she was having trouble trying to find something good about the woman in front of her; she always liked to find the good in everyone except Phoenix of course.

'Never thought of it like that,' Jack mused.

Then Karla got the bit between her teeth, 'Perhaps if you were allowed to take part in a mission you would understand.'

'I was thinking the same about you,' Tannis said stiffly.

'Oh, I intend to be out there doing my duty, not taking up desk space.'

The whole misunderstood conversation came to a head at this point as Tannis instantly leapt to the defence of her absent brother. 'Ned does an outstanding job, what he briefs the teams with saves their lives and before that, we were both out there with our brothers and sisters doing our jobs,' her eyes flashed now, 'and NO none of us volunteered, we all wanted to run a bloody mile!'

Karla's jaw dropped, but she didn't have the opportunity to reply as Ben took his wife by the arm, 'Let's check out the grounds, shall we Babe?' He glared at Karla.

Dr O'Brian gave Jack a knowing look, 'I thought basic training tells you not to make assumptions?'

'It does Doc,' Jack concurred but his attention was drawn to the Admiral, he had excused himself from the Joint Chiefs and was heading in the same direction that Ben and Tannis had taken toward the maze; not like his CO to wander off on his own Jack decided to follow and detached himself from the awkwardly silent group.

Although it had been a sunny afternoon it was still springtime fresh, but now as Jack entered the maze he felt a warm breeze on his face, and the smell of the nearby roses had been masked by an earthier scent, something wasn't right here. He picked up the pace and caught up with Hennessey. 'Taking a moment sir?' he asked.

The Admiral seemed a little confused, 'I thought I heard someone calling me,' he confided, both men paused and listened, 'nothing now,' he confirmed, somewhat annoyed.

'Jack!' They both heard Tannis calling.

'Here,' Jack called back and remained in position so that she and Ben could follow his voice.

'It wasn't Tannis that I heard,' Hennessey frowned at himself.

A few moments later both Tannis and Ben rounded the corner ahead of them. 'Sir something weird is going on,' Ben explained to his senior officers, 'the walls of the maze keep moving, it's as if we're being forced in a particular direction.'

Hennessey was back to himself 'Phoenix?'

Tannis shook her head, 'No...' she said no more as they all quickly turned and looked behind them, the maze had moved, cutting off their only way back; then as if growing impatient the wall of the hedge behind them began to move again, driving them forward.

'Move out,' Jack took command and motioned for them to get going. 'I'll take point, you two cover the Admiral.' Ben acknowledged their orders, and he and his wife dropped back behind Hennessey. They had little choice but to let the moving foliage lead them and lead them it did. Right into what looked like a clearing in the centre of the maze, it was however not as they would've expected it to look like; instead of a small lawn with perhaps a bird bath, or a statue in pride of place, there was dry and cracked soil, almost red in colour and standing smack in the middle of it right in front of them was a man. He appeared to be an Aboriginal Australian, the full Monty too, face painted with a loin cloth leaning his weight against a long thin spear. 'G'day,' he grinned as he held up a hand in greeting.

Alpha team and the Admiral now stood side by side as Jack looked across at Tannis, she knew he wanted confirmation that this guy wasn't a threat, 'He's not Phoenix,' she said confidently as she looked back at the stranger.

'Who are you and what are your intentions?' Hennessey took his rightful command.

'You can call me Billy mate,' the stranger grinned again 'and my intentions,' he looked up thoughtfully at the sky. 'There's a storm coming, bad things are going to happen to my people and yours, your Phoenix fellas have been messing with their timepieces, gone too far back they have, and got stuck in Dreamtime,' he nodded toward Alpha team 'and you're the ones who put things right.'

'I don't follow; I thought Dreamtime was a spiritual place in your culture?' Ben frowned.

'Too right mate but just cos you can't see it don't mean it ain't there,' Billy replied then looked skyward again, 'when the storm comes you meet Billy at Uluru in the now time, your fight will be in Dreamtime, and you'll need Billy's help to get there.' And with that he was gone as was the dirt floor; they were still in the centre of the maze, but now it was grass covered, and a sundial stood in the place Billy had recently occupied.

'You see that's why I love living on Atlantis, strict entry rules,' Jack broke the silence.

'Humph I let you in,' Tannis muttered as she walked over to the sundial and touched it just to make sure it was real. The hedge had returned to normal too revealing their exit, and although they were in the shelter of the maze a breeze blew around them and the sky quickly clouded over. Tannis stopped in her tracks and turned to face the others, 'We need to leave now!'

Ben looked around them, his view of the outside was obstructed by the tall hedges, but he knew something was wrong as he could no longer hear the sounds of the garden party 'Time's changing,' he quickly set his timepiece as his wife nodded. They had no time to warn Sam and Dr O'Brian or the Joint Chiefs for that matter; it was all they could do to get themselves out of there and back to The Eldridge. Their hasty leap back to Atlantis startled the crew in the hold as they quickly trained their weapons on the unscheduled arrivals, 'Stand down!' Hennessey ordered, 'and have Ned report to the briefing room asap,' he barked to the deck officer as he and Alpha team hurried out of the door.

Ned was already in the briefing room when they got there, the screen on the wall showing images of the time screens in the comms room; they were going crazy. Ned shook his head in disbelief 'They're changing every two or three minutes, I can't even get a fix on the first change before it alters again, this is unprecedented,' the stress showed in his voice.

Hennessey nodded his understanding, 'Sit down Ned, we'll tell you what we know, and hopefully we can make some sense of the situation.'

So, the four of them briefed him on their meeting with Billy. 'You're sure it wasn't Phoenix?' Ned looked across the table at his sister.

'If he were, he would be dead by now, wouldn't he?' Tannis gave her brother a hard stare for questioning her.

'Hmm,' he thought for a moment, 'sounds like a Totem' then realising he was getting blank looks from all present he added, 'a Totem is believed to be an entity who watches over a group or tribe of people. Not just Aboriginal Australians either, but that's not my primary concern,' he looked grave now. 'What the hell were Phoenix up to with their timepieces to get sent back so far, they don't have the power for that reason?'

'I'm working on the assumption that Dreamtime could exist on another level almost like a parallel universe,' Ben threw his theory into the mix, 'maybe that's what Phoenix was messing with.'

'Possible,' Ned was impressed with his brother-in-law's train of thought.

'Have you ever tried to leap back that far?' Jack turned to Tannis; she just shook her head. 'Actually, I'm a bit lost with the whole Dreamtime thing,' she confessed.

'Ned perhaps you could enlighten us all,' Hennessey sat back in his chair.

'Of course,' he concurred. 'Aboriginals believe in two forms of time, twin parallel streams of activity. One is the daily objective activity, the other the infinite spiritual cycle they call Dreamtime; more real than reality itself, what happens in Dreamtime establishes the values, symbols and laws of their society; they say that some people of high spiritual power have contact with Dreamtime.' Ned's mini lecture was cut short as everyone's attention was drawn to the screen on the wall, the time screens had settled down. 'Looks like Phoenix have finally made their minds up,' Jack exhaled slowly as he and the others read the new description of the real world. It seemed that it was now ruled by a master race of elite warriors, Aboriginal warriors who possessed psychic powers with which they could control the whole population.

'My God those bastards have altered them at DNA level, they're an army of Phoenix!' Tannis shivered.

'Yeah, with the original Phoenix in control,' Ned glared at the screen.

'So, Uluru it is then,' Jack looked at his team. But Hennessey was still uncomfortable with the idea, 'We are placing an awful lot of trust in a being that we briefly met, Colonel.'

'Unfortunately, he's the best bet we have, sir,' Jack replied.

'From what you have told me about him he has special powers of his own, and experience tells us that if he had meant you any harm, he would've made his intentions very clear then and there,' Ned added.

Eventually, it was agreed that Alpha team would make the leap to Australia. But with Ned's dire warning ringing in their ears, 'Get there and find Billy quick, you need to be in Dreamtime fast; if you're caught in an altered timeline and Phoenix decide to change it again, you who leapt into it will cease to exist.'

So, as they were leaping into an already altered timeline Alpha team wore their combat gear and were fully armed, they made the leap as close to the rock as possible under cover of darkness.

'Didn't look like this in the brochure,' Jack whispered as he and his team took in the sight in front of them. Huge shabby high-rise blocks of flats were all around them, litter and burnt-out vehicles were scattered all over, and in the distance, they could hear the occasional volley of small arms fire. They were alerted at once to the sound of footsteps approaching and hid in the shadows, their weapons at the ready.

'G'day, glad you could make it,' Billy grinned at them as he came into view, 'told you there was a storm coming,' he said thoughtfully as he took notice of the slum. Above them a light came on in a window illuminating their presence, then a shadow then fell across them, they were being watched.

'We better go, guards will be coming now,' Billy turned and walked towards the rock.

'How do we get there?' Jack asked as they turned their backs on the slum and followed their guide.

'We're already there mate,' Billy continued on his path. 'Dreamtime's not just a place, it's a state of mind.' It was as if they were taking in their surroundings with fresh eyes as they looked around now, the slum was gone, and as they walked through the dry grass, they could hear crickets and the air smelled clean and fresh once more.

They came to a stop right in front of Uluru all except for Billy that is, he continued on his way; all three team members winced and waited for the thud, but he just vanished into the rock. Jack walked cautiously to where Billy had disappeared and rested the palm of his hand against the warm stone. As if to prove it was solid, he slapped it, then turned to his teammates and opened his mouth to speak. But before he could get a word out a dark-skinned hand came through from out of the rock and grabbed his wrist pulling him in. Quickly Ben took hold of his CO's arm and tried to hang on to him, Tannis too held her husband around the waist; but their efforts were futile as they were all pulled in. Jack was first through; Billy had pulled hard and fast so when he stepped out of the way Jack fell flat on his back closely followed by Ben who landed next to him but with Tannis on top of him.

'Makes a change,' Jack smirked as he offered Tannis a hand to get up, Ben lay there for a second or two longer still a little winded.

They appeared to be inside a cave but a cave with no opening except for the one in the roof that acted as a chimney for the fire that blazed in the centre of the room. Billy stood opposite them now on the other side of the fire and watched in silence for the moment as Alpha team shrugged off their jackets. 'The middle of Australia, in the middle a heatwave and you have a fire?' Ben gave Billy a stare.

'You can leave your weapons with your jackets too,' Billy told them, 'Won't be any use in Dreamtime.'

'And what do you suggest we use to defend ourselves, give them a hard stare?' Jack shot back sarcastically, 'we are only flesh and blood after all.'

'Your flesh and blood will stay here mate; it's your spirits that will do battle with the darkness that has tainted my people.'

'Even better,' Ben's tone matched that of his superior, 'now we have to jump out from behind a rock and shout BOO! Scare em away!'

Billy looked at Tannis now, 'You're very quiet Missy, don't worry you'll always have the gift your Mother Nature gave you.'

'And what about Ben and Jack?' She found her voice now.

Billy walked over to them carrying a small bowl made of clay that contained a white paint-like substance into which he dipped his finger and drew a line on his face. Then standing in front of Tannis he did the same to her and then to Ben and Jack, as he marked them all he said, 'You will each have to face a test they put before you, how you react will determine your team's fate in both Dreamtime and the real world.'

Tannis stared into the flames, 'So we'll be fighting their spirits too?'

'That's right Missy, if you make your choices wisely, you can banish them from Dreamtime, and both our worlds will be as they should be.'

'And what about the Phoenix agents?' Ben asked.

'The link between our worlds will be severed; they will be able to return as they were.'

'Hang on a minute, we can't even kill them?' Tannis glared at Billy.

'This is a time to restore balance; your revenge will have to wait,' Billy fixed his gaze on her, 'oh your day will come, don't worry about that. It has been foreseen; with his seed growing strong in your belly,' he nodded toward Ben, 'Alpha team will defeat Phoenix.'

Ben looked across at Tannis and winked, she gave him a quick smile before Jack cut in, 'You still haven't told us how the Major and I are supposed to defend ourselves?'

Billy looked at the two men as he gently touched Tannis on the forehead, instantly her eyes closed and her head fell forward, but she didn't fall, she seemed to be suspended in the air, her feet a few inches from the ground. Ben hurriedly grabbed his sidearm, 'What did you do to her?'

'No worries mate, she's good, she's in Dreamtime,' Billy reassured him and watched as Ben lowered his weapon, 'and in answer to your question Colonel,' Billy seemed to summon a golden stream of light from Tannis' mouth, 'I'm sure she won't mind sharing what she has for a little while,' he said as he guided the stream towards them and before they knew it they were both in the same state as Tannis.

I don't feel any different Tannis thought as she made her way through the bush, although her surroundings were certainly different; there was no sound at all, not even her footsteps and the light all around her was a sort of amber haze, almost like being in an old sepia photograph she pondered. Her eyes were everywhere, her thoughts on her team.

As she continued cautiously on her way, she noticed that the trees and the dry grass beneath her feet had vanished. And as she looked down, she was standing on a carpet, raising her gaze she was in the old dining room on board The Eldridge as it was before the coalition as it was when *DE-173* were alive. Then there they were, her former team all seated around the table except Ned; eyes closed and motionless. She looked at them all in turn, and her heart ached for the ones she had lost. Then he appeared, Jefferson stood behind Cole at the head of the table, 'You have the power to bring them back,' he said calmly, 'join us, and you can control time any way you wish, the final battle need never happen.'

Tannis walked slowly around the table looking at each of her dead siblings and came to a stop behind Will, then looked across the table to Meg the memory of her murder still raw in her mind; she reached out to touch her brother, her hand passed right through his image as if to remind her she was still in Dreamtime.

'Just sit and join the feast,' Jefferson spread his hands out.

'And allow all of Phoenix to exist once more,' she sneered as she turned her back on the scene saying as she left, 'they died so that others could live free, I wouldn't tarnish their memory by giving this sham the time of day.'

Ben too experienced the same change in his surroundings as he made his way to wherever the hell he was going, also wondering where and how his teammates were; that was when he too noticed his environment had changed once more. The sight that greeted him though was worlds apart from that which Tannis had witnessed. He was standing in what could only be described as a palace, in front of him were two thrones made from solid gold, upon one of which sat Tannis in a long flowing white robe made of silk. She smiled as she looked towards him, at her feet sat two small children, a boy and a girl who were quietly rolling a ball to each other, then noticing his presence, 'Daddy,' they chorused. He couldn't help but return their smiles even though he knew the scene being played out in front of him wasn't real, and as if to clarify the fact and ruin the moment, Kaitlin stepped out from behind the throne Tannis sat on. 'All of this is yours for the taking Ben,' she moved silently toward him holding a crown made of crystal in her hands. 'You and Tannis can rule time together, no more threats, no more missions,' she soothed in his ear now, 'crown your wife, join us and secure your future.'

He was taken by the whole scene as she placed the crown in his hands, allowing himself a moment to enjoy the sight in front of him. He then turned to look at Kaitlin as he did, letting the crown slip from his hands and shatter into a million pieces at her feet, he knew by crowning Tannis in this reality he would be taken away and either killed or reprogrammed. He turned and walked away, 'It's not real, it's only a mission, we're the only thing that's real.'

Not very tempting, Jack thought to himself as his test opened up before him. He was standing in a dungeon and not a pleasant smelling one either. Straw covered the floor in a half-hearted attempt to mop up some of the blood that covered it. Before him on their knees, their heads bagged were he assumed two prisoners; a shadow fell across him and from that darkness stepped Rafe, 'I have a proposition for you Colonel,' he said in his arrogant tone, 'how would you like to be supreme ruler of Atlantis? You and yours would live in continued safety, but with no more dangerous missions condemning all those innocent people in the past to death,' he sneered. 'It hurts doesn't it, that feeling of helplessness when you have to change things, how many is it now Jack, how many men, women and children have you allowed to die?'

Jack said nothing, just glared at Rafe as he continued, 'you will rule Atlantis, no coalition all you have to do is terminate our captives here. Jack's eyes widened as Rafe removed the bags covering the heads of his prisoners; it was Tannis and Ben, and his horror was compounded as he realised that he now held his sidearm in his hand and had it pointed at Tannis' head.

Rafe smiled cruelly, 'Join us, when your training is complete Atlantis will be yours,' he paced around the three of them trying to wear Jack down, 'how long do you think you can last out there before that final mission, the one you don't make it back from? You've been given a special gift; your family was saved and brought back to you, finish them Jack and live your life safe and happy where you belong,' he raised his voice now.

Jack dropped his weapon and turned to walk away, 'I would never harm them, we're a team, we take care of each other, it's what we do.'

As Tannis picked her way through the bush she suddenly became aware that sound had filtered back into the world, she could hear the crickets again and the birds as they flew from tree to tree; and a warm breeze blew her hair gently as she stepped into a clearing.

Sensing someone approaching she turned quickly, it was Ben walking towards her.

'You are you, right?' She eyed him cautiously as they came to a stop in front of each other, 'I mean this isn't another test or anything?'

'No, I'm me,' he smiled.

'Prove it,' she teased.

He gave her a grin as he put his arm around her waist and pulled her firmly to him and kissed her. They stayed like that for a moment or two; pulling away quickly when they heard Jack's voice.

'Well, you're just going to have to take my word for it,' he said dryly as he joined his team, 'so I suppose we've been brought to this spot for a reason?' He continued as he looked around.

'That's right Colonel,' Billy stood with them now.

Jack frowned and poked Tannis on the shoulder, 'Just checking.' 'The dark souls are on their way, you passed your tests well, Billy made the right choice for you to put things right,' he grinned, 'just remember what you are, and you'll be alright,' and once more before anyone could say a word he was gone again.

'And what would that be then, unarmed and about to get the shit kicked out of us?' Jack shouted at Billy's vacant space.

'Back in the cave just after he put Tannis under he said she could share her powers with us,' Ben remembered now.

'I'm under?' Tannis folded her arms defensively.

'I should think we're all in the same state,' Jack's memory stirred now too.

'If he did give us some of your powers, I don't feel any different, not like before,' Ben looked at his wife.

Tannis looked from one teammate to the other in impatient disbelief, 'Oh for goodness sake just try something.'

Jack went first, it was decided that he should try and blast a tree on the other side of the clearing, he concentrated as hard as he could but to no avail. 'Maybe you have to be angry, that's how it started for me, and Ben,' Tannis tried to help.

'Well, I can't just make myself angry,' Jack folded his arms and looked at his teammates.

It was at that point Tannis decided to take matters into her own hands, so she kicked him hard on the shin.

'Ouch!' he yelled as he hopped on one leg holding the other as it throbbed painfully, 'what the bleedin hell did you do that for?'

'Just trying to help,' she shrugged.

Jack tried gingerly to put the weight back on his sore leg and noticed Ben frowning as he did so, 'What?' He looked around.

'Us,' Ben replied.

'Major, I know I usually like words with few syllables when given an explanation, but feel free to elaborate on this one,' Jack said sarcastically.

'That's what I mean, listen to us; we're not like we usually are. I haven't called you sir once, you haven't taken command, and Tannis would never lash out at you like that,' he looked at his wife now, 'and we would never behave the way we just did on a mission.'

'Smart,' Billy had appeared again, 'the darkness surrounds you before you see it coming.'

'Phoenix are trying to use their powers on us?' Tannis fixed Billy with a stare, 'so how come I can't sense them or block them?'

'Your powers had to be shared with your two fellas.'

'But we don't have any powers,' Ben frowned.

'Don't know what you've got until you need it,' Billy winked as he disappeared again.

'That is beginning to get on my nerves,' Jack sighed as he turned to his team. 'Come on, we're not hanging around here while Phoenix plays mind games with us. If it's a fight they want, we'll take it to them.'

'Yes, sir,' Ben smiled, Alpha team were back.

They walked on in silence, their senses working overtime searching for any imminent threat. Another clearing opened up before them and at the far side stood the three Phoenix agents. As the two opposing forces slowly advanced on one another they chose their respective targets; Ben made it clear he was heading for Rafe who seemed to have the same idea. Tannis narrowed her eyes with hatred as she made a beeline for her sister's killer.

'I suppose it's pointless telling you two not to make this personal?' Jack said eyes front, when neither of his teammates replied he looked across at them, they were both focused on their targets and the fight ahead, 'fair enough I'll take tubby then.'

Both sides had quickened their pace as they got closer to the centre of the clearing until they were almost at a run.

Rafe and Jefferson had begun their attack already, Rafe thrust his hands out sending a surge of energy at Ben, he was nowhere as strong as Tannis, but it was enough to take a man off his feet. It hit Ben square in the chest, but instead of disabling him his body seemed to absorb the power, he could feel his fingers tingle now, and he knew what that meant. He'd had that power before; his whole body surged with the energy as he hurled himself toward Rafe grabbing him around the throat as the two men vanished.

Jefferson's attack came from his mind straight into Jack's; his plan was his usual MO to torment his quarry into suicide or to render him so brain dead that he would just slip away. Jack couldn't stop the force entering his head, but he too absorbed the power, and as he did, he could sense everyone's thoughts around him. He knew exactly what move Jefferson was going to make before he made it, so Jack floored him quickly, but as with Ben and Rafe as soon as he made contact with his opponent they vanished.

It was no different for Tannis, Kaitlin began to make multiple images of herself, but Tannis stayed on course and lunged and simultaneously with her teammates and their adversaries Tannis and her foe disappeared too.

The six of them reappeared at the same time, so embroiled in their own fights to pay too much attention to their new surroundings; Jack found Jefferson harder to tackle than he had imagined, physically he was a pushover, but his mental strength was great as he inflicted torturous pain on Jack who fell to his knees, but soon found his gift from Tannis as he was able to send the power and suffering straight back to his portly adversary. Realising their powers were a match for one another both men looked around their surroundings. There were still only the six of them, and once more they were in a clearing, but this time one in a forest, three or four white tents were dotted about, it seemed strangely familiar to Jack although he knew he had never been there before. On the ground were an assortment of weapons, swords, daggers and the odd crossbow. Jefferson dived for a sword and Jack knowing his opponent's thoughts did the same with both of them beginning a fight to the death. Jefferson was an accomplished swordsman and why wouldn't he be Jack thought, Phoenix had seen pretty much the same action as *DE-173*.

Ben and Rafe fought bare knuckles; they too had realised that their powers were equal and besides Ben thought to himself he preferred kicking his ass this way. A short distance away Tannis and

Kaitlin were going at it hell for leather although Tannis had gained no powers whatsoever from her attacker, she still managed to land a punch that split her lip and sent her bowling backwards, that was when Kaitlin noticed her surroundings as she wiped the blood from her mouth, 'Oh how appropriate,' she laughed. 'I get to kill you in the same place I killed your sister.' A chill ran down Tannis' spine as she too realised where they were, but she wouldn't give this bitch the satisfaction of seeing her fear, 'Have you forgotten what else happened here?' Tannis glared, 'did you have fun in the dimension I sent you to?'

The last comment had the desired effect; it had hit a raw nerve with Kaitlin who then let her anger take over. She charged at Tannis who just grabbed her and threw her to the ground reaching for a nearby dagger as she did. But Jack was in trouble, although he was good with a sword Jefferson was able to fight and use his mind powers at the same time, something Jack didn't have the time to practise, he was forced to his knees momentarily stunned as Jefferson raised his sword ready to behead him. Tannis made the split-second decision, and instead of finishing her fight she threw the dagger at Jefferson, it stuck in his neck, and he vanished instantly.

'That was a foolish mistake,' Kaitlin hissed as she freed a hand and knocked Tannis off her, she then proceeded to make three more images of herself to surround her prey. Tannis stood alone and defenceless, 'You'll never win,' she said defiantly.

'Oh, and why is that?' Kaitlin sneered.

'Because we are something Phoenix will never be,' Tannis replied.

'And what's that?' Katlin asked as she picked up a crossbow and took aim.

'A team,' Jack's voice came from behind the agent as he drove his sword into her back and watched as she and her other images vanished.

Jack and Tannis looked over now to where Ben and Rafe were still slugging it out, both men were bruised and bloodied but showed no signs of wanting to slow down.

Jack knew his subordinate was just taking his time, playing with his enemy and let him have his fun for a while, but this was a mission, 'Finish it Major,' he ordered.

Ben's acknowledgement was to punch Rafe to the ground. As he did so the agent fumbled for a nearby dagger and threw it at Ben, it all happened in a blink, no one had time to react. Instinctively Ben thrust a hand out to defend himself, the weapon stopped in mid-flight and turned itself back on Rafe, it hit him in the chest, and he vanished.

Tannis walked over and picked up the knife where it now lay on the grass, she turned it over in her hand and looked at the blade, then gave it to her husband and walked away from her team.

Ben looked down at the knife; there was an inscription on it; Jack gave him a curious look, he turned it so that his CO could see it, it read *DE-173*. The two men looked around them realising why the place seemed familiar; they had seen it when Tannis had allowed them to see her memory of the final battle.

There were no bodies, just stains on the grass, and Tannis stood looking down at the largest patch of bloodstained earth, her teammates joined her and knew that this was where Meg had been murdered. They both put an arm around her and led her away. 'Come on Billy, job's done!' Jack called out angrily.

Back in the cave Alpha team gasped as they woke and dropped to their knees from their elevated positions, as they got to their feet, they rearmed themselves and picked up the rest of their kit. From his side of the cave behind the fire, Billy nodded to them, 'All's well.'

'And Phoenix?' Jack knew he wasn't going to like the answer. 'Back in your world now.'

'And where are we?' Ben asked.

'Back in your world too,' Billy's voice faded as the team shielded their eyes from the bright sunlight, they were outside again standing in front of the rock, it was a beautiful sunny day and not a high rise in sight.

'So, we kicked Phoenix's arse but didn't,' Tannis tried to fathom the point of it all.

'Killing them wasn't the mission you knew that love,' Jack too was pissed off at the outcome. 'Suppose' Tannis sighed as she thrust out her hands and blasted a nearby tree, making her teammates jump 'just testing,' she smiled, 'I only let you borrow them, you know.'

'I couldn't do that,' Jack thrust his hands out to demonstrate, as he did so he felt the power surge through him. The energy burst from his hands, and he blasted a distant tree into oblivion, 'Oh yes,' he grinned and had another go, Ben flashed his wife a smile as he too tried his luck with much the same effect.

'Err I'm sure some of these are protected, you know,' she called after them as they wandered off blasting any tree that stood in their path.

'Let them have some fun, it'll wear off in an hour,' Billy's voice whispered in her ear.

'Christ, will you cough or something next time,' Tannis almost jumped out of her skin. Billy gave her a grateful nod, 'You know where I am now,' and he was gone.

'Hey, Tannis, come here, I wanna try a leap,' Jack called to her.

Chapter Two

'This mission sucks!' Tannis grumbled as she lay on her front and looked down the sights of her sniper's rifle. As if it wasn't bad enough it had rained for a week, and the ground was nothing but mud, it was still raging a monsoon now.

'Well, it can't all be fun, fun, fun!' Jack's voice came through her earpiece tinged with the same pissed off tone she had used, he was hidden, his position much the same as hers some distance away.

'Oh, it's not so bad here,' Ben spoke now, he was dressed in the finest clothes from the fashion of 1867 as were all of those he mingled with on board the paddle steamer. His teammates watched him through their sights as he drank champagne and paid court to a beautiful young woman who at present was chatting animatedly to another couple, she soon however excused herself and took Ben's arm as he escorted her out onto the deck.

'Make me nervous if my wife was watching with live rounds aimed in my direction,' Jack replied smugly.

As Ben sat with his mark, Tannis and Jack scanned the area; she saw the threat as soon as he poked his head above the water line and began to edge his way along the hull.

'Threat identified,' she said as she lined up to take the shot. 'Phoenix?' Jack wanted confirmation.

'Negative hired help,' she informed her team, 'he's carrying an explosive device.' It was not unheard of for Phoenix to hire paid assassins to carry out their dirty work on less crucial hits. 'Permission to fire?' She was speaking directly to Jack now.

'Take the shot,' her CO confirmed.

Tannis hated this sort of work; she preferred a straight fight but needs must, she squeezed the trigger, and the bullet spat toward its target. Only his trained ear told Ben that the shot had been fired. 'Kill confirmed,' he heard his wife's emotionless tone. He along with his teammate knew how she felt about this sort of work too but at least now the mission was over, and they could get out of there. 'Ok, you two let's wrap it up, be at the meeting place 2200 hrs,' Jack gave the order.

'Confirmed,' Ben muttered as he stood and excused himself from his companion, she was safe now, job done.

'Confirmed,' Tannis too was getting up, she looked down at her soaking wet mud-covered combat greens and shook her head as she slowly began to make her way to the meeting place.

Her team was already waiting for her when she arrived; Jack was soaked and covered in mud and camouflage face paint just as she was, her husband, however, was just wet from the rain, 'Well it makes a change,' he tried to defend his pristine clothing.

The two men set their timepieces ready to make the leap, but Tannis was on the alert. She quickly picked up her weapon and took aim at something in the bushes, 'Show yourself,' she hissed; her teammates too took aim as from out of the damp foliage walked an old man his hands raised above his head. 'Don't shoot, I mean you no harm,' he stammered.

'But I mean you some,' Tannis answered coldly. 'You can sense me?' The old man was impressed. 'He's Phoenix?' Jack glanced briefly at Tannis. 'How?' Ben hadn't seen this one before.

'I came back from the future, didn't agree with the ruling classes there,' the old man didn't take his eyes off Tannis.

'If you leapt back here before the electromagnetic shift, why haven't we met before?' Tannis was naturally suspicious. 'My timepiece was damaged,' he twisted his wrist to show them its shattered face. 'Tough,' Tannis armed her weapon.

'No, you don't understand I have information for you, I can help you,' he gabbled nervously, 'I just want the chance to return to your timeline and live out my life in peace.'

'Bull, what do you lot know about peace?' Ben snapped.

'I know there is none in the future and soon it will come back to your timeline,' he bargained.

'Explain,' Jack allowed his finger to relax a little on the trigger, lowering his weapon slightly.

'Before the electromagnetic shift was ordered I and three others were sent back to the past on a mission to ensure it would not take place. If you kill me the world as you know it will be ruled by

Phoenix in both past and future,' he tried to lower his hands slowly but soon raised them again as Jack took his aim once more.

'How?' Tannis stepped closer to the agent, her weapon still trained on him. 'Take me back to your timeline, and I'll tell you,' He stood what little ground he had, 'if I had meant to harm you and your team, I would've done so one by one when you were alone,' he gave her a hard stare that phased her not.

'How about you tell me, and I kill you quickly, you don't tell me, and I take my time about it?' She sneered. It was then he broke eye contact with her and looked directly at Jack, 'You are in command Colonel, it's your call,' he looked back at Tannis again, 'you can sense I am not controlling him.'

Jack thought for a moment, and even though it went against every fibre of his being he gave the order that they would take the agent back to their timeline, although he couldn't go to Atlantis, he would be taken to a secure location the coalition had in England.

Tannis was furious, her anger showed as her eyes flashed when Jack gave the order. She knew he was right, the future, and the past may well be in danger but how would they sort the truth from the lies the agent was going to tell them.

So, they made the leap to the safe house where the agent introduced himself as Silas, and it was at that point that Tannis told him in no uncertain terms that if he started anything, she would most definitely finish it. A short while after they arrived Admiral Hennessey joined them; Silas had requested that Ned be present also so that he could hear what was said as it would help their mission. Tannis didn't need to object as Hennessey refused point blank. Ned had remained on Atlantis, and he hadn't been keen on his sister being present either. But as Hennessey had said Silas had more to worry about from Tannis than she had to worry about from him and besides she was needed there in case he tried to use his mind powers; she was their only defence against that.

The five of them now sat around a table in a nondescript room with no windows and only one door which was guarded from the outside. Tannis sat opposite Silas and glared at him the whole time. 'You know she makes me nervous when she does that,' he complained to Hennessey. 'As long as you are not a threat to us,

Tannis is no threat to you,' the Admiral replied bluntly. He had no time for Phoenix, had had personal dealings with them in the not too distant past and knew only too well what they were capable of, 'you approached us, so I suggest you make your bid.'

Silas cleared his throat nervously, 'As you know some of us made a leap to the future closely followed by Tannis' parents and Ned's father.' He paused and looked at them all, 'Well when we got there all hell let loose, most were killed,' he shuddered at the memory. 'In the future they have a device that can track us from our DNA. We were like sitting ducks,' he looked directly at Tannis now, 'your folks hunted us down like animals.'

Tannis sat back in her chair and folded her arms across her chest 'Your point?'

Realising he was getting no sympathy he continued 'We found out that the powers that be were going to create the electromagnetic shift. We had to stop this, so we looked into the life of the scientist responsible for the creation of the machine. The same woman responsible for sending The Eldridge back to Atlantis and removing you from the real world,' he rested his arms on the table in front of him as he looked at Tannis once more, 'yes the one who helped make you and yours guardians of the past.'

'Get on with it!' The whole thing was giving Ben an uneasy feeling, and he didn't like the effect he knew it would be having on his wife. Silas nodded, 'The powers that be already had this covered; they had their own people erasing records of her past, protecting her family.' His guard dropped for a moment as he allowed himself a cruel smile. Showing his real Phoenix side. 'But we managed to trace her father to where he would be unprotected, we were able to read the thoughts of one of those in charge of the cover up,' he didn't take his eyes off Tannis, 'as I told you when we first met myself and three others were sent back to kill our mark, but I couldn't do it, I am like your mother, I just want to live in peace.'

'You are nothing like my mother!' Tannis yelled as she threw herself forward, 'I don't know what your mission was, but my guess is you bottled it because it was too dangerous or you knew you'd come up against *DE-173*, and we'd kick your arse!'

Ben and Jack who sat either side of her put a hand each on the shoulder closest to them easing her back into her seat.

'I think you should get to the point,' Hennessey said dryly, thinking how lucky Tannis was to be allowed the luxury of an outburst, an outburst he too would like to unleash. 'Very well,' Silas agreed, clearly shaken by Tannis' hatred 'the powers that be didn't need to erase records too far back to look after Doctor Clunes and her forefathers because they could only trace them to 1945.'

'How come?' Jack didn't trust this smarmy little git one bit; this had to be a trap of some sort.

'Because her father was orphaned in the closing months of the second world war. There was no record of who his parents were and being a babe in arms he could tell them nothing.' He looked at them all in turn now, allowing his gaze to rest on Ben a little too long for Tannis' liking; she sat forward the static charge crackled as it built up in her hands ready to dispatch him should he make a sudden move.

'So, our mission was to terminate the infant the night his family was killed,' he sighed as he sat back in his seat now removing his gaze from Ben, 'I could not bring myself to take the life of an innocent child, so I made a break for it. As I struggled with my team my timepiece was damaged, and I was sent back to a random time and place.'

'I knew something was wrong about our last mission; it wasn't Phoenix style to kill the girl; her death didn't change history that much.' Tannis said aloud to no one; she didn't have to address anyone; her team and Hennessey were well aware of her thoughts as she had given it to them straight when the mission first arose. Ned too had been sceptical, but these things had to be followed up no matter how seemingly trivial. 'You staged the whole thing, you were prepared to kill all of the people on the steamer just to get us there,' Ben shook his head in disgust.

'I had to make contact with you somehow, and I knew you would save them,' he smiled an oily smile 'you're good at what you do.'

'Not that good, you're still breathing,' Tannis hissed 'you made me kill an innocent man.'

'He was prepared to kill everyone on board for a small fee; I really wouldn't call him innocent,' Silas replied, his tone as emotionless as his expression.

'Getting back to your story,' Hennessey prompted he didn't trust Silas one bit, but if there was a threat it had to be recognised and dealt with as Silas would be in due course.

'Certainly, Admiral, that's why I'm here,' the agent fawned 'as I said it was impossible for them to protect the infant the night he was orphaned, so we were sent back with orders to terminate.' He kept his attention on Hennessey, 'You must send a team back to stop this Admiral, or the past and future will be open for all to travel, and I think you will agree it's bad enough as it is.'

'Where and when was the child orphaned?' Jack was getting sick of Silas' cutesy act.

But it was towards Tannis that Silas directed his answer, 'January 30th, 1945, Baltic Sea, probably the worst shipping disaster ever?' He paused and seemed to enjoy the look of dread that washed over her face as she almost whispered 'Jesus Christ, *The Wilhelm Gustloff*.'

Silas sneered, 'Tell me Tannis, have you ever been on a ship that didn't sink?' He listed the names '*Titanic, Lusitania* and let's not forget the *Arizona*.'

But Tannis was not for riling. 'Let me tell you a few things 1, you don't know dick about me, 2, technically the *Arizona* was still afloat when I jumped off it and 3, if you've such a keen interest in my nautical missions. Maybe you should've taken the *Titanic* instead of Moira the old hag.'

It was Silas who flinched back in his seat now, his eyes full of tears, 'They never told me,' he choked, 'she went down with the ship?' He gasped.

'Oh, I made sure of that, the evil bitch!' Tannis held his stare.

'She was my wife,' he sobbed.

'They were my brothers and sisters,' she snapped back, 'you lot should've learned not to start what you can't finish.'

Hennessey nodded to the waiting medic who had been standing in the shadows, and the young man stepped towards Silas, a syringe in his hand.

'What's that for?' Silas sniffed.

'We need to keep you sedated while we discuss the mission further, I'm sure you understand,' Hennessey's tone was as blunt as it had been from the start.

'Anything else you want to tell us before you go bye-byes?' Jack asked.

'The infant was the last survivor to be found seven hours after the ship went down. Everyone else in the lifeboat was dead, the child had been wrapped in a woollen blanket.' He reached into his pocket and pulled out some photographs, 'The blanket and the agents you are looking for...' was all he said as the medic administered the injection and the agent slumped in his chair unconscious.

Back on The Eldridge Alpha team along with Hennessey and Ned sat in the briefing room. A stunned silence had fallen when the Admiral had informed Ned about the proposed mission, Tannis too had remained quiet for most of the time, Ben knew it wasn't Silas' presence that had made her feel this way, it most certainly had something to do with the mission the agent wanted them to undertake.

Ned finally spoke, 'And how do we know the threat is a credible one? I wouldn't trust these bastards as far as I could throw them.'

'We don't,' Hennessey was truthful, 'but you know we must react to all possible threats, if you're worried that it's a trap, you know your sister will be with her team...'

Ned didn't give him the chance to finish his sentence, 'Admiral, with all due respect I have watched my sister go on missions that would make the best of us turn tail and run for the hills, and I also know that Alpha team would go the distance for each other, they are an extension of *DE-173*.'

Both Jack and Ben looked up at Ned when he made this comment; it was a fantastic compliment. Which they both acknowledged with a respectful nod as Ned continued along a different line. 'Except for Tannis no one here can comprehend the scale and well almost suicidal task of this mission,' for once he was lost for words, his concern for his sister and his friends was playing hard on his mind. Ben understood and tried to bring him back with a question. 'Sylas said it was one of the worst shipping disasters ever, so how come we've never heard of it?'

'It was almost the end of the second world war, and it was a German liner,' Ned shrugged, 'to be blunt it happened to the ones who started the whole thing, so no one was really that interested.'

'It was still brutal, all of those babies and children, it's always the innocent who suffer,' Tannis wrung her hands as personal memories of *Titanic* came back to her.

'From the beginning, if you please Ned,' Hennessey sat back in his seat as Ned told the story of *The Wilhelm Gustloff's* last voyage.

'It was January 30th, 1945, and *The Wilhelm Gustloff* was at the Baltic port of Gdynia near Danzig as thousands of German civilians were trying to flee Prussia from the advancing Russian army. They travelled for days in freezing temperatures heading for the port in the hope of escaping to safety. Although the passage itself was going to be a rough one with gale force winds, snow and hail and waves metres high, even that was preferable to the fate that they would face when the Russians reached them. The liner itself since the beginning of the war had been used as a hospital for the troops, then more recently as a training ground for submariners; although it had never left port since the war started, it had been fitted with large guns on the deck.

Its maximum capacity for passengers and crew was 1880, but that day terrified refugees, naval personnel and wounded soldiers crowded into every nook and cranny they could find bringing the total to approximately 10814.'

'So many?' Even Hennessey was shocked.

'Yes, Admiral and the fact that will make the mission difficult, to say the least, was the number of babies and children on board,' Ned looked at his sister who added, 'Around four thousand.' Ben slumped back in his seat as opposite him Jack rubbed his hands over his hair 'We're going to need more than one team sir,' he looked at the Admiral who merely nodded seemingly still processing the huge number of people his teams would have to make their way through to find the baby.

Ben too was still trying to get his head around the numbers, 'So how did it sink?'

Ned gestured to his sister to speak; he wanted to know exactly how much she knew as her life really would depend on it this time probably more than ever.

She didn't let him down, 'Three torpedoes just after 2100 hrs about eight and a half hours into the voyage,' she closed her eyes now concentrating hard, 'the first struck the front on E deck compartments two and three, the second again on E deck but in the middle, compartments four and five; the swimming pool which had been drained and was full of navy nurses. The third hit the rear in the machine room; as it begins to go down bough first, the Captain gives the order to seal the doors in compartments two and three.' She opened her eyes now and looked directly at her husband as she recited the fate of the ship, 'This sealed the crew compartments killing most of the crew members whose job it was to lower the lifeboats. He also gave the order to seal the machine room, but some of the men managed to get out of there by climbing the smokestack.' She finished, and looked over to her brother who was looking at everyone around the table, the gravest of expressions on his face as he continued to fill them in on the details of the ship's last moments. 'As soon as the ship began to go down bough first it also listed heavily to port so the lifeboats on the starboard side were resting against the vessel and rendered useless and the ones on the port side just dangled out of reach, as a result very few boats were lowered.'

Tannis put her head in her hands, 'Is it true parents were shooting their own children when they knew it was hopeless?'

Ned just nodded slowly, 'It was sheer panic, people were trampled to death in the stairways and shoved overboard into the freezing water. Those parents that didn't kill their children by their own hands strapped them into life jackets and dropped them into the sea. But in those days, there were only life jackets for adults, no children's sizes so when they hit the water, they were turned upside down and drowned before they could freeze to death,' he blinked hard, 'later rescuers reported seeing hundreds of little legs of the upturned children bobbing in the water.'

'Jesus, how many survived?' Jack felt sick to his stomach.

'There were 996 survivors,' Tannis murmured.

'My God,' Ben muttered, Tannis saw his eyes widen as he did the math's.

'9618 died,' she almost whispered.

'Who did it?' Jack turned to her now, 'who fired the torpedoes?'

She knew he meant British or American and she could see Ben wanted to know too, 'In his defence, *The Gustloff* was still armed on deck, the Captain of the sub may not have known civilians were on board.'

Jack didn't ask again; he just gave her a look to answer him. 'It was a Russian sub,' she eased their thoughts a little.

'How long did it take to go down?' Jack was focusing on the mission now.

'Less than fifty minutes,' Ned confirmed.

'So, we have eight and a half hours to locate three Phoenix agents amongst over ten and a half thousand people and neutralise them before the torpedoes hit,' Hennessey mused uneasily 'as well as identifying the baby from the blanket it was wrapped in.'

'Needle in a haystack,' Ben said aloud, everyone nodded.

'So basically, if we manage to neutralise the agents but don't find the baby when the torpedoes hit, we have to check all the lifeboats which means staying on board until the end,' Jack sighed.

'Provided it's not a setup, we should have the advantage of them not knowing we're coming for them,' Ben added.

'Yes, getting back to it being a setup when can we off Silas?' Tannis fixed Hennessey with a stare.

'Tannis, he has been no threat to us so far, maybe even a help,' Hennessey chastised gently.

'He's Phoenix and therefore by definition a threat,' she wasn't going to leave it there.

Ned backed his sister up, 'I've looked him up on our records, and there's no trace of him.'

'Let's get the mission out of the way, then I will discuss the matter with the Joint Chiefs,' Hennessey turned his attention to Jack now 'Colonel I want two teams on this mission, I will leave the choice of men to you, we will meet back here at 0900 hrs tomorrow,' and with that, he began to rise.

'Ned I'll need to go through a few things with you,' Jack collected his paperwork then turned to the rest of his team, 'you two may as well get out of here, I'll see you in the morning.'

Ben knew his wife so well so spoke for the both of them, 'If it's ok with you sir we'll hang out here a while longer, we're gonna need all the info we can get on this one.' Tannis smiled at her husband as Jack gave the ok, then almost startled, she quickly turned to Ned,

'And don't be sending us back as Nazi's I refuse to die in that uniform!'

Ned tutted, 'Blonde hair, blue eyes you'd make the perfect Aryan.'

'There are people I plan to haunt when I die, I have a list,' she glared.

Jack gave the both of them one of his looks that meant the conversation was over, he didn't get how they could joke about things like this, and he knew Ben didn't like it either, although he had to agree with Tannis on the uniform thing.

Later that afternoon Alpha team walked down the gangplank with Ned making their way to their respective homes. As they walked on in silence Ned tried to lighten the mood, 'You know I bet the powers that be in the future look back and see you as a bit of a maritime nightmare, every ship you go on bloody well sinks,' he nudged his sister. Tannis was walking arm in arm with her husband and didn't even break her stride, 'Bugger off, I've already had the have you ever been on one that didn't sink today from Silas.'

Ned's interest piqued, 'What did he say?'

'What I just said,' she frowned.

'Exactly,' Ned insisted.

'He just reeled off the names, *Titanic*, *Lusitania* and *Arizona*,' Ben added.

With the mention of *The Arizona* Ned made eye contact with his sister and winked giving her a knowing look. Jack and Ben both picked up on it, 'Care to share that little moment?' Jack raised an eyebrow.

'Oh, it was just a mission,' Tannis shrugged.

'Don't be so modest dear sister; it was the end of a mission the night before the attack on Pearl Harbour. But mine and Will's part went wrong, and we ended up in the brig on *The Arizona*, somehow Tannis found us and ran on board just as the attack started and busted us out literally with minutes to spare, we managed to run out on deck and jump overboard.'

'Past History,' Tannis grumbled.

'That's it,' Ned knew there was something wrong, 'Sylas never mentioned *The Wind Dancer*.'

Tannis glared at her brother, 'That's because it didn't happen and I wasn't even there at the time it didn't happen,' she said it as if she had rehearsed it many times.

'Exactly,' Ned looked at Jack now, 'sorry but bear with me, the Admiral and the Joint Chiefs erased all files on Tannis going back for Caroline and the kids in case others would use it to set a precedent.'

Tannis followed her brother's train of thought, 'So Silas would've only known about my logged missions if he had read about them when he was in the future.'

Ned nodded, 'Jack, what was the first thing that came into your mind when Silas reeled off the names of the ships?'

'*Wind Dancer*,' he admitted.

'And you Ben?' Ned turned to his brother-in-law.

'Yeah, me too, like it was a rerun of the satellite link we saw,' he held his wife a little closer at the memory.

'Any Phoenix worth their salt would've picked up on those thoughts,' Ned pondered.

'Unless he was using his powers somewhere else,' Tannis sneered, 'I knew I should've killed the little bastard before we left.'

Ben thought for a moment, 'But where else was he using? He wasn't controlling anyone, Tannis was there to make sure of that.'

'This requires more thought, let's get the mission out of the way first,' Ned looked at them all for agreement.

'Ok I'll have a word with the Admiral in the morning, no one wakes the little git up until we get back.' Jack added.

'The Eldridge,' Tannis piped up.

'What about it?' Ben slipped his arm around her shoulders now. 'Just proving there is a boat that hasn't sunk under me,' she smiled triumphantly.

'Ship,' her companions chorused.

'Whatever,' her moment of satisfaction was short-lived.

Ben and Tannis sat on the balcony of their apartment watching the sun go down, 'Never get tired of seeing that,' he said softly. 'So long as you never get tired of me,' Tannis teased as she stood next to where he sat, he took her hand and pulled her down towards him, she straddled him, and his lips were on hers as he unbuttoned the front of her dress and slipped his hand inside caressing her breasts. His tongue was in her mouth as she reached down and opened his trousers taking his hardness in her hand and guiding it inside her, he groaned and leant back savouring the pleasure as she began to move on him.

Leaning forward now he ran his tongue over an erect nipple, gasping at the sensation she held him to her as her movements became more vigorous, his mouth sought hers as they climaxed together. They stayed like that for a while after just holding each other both knowing that the other was thinking about the impending mission but neither speaking a word, there was no point paying lip service to their fears, it had all been said before, nothing had changed.

Jack had called for Ben and Tannis that morning so they could walk to The Eldridge together and talk off the record before they got to the briefing. Along the way, he told them that he had chosen Bravo team for backup, his first choice would've been Delta team, but they were carrying injuries from their last mission. Sure, there was no love lost between Ben and Harmon. But that was always put aside on missions, they were both professional soldiers, and even Ben had reluctantly agreed Harmon was good at his job.

It came as a surprise to them all though when Harmon himself was waiting for them at the end of the dock. 'Sir,' he saluted Jack, acknowledged Ben with a nod and winked at Tannis. Ben didn't let this get to him though as they were still off duty and not on board he slipped his arm around his wife's waist, and she leaned into him.

'Sir,' Harmon continued, 'permission to speak with you off the record?' He seemed a little cautious, not his usual overconfident self.

'Very well Major,' Jack frowned, wanting to get to the briefing.

'It's about Lieutenant Anderson,' he referred to one of his team members; the Lieutenant had been brought in as a temporary replacement for his usual second in command who had been wounded a couple of months ago and was still undergoing physiotherapy.

'What about him?' Ben folded his arms also wanting to get on.

Harmon looked back to Jack 'Well sir; it's nothing concrete, I mean we all just passed our latest psych evaluation and all.'

This was a test all team members had to take regularly to keep an eye on their mental state; missions took their toll both physically and mentally on some people. 'And the Lieutenant has fitted in well with us as a team but…' he paused trying to find the words, 'well lately he's been questioning the missions, you know why should so many people die when we return the timeline to how it should be.'

'Have you spoken about it with him?' Jack didn't like the sound of this.

'Yes sir, as soon as we had the conversation his comments stopped. But I don't think his thoughts have,' the Major said truthfully. 'I know a gut feeling isn't enough to go to the Admiral with, especially when the Lieutenant passed his evaluation with such flying colours. But I'm not sure he should be going with us, I know we're all having difficulties with the numbers on this one, but I think it might be too much for him.'

Jack thought for a moment, 'Point taken Major. But you're right, I'll need more than a gut feeling to have him stood down, and with all other teams away or on sick leave we couldn't get a replacement with any experience,' Jack's tone changed as his darker professional side kicked in, 'keep a close eye on him Major, the mission must not be compromised at any cost.'

So, the briefing went ahead, it had been decided that they should leap aboard just as the ship was about to leave port. It would be busy enough with people jostling each other trying to get below decks in the foul weather; they would work in teams of two, one team would be in the bough section the other in the midsection, then the last in the rear.

As requested, or rather demanded by Tannis they were going to be sent back as civilians, their brief sounded a lot simpler than it was, 'Find and eliminate the three Phoenix agents and make sure the baby is safely on the lifeboat before they leap.'

'Don't take any unnecessary risks on this one people, we don't even know if the threat is real, get in, get the job done and get out,' Hennessey said as he dismissed them to go and change for the mission.

Tannis waited outside the locker room for her team, Bravo team came out first and nodded to her as they made their way to the hold, all jokes were off now, they were all focused. Shortly after Ben and Jack joined her in the passageway, Tannis hugged Jack and buried her head in his neck; he returned her embrace, 'Stay safe Jack,' she whispered.

'You too,' they moved apart, and Jack looked from her to Ben now, 'no heroics, if it can't be done, get out of there,' the two men shook hands, and the three of them walked to the hold.

At the far end of the passage, Barbara stood with the Admiral; she had followed him on his way to the hold with some last-minute papers to sign, 'Admiral isn't that against regulations?' she rasped.

'Tannis is not military personnel Barbara, so she doesn't fall under the rules of fraternisation. But rest assured should I see the Colonel and the Major embrace I'll be sure and step in,' he allowed himself a grin as he left her standing while he continued on his way, he could almost feel her scowling behind him.

The teams were assembled in their pairs when Hennessey walked in; Jack was with Sgt Sawyer of Bravo team, Harmon was with Anderson and Ben was with Tannis, although at present she was struggling to free herself from the bear hug Ned was giving her. Finally, he released his grip and stepped back standing at the Admiral's side as he addressed his teams 'Alpha team, Bravo team, good luck!'

The sub-zero wind cut into them as they appeared on deck, hidden between the extra lifeboats that the crew had hurriedly stacked there.

Tannis blinked hard as the snow and hailstones stung her face. Their voices were lost in the howling of the wind, but they didn't need to say anything; they just made their way to their allocated parts of the ship, it would be a slow task as almost every inch was crammed with people trying to find respite from the weather. As they sought to make their way toward their aft position Ben and Tannis observed everyone they could. The ship had raised the gangplank now and was moving slowly away from the dock as it did so they could hear the cries of desperation from those left behind as they begged the ship not to leave them. *If only they knew they stand a better chance*, Ben thought to himself, he held Tannis tightly as he stood behind her while she leant against the rail, terrified people pushed past them trying to get below decks; there was no order, it was everyone for themselves.

'We should get below,' he had to shout to be heard. She nodded and holding his hand tightly they began to shove their way through checking every face and babe in arms as they did so. It took them an hour just to make their way to the first level; the other teams were having the same problem too. For this mission, they had all been allowed small earpieces that doubled as transmitters, and they were all communicating the same issues and another fact they had all stated, no one had seen either an agent or the baby for that matter.

Time was against them, and it was Jack's call, 'Split up, we'll cover more ground that way, arrange a meeting place with your teammate if we have to be on board for the sinking and be there,' he ordered, 'and for God's sake stay sharp.'

Both teams acknowledged their orders.

'We'll meet back here if we need to,' Ben touched Tannis' face gently then kissed her softly, 'be careful,' he couldn't say too much as they had open mikes, she winked back at him and began to pick her way along the crowded passage.

Jack exhaled a deep breath, he was only just on his second deck down and already the heat generated from all the bodies crowded down there was unbearable, he looked on helplessly as people took off their life jackets and cast them aside with all of their warm clothing. He too though was forced to remove his topcoat and jacket and, rolling up his shirt sleeves, continued on his thus far fruitless search.

They were five hours into the voyage when Sergeant Sawyer reported sighting an agent on E Deck midsection not far from the swimming pool. 'Keep him in sight but do not engage,' Jack ordered 'I'm on my way.'

'Roger that,' Sawyer replied as he maintained a discreet distance. From past experience, Tannis and Ned had told them that with so many souls on board the agents wouldn't try to read any thoughts as it would be too much for them to cope with.

The issue of dealing with an agent in such a densely populated area had already been addressed, and each team member had been given what looked like an ordinary pen. But the nib had been replaced with a needle that delivered such a fast-acting poison that the agent would be well on the way to death before they even realised, they had been stuck with it, and all anyone would think was that the victim had suffered a heart attack.

Jack made his way closer to his quarry, was it going to be this easy? He thought, these bastards usually put up a fight with whatever their nasty little speciality was. So, he put these thoughts out of his mind for now as he drew closer to the agent and just in case, began to think about the Russian advance on Prussia. Sawyer was feet away from the target too but followed his orders and held back if the Colonel failed then he would have to take over. But he didn't fail; he casually walked past the agent who just slumped to the floor as Jack passed by, 'Midsection threat neutralised,' he confirmed.

Major Harmon had followed his orders and split with Lieutenant Anderson, but he wasn't comfortable with the idea, 'Anderson sitrep?' Harmon requested 'Anderson report,' Harmon ordered but still no answer.

'Sir I think we have a man down,' he spoke to Jack now, but it wasn't Jack who replied. 'Not a man down Major, a man reborn,' it was Anderson.

'Lieutenant, get to your meeting point with Major Harmon,' Jack hissed.

'I'm sorry Colonel, I can't do that, you see I can't just stand by and watch over nine and a half thousand innocent people die when I have the power to do something about it,' Anderson's voice was eerily calm as he spoke.

'Just get to the meeting place, and we'll talk about it there,' Jack clenched a fist as he replied.

'Can't do that sir, I've got my target in sight shhh!'

'You've located an agent?' Jack wanted confirmation. There was the sound of a body having the breath knocked out of it followed by a thud as it hit the floor.

'Threat neutralised,' Anderson's tone carried a smile with it.

'Lieutenant Anderson, confirm Phoenix agent neutralised?' Jack ordered.

'No Colonel, I said the threat was neutralised, she won't be any trouble now.'

Jack's mind raced, 'Tannis call in…Tannis call in.'

'Colonel didn't you hear me; I said I had neutralised the threat?' Anderson seemed confused at Jack's lack of understanding.

'TANNIS!' Ben yelled, but there was no answer, 'you bastard, what have you done to her?'

'Oh, don't worry Major Rhodes, my killing days are over. She will have a sore head when she wakes up, but by then it will be too late, I will have saved all these souls,' Anderson was almost preaching now.

'Teams report positions,' Jack called out, this nut job was on his way to the bridge it didn't take a genius to work that one out.

'C deck aft,' Ben reported.

'B deck forward,' Harmon was next.

'Major Harmon, you're closest, stop Anderson getting to the bridge at all costs,' Jack knew he didn't stand a chance of getting there first he was still on E deck with Sawyer.

'Yes sir,' Harmon acknowledged.

'Shit!' Jack leant back against the wall, 'Sgt you maintain the search here I'll take over from Major Harmon.' Sawyer gave Jack a nod as the two men parted, this was all they needed Jack thought to himself, so much for psych evaluation, sure Harmon could be a dick at times and especially liked winding Ben up, but he was a good soldier, and he knew his men.

In the aft section, Ben hurried as best he could along D deck to where Tannis had been searching before she had been assaulted. But he found nothing and nobody, at least no one he wanted to, just hundreds of refugees huddled together; they seemed more confident now some of them sang and joked and toasted the Fuhrer, but the irony of the situation was wasted on him he was too busy. Up on deck Harmon waited in the shadows at the bottom of the stairs that led to the bridge, it would be Anderson's only way in as he was dressed as a civilian so would have to sneak in that way unobserved. Harmon hoped it would be sooner rather than later as he, like the others, had shed his topcoat and jacket below decks and now he was being battered by a gale force wind with a chill factor of at least minus twenty, not to mention the snow and the hail. His teeth chattered as he shoved his hands under his armpits to try and thaw out his fingers.

'I know you're here John,' Anderson's voice whispered in his earpiece. 'I don't want to kill you, but if you try to stop me, I will have no choice, I'd rather have one death on my conscience than thousands,' he stepped into the light now. Harmon too showed himself prepared for a fight, 'Lieutenant relinquish your timepiece and get back down to the meeting point,' Harmon forced his teeth not to chatter as he faced up to his target. Time was against them; they were almost six hours into the voyage.

'I'm going to the bridge now John, don't try to stop me.'

Harmon just shook his head as he stepped toward his adversary, the struggle was intense. Both men were highly trained and had fought side by side before, so they knew one another's capabilities.

'You shouldn't be wasting time John, Tannis is down on E deck sleeping like the baby we're all looking for, very close to the machine room right in line for the third torpedo, so you see if you don't let me do what I need to she will indeed die.'

'Rhodes, did you get that?' Harmon called out as he dodged a punch from Anderson.

'Got it, I'm on my way,' Ben shoved his way toward the stairs. 'You fool you know they are still able to communicate,' a voice from the shadows spoke harshly. 'The Eldridge brat must die no matter what,' it was one of the Phoenix agents.

The scuffle stopped abruptly 'You son of a bitch you sold out to them?' Harmon was aghast.

'No, you don't understand this agent doesn't want the ship to sink either, he read my thoughts when we were in a quiet place below decks and approached me with an alternative. We can save all these people John, so what if time changes a little, this guy isn't like the others, he wants peace too,' Anderson explained. But before he could go any further, he screamed and clutched his head in agony as blood ran from his eyes and nose, then gushed from his mouth Harmon had seen this before when Tannis' sister had been executed by Phoenix during the final battle.

Anderson's corpse dropped to the deck. 'You, humans, are all such a waste of time, like cattle easily led and easily discarded,' the agent sneered at Harmon. 'Yes, the fool told us your plan, you will fail, and now it's your turn to die, I think a suicide overboard, I can't be bothered dragging two bodies, you can do it yourself.'

Harmon wasn't going to give the agent a smooth ride, instead of running from him, he moved toward the agent and pushed him over the handrail. But as he fell, he grabbed onto Harmon's wrists, 'Pull me up, or you die too. Killing me will not help if my fellow agent loses contact, he will just wait by the lifeboats and kill the infant then, you can't win,' in his struggle to hold on he couldn't use the full force of mind control, but he could still kill.

'Then it looks like we're both going for a swim,' Harmon struggled to get his words out with the strain of the agent's weight pulling him; then he gasped in pain as his head began to feel like it was going to implode and he slowly began to slip further over the edge; he was almost unconscious when he felt someone holding him around the waist, then from over his shoulder he saw an ice pick fly past him as it was plunged into the agent's skull and his grip was released immediately as he fell into the water below, Harmon almost followed, but his rescuer pulled him back to safety.

'That was a very brave thing you were about to do,' it was Tannis, she gently wiped away the blood from the split lip Anderson had given him.

'Ben, get away from E deck I'll see you at the meeting point,' she said.

'You, ok?' Her husband's voice was full of concern.

'I'm all right, I couldn't let you know earlier, Anderson would've heard, I saw him talking with the agent when I woke up, so I followed them,' she explained.

'Good work, now Major Harmon meet with myself and Sergeant Sawyer forward on A deck. Tannis and Major Rhodes to your meeting point A deck mid ship,' Jack's voice cut in.

They all acknowledged their orders as Tannis helped Harmon to stand, they had to get Anderson's body out of sight, so they dragged him to the stacked lifeboats near to where they had made their leap. They turned to leave, but Tannis faltered, Anderson wasn't dead, he had grabbed her ankle releasing it as she knelt by his side, he said nothing, just handed her a small brass key before he died.

'Someone's coming,' Harmon looked over Tannis' shoulder. 'They can't find you with the body, act like you're making out.' Jack ordered.

Ben opened and closed his mouth without saying a word, he thought better of it.

Harmon didn't need telling twice he pulled Tannis to him and kissed her, two sailors walked past, and one nudged the other 'I don't blame him, not even this weather would cool my passion if I had a woman like that.' The sailors were out of view when Tannis gently pushed Harmon back, 'They're gone,' she told him, he pulled her close again, 'Yeah but they might come back.' Tannis shoved him harder this time and backed him into a stack of lifeboats, 'By which time we'll be gone,' she moved away towards the hatch that led below decks. 'Good luck Major.'

As she waited for her husband to make his way to her on A deck, Tannis fiddled with the key in her pocket. She had told them all about it over their earpieces, but no one had any clue as to what it was for. Hitler's speech was being played over the ship's intercom system when Ben finally reached her. Hugging her tightly then taking her face in his hands he kissed her lips, 'You, ok?' he whispered, she nodded and kissed him quietly after all they had unwilling eavesdroppers, then they just stood holding each other there was nothing else they could do now but wait.

Tannis put her hand in her pocket and pulled out the key, still trying to fathom out what it was for. 'If it were a room key it would have a number engraved on it,' Ben took it from her and looked closer; there were no markings at all. They both stepped back a little to let a crew member get by and as he passed, he noticed the key in Ben's hand, 'Are you lost sir, I see you're missing the fob from your key, your stateroom is all the way forward that way,' the helpful man pointed out.

'Yes, so it is, thank you crewman,' Ben adlibbed, then he noticed the small handful of blankets he was carrying, they were all identical to the one the baby was found in; Tannis followed his gaze 'Crewman where are you taking those blankets?' She pretended to shiver.

'These are children's blankets ma'am only for issue in the staterooms. If you like, I can have some more adequate ones delivered to yours?' He replied helpfully.

'Oh, no that won't be necessary, thank you, I'll be fine,' she smiled as he gave them a small salute and went on his way.

'Anderson must've found the baby and locked it in a stateroom,' Ben looked down the crowded passage that led forward.

'We've got to get to them fast, everybody,' Jack ordered.

But Tannis stopped them all in their tracks, 'It's too late Jack, the speech has finished,' she looked at her husband her eyes wide as he wrapped his arms around her, she did the same to him, and they held on tightly to each other.

'Good luck everybody, brace for impact then make your way to the staterooms a.s.a.p.' Jack took a breath and steadied himself against the handrail.

'I love you,' Ben mouthed the words, Tannis reciprocated, and his lips were on hers. They felt the whole ship move as the first torpedo hit the bough, then it was their turn midships, it was so violent it knocked them to the floor. Ben was first up he pulled Tannis to her feet, and they forced their way to the stairwell along with the terrified passengers now all heading for the lifeboats. Tannis gasped for air as they made it out on deck it had been one mad crush.

'Jack!' She yelled above the screams.

'We're ok all out on deck, you two?' He had to shout too. 'Both out on deck trying to get forward,' Ben confirmed.

The deck was covered in ice and Ben had to quickly grab Tannis as she slipped towards the far side of the ship as it began to list, the bough was already going down. They pushed their way roughly, and as fast as they could, the lifeboats were swinging away from the ship, and there was no one there to lower them. They caught up with Jack and the others as close to the now submerging bough as they could get, Tannis flinched and turned quickly as a shot rang out, and her hands went to her mouth. A German officer had just shot his toddler and was now turning his gun on the infant his wife tearfully cradled in her arms. Ben quickly pulled his wife into him so that she wouldn't have to witness the horror that was about to happen, the shot rang out, and Tannis gave a muffled scream, the teams moved on as the officer turned the gun on his wife.

Two decks were already under water at the bough when they reached the entrance, and for the moment all hopes of getting through were halted by the mass exodus from within. People now began fighting amongst themselves, and the bodies of the trampled dead strewn across the frozen deck slipped silently into the sea as the ship listed even more in the darkness.

'Just shove through,' Jack called out to his people then there was another pistol shot, but this time Tannis spun around to try and catch Harmon as he fell backwards and slid over the side. He had been hit in the shoulder, instantly Sawyer jumped overboard after his CO, in their earpieces they heard Sawyer's voice, 'I've got you, sir, just hang on,' then in the darkness Alpha team saw a small bright blue flash. Tannis glared as she scoured the area for the culprit, he was nowhere to be seen, but she sensed him, 'It's the last agent,' she looked at Jack 'and if he read anyone's thoughts he'll be heading for the staterooms.' It was a hard slog pushing their way through the throngs of frightened passengers, but eventually, the crowds thinned, and the passageways grew quiet as they picked their way through the trampled bodies of men, women and children none had been shown any mercy.

They were practically running downhill now, the bough was going down so fast, and the icy cold water was already up to their knees. That was when they heard it, the sound of a baby crying, they hurried down the passage stopping at every intersection to listen, the water rising ever quicker; it was down one such passage that they saw the last surviving agent trying to force open the door in front of him. Alpha team looked at one another, none of them was armed, Tannis reached into her pocket and pulled out her poison pen. 'I'll do it, I'll swim up close behind him.'

'You'll freeze first,' Jack whispered through chattering teeth.

'I'll do it,' Ben volunteered.

'This isn't the time for gallantry, you both know I'm stronger if any of us can make it it's me,' she looked at Jack who reluctantly nodded as she lowered herself into the icy water.

The bodies of the dead floated along the passageway bumping into the agent; he paid no attention to them as he continued trying to smash the door down.

The coldness of the water sliced through Tannis at first as she made her way toward the agent, she was so tired now all she wanted to do was just close her eyes for a second and the water didn't seem so cold anymore, she could hardly feel it now.

'Move your arse Tannis,' her inner voice took on Jack's.

'She's taking too much time,' Ben whispered to his CO who nodded, they were about to resort to plan B when the agent suddenly collapsed and fell beneath the surface.

The two men hurried down the passage as fast as the now chest deep water would allow, bodies still floating by. Ahead close to the half smashed in door Tannis slowly stood, she was hunched over shivering uncontrollably when Ben reached her and pulled her to him rubbing her arms trying with little effect to get the circulation going, who was he kidding he was borderline hypothermic as he was sure was Jack.

Hand numb with cold, Jack put the key in the lock and opened the door, he stepped inside briefly then returned cradling a very opinionated baby in his arms wrapped in the much sought-after blanket. 'The parents are dead, tied up with their throats cut,' he stammered with the cold. 'Let's get him to the lifeboats.'

They tried to go back the way they came but a loud creaking noise alerted them, the floor was buckling and ahead of them at the far end of the passage it burst, and water gushed through straight toward them. 'That's the only way out,' Ben yelled over the roar of rushing water.

Tannis grabbed her teammates ready to leap.

'We can't; the mission fails if we don't get the baby out,' Jack held the infant higher.

'The child was found seven hours after the ship went down, I can leap back the time gap should be long enough for it to be safe if I'm careful,' Tannis' numb fingers were losing their grip on her team.

'You're sure?' Jack looked at her now.

'It's our only chance sir,' Ben answered for his wife.

'Do it!' Jack shut his eyes; the torrent was seconds away from them.

The next they knew the four of them were huddled together in the hold on board The Eldridge, Tannis collapsed taking Ben to the floor with her, the medics rushed in.

Jack's eyes flickered open, he could hear a baby crying, his mind snapped back to the present as he sat bolt upright, he was in sick bay Ben was sleeping in the bed next to him and Tannis in the bed next to his.

'Ah Colonel, good you're awake,' Dr O'Brian stood in the doorway. 'The Admiral wants a word.'

'They alright?' Jack looked across at his sleeping team.

'They'll be fine, just waiting for the lazy devils to wake up,' the doctor grinned.

'And did Harmon and Sawyer get back ok?'

'Yes Colonel, Sgt Sawyer is waiting outside in the passage, Major Harmon is still sedated from surgery; he won't be going on any missions for a while, but he'll make a full recovery.' The Irishman passed Jack some clothes, 'And if you're interested, you're fine too.'

Jack dressed and made his way to the briefing room to meet with the Admiral and Ned, and when he entered the room, he could see by the look on Hennessey's face that the reason for bringing the baby back with them had better be a good one and delivered quickly, so he took a breath and …

'Is it possible for Tannis to make a return leap with only a seven-hour delay and not cause a paradox?' Hennessey growled at Ned; he understood that Alpha team had no choice, and he wouldn't for one minute expect them to lay down their lives unnecessarily, but this was a huge risk with so much at stake.

'Well, the shortest she's ever done was eight, so I don't see why not, I know that we were told never within the twenty-four-hour time frame. But Tannis doesn't chuck energy around like the timepieces do, so she'd have to take you all back using her own power,' Ned looked at the Admiral, 'but these things should be done rarely.'

'Very well,' Hennessey agreed; 'but this time you will return prepared,' he stood and made to leave, 'let me know when your team is ready.'

Jack walked back down to the infirmary with Ned; he was concerned about what his sister had gone through on the mission after all Jack's debrief had been short, and to the point, he knew he would have to wait until they were back from the next leap until he heard it all.

'Was it as bad as it read?' Ned looked across at his friend. 'Stuff of nightmares,' Jack sighed, the memories still raw.

'I'm sorry Jack, I know you don't want to talk about it, I just worry about Tannis, *Titanic* changed her for a long time after.'

Jack stopped and put his hand on Ned's shoulder, 'Ned, I don't know what it was like on *Titanic*, Tannis was a kid back then. *The Gustloff* was a hard mission, and I don't doubt not one of us will have issues when it's all over, but we'll get through it as a team, as friends and as family, she'll be fine she's got Ben now, she's not alone anymore.'

Ben and Tannis had woken and dressed by the time Ned and Jack got there, Tannis was cradling the baby in her arms giving him a bottle feed while Ben was talking with Dr O'Brian. Jack found it a little surreal briefing them on their imminent mission while Tannis fed then winded the baby, she was an old hand at such things as she'd had a lot of practice helping out with her nieces and nephews.

'Oh, back out in the cold again Joseph,' Tannis cooed at the baby. 'Joseph?' Jack raised an eyebrow.

'That will be his adoptive name,' Ned informed him.

'Yes, we'll keep you safe until the big rescue boat finds you,' she smiled down at the infant.

'Ship,' Hennessey corrected from the doorway before the others could. Tannis frowned but ignored the comment as she continued 'Then when you're safe and sound, we will come back and get rid of the nasty little man who wanted to hurt you.'

'Joint Chiefs still need proof of malicious intent Tannis, so far Silas has only helped us,' the Admiral admitted reluctantly.

'Oh, give him enough rope, and I'll hang him with it,' she passed the baby to the nurse now.

'Don't you mean he'll hang himself?' Hennessey folded his arms. 'No, I know what I'm saying,' she smiled sweetly then turned to her CO, 'well I'm ready when you are Jack.'

As they would now be leaping straight into the Baltic Sea, they had been issued with survival suits that should give them long enough to find a lifeboat and stay with the baby until rescuers found him. The baby himself would be cocooned in a thermal floating device safe against the elements until rescue arrived.

'Alpha team, good luck,' Hennessey gave them their permission to leap.

The only exposed parts of their bodies were their faces, and as the icy choppy water splashed against them it felt like a slap, all around was silent now, the storm had had its way and moved on. The bodies of the dead floated all around as far as the eye could see. Alpha team gently pushed the corpses aside and made their way to the nearest lifeboat. 'They're just sleeping,' Tannis whispered to the baby, but her team noticed that she was reluctant to look around and who could blame her. Ben lost count of all the pairs of little legs that dangled frozen in the air of the children who had been put in life jackets designed only for adults, and as Ned had explained, as soon as they hit the water, they were turned upside down and drowned.

The sight too was etched into Jack's mind, but he couldn't let that distract him now they had one little life to save here, a life whose descendants would save millions of lives. Upon reaching the lifeboat Jack checked for signs of life, but all aboard were dead, in the distance they could hear the cries from rescuers still combing the scene for survivors, but their calls remained unanswered as the dead slept on.

Tannis hurried to put the baby in the lifeboat making sure he was tightly wrapped in his blanket, then after lowering herself back into the water, she reached out her cold, gloved hand and touched the sleeping baby's nose. It had the desired effect little Joseph put his healthy set of lungs to good use and screamed for all he was worth. Alpha team pushed the lifeboat away as the search light from the rescue boat shone upon the wailing child.

The team swam to a safe distance and watched as the baby was taken on board the rescue vessel, it was then Tannis heaved a sigh of relief and thinking Ben was resting his hand on her shoulder, she turned to him only to find it was one of the dead. She didn't scream but as she pushed the body of the young man away more seemed to close in around her; she began to thrash in the water now trying to get away. Then a hand was on her shoulder again; it was Ben, he turned her to face him, she was shivering with cold as they all were, the suits wouldn't protect them forever. Tears ran down her face as she fixed her eyes on him like a frightened rabbit caught in headlights. He rested both hands on her shoulders now, 'Just keep looking at me,' he whispered, 'it'll be ok.' The two men were both getting the creeps now too, so satisfied the baby was safe Jack gave the order for them to get the hell out of there, he had one last look around at the horrific sight and shook his head as he shivered 'Such a tragedy and hardly anyone will know.'

Back in the hold Alpha team appeared, Tannis had brought them back safely, Jack was holding on to her arm while Ben still held onto her shoulders, her eyes still fixed on his, 'Let it go now love, job done,' Jack whispered.

'Congratulations on a mission well-done Alpha team,' Hennessey welcomed them back, 'Please change and report to the briefing room a.s.a.p.'

Ned stepped up to them, he knew his sister wasn't right, he also knew there wasn't a damn thing he could say or do about it either, so he did what Ben couldn't and hugged her tightly then led her out of the room.

An hour or so later after very long hot showers they all reconvened in the briefing room and were debriefed.

'Dr Nichols has asked that both Alpha and Bravo team undergo another psych evaluation,' Hennessey added as he was bringing the debrief to a close.

'We just had our brains felt by the thought police,' Tannis rolled her eyes.

'Due to recent events, he thinks it's for the best,' Ned put in. 'Shouldn't it be him being reassessed, after all, he passed Anderson fit for duty?' Ben looked pissed off.

'Yeah, I'd rather talk to Dr O'Brian anyway,' Tannis grumbled.

'Dr O'Brian is not a psychologist, he's not qualified, although…'

Ned didn't get the chance to finish as his sister gave him a gentle warning, 'Steady on, national treasure, tread carefully,' she wouldn't have a bad word said against the man.

'I was going to say, although he probably knows more about the teams than anyone else, you all confide in him.'

Tannis gave her brother a smug nod in reply, 'That's because we trust him, he's a cross between a confessional and a fountain of wisdom.'

'Have the Joint Chiefs made a decision about Silas yet sir?' Jack changed the subject, making Tannis sit up and stare at the Admiral.

Hennessey took a breath he knew this wasn't going to go down well; hell, he had almost exploded with rage when he heard the news too, 'While you were away Dr Nichols was granted permission to evaluate Silas.'

'They woke him up?' Tannis banged a fist on the table, 'how could you let them?'

'I have my orders too Tannis,' the Admiral gave her one of his looks telling her she was on thin ice, 'and for what it was worth I made my doubts clear, the only reason they granted access was on the understanding that Silas would remain partially drugged.'

'Jennings hit Tannis with a dart filled with enough juice to knock an elephant out for a week and how long did it last?' Jack looked at Ben.

'About an hour,' Ben confirmed, smiling at his wife remembering how they first met.

'Tannis has extra chromosomes that makes her system different to ours and that of Phoenix agents, Silas may not react the same,' Ned tried to show support for the Admiral, but his heart wasn't in it.

The room fell silent; no one trusted themselves to speak; they all waited for Hennessey who didn't let them down, 'Well, now that the mission is over and Silas was telling the truth I see no reason why we shouldn't pay him a visit, see if there's anything more, he'd like to tell us.'

Tannis raised a cruel eyebrow and smiled, 'Yes I'd like to see him one last time, much as I love The Eldridge, I'm a bit fed up with boats at the moment.'

'Ships!' They all corrected.

Tannis sighed, 'Whatever.'

'You behave and follow Jack's orders,' Ned warned his sister.

'Or mine even,' Hennessey frowned.

'Well, those too,' Ned looked sheepish.

So, Alpha team along with the Admiral made the leap back to England, everything seemed fine. Dr Nichols told them that Silas had been cooperating well with them and that it was his opinion that his offer to help the coalition was genuine. The look on Tannis' face said it all, but it was Jack that put voice to her thoughts, 'You mean like Anderson was fit for duty, you don't know these guys like we do, and no one knows them like Tannis.'

'Yes, well with respect Tannis' past experiences have left her a little biassed,' Nichols said, almost looking down on her.

'We'd like to see Silas now please Doctor,' Hennessey used a tone that told the psychiatrist it was an order, not a request.

'Very well, but Silas has asked that Tannis not be present, it makes him uncomfortable.' Nichols almost glared at her now. Tannis opened her mouth to protest, but Nichols got there first. 'He's unconscious so no threat at all if that's what you're worried about.'

'Well if he's unconscious he won't know I'm there to make him feel uncomfortable will he,' she retorted.

'Those are the rules, you do understand what rules are for don't you?'

'I'm the youngest sister, I'm the reason for rules.'

'We'll just go down and make sure everything is as it should be,' Hennessey nodded to Jack and Ben, 'Tannis you wait here with the good Doctor.'

She opened her mouth, but one look from Jack and she closed it.

Alone in the office with Nichols now Tannis decided to make herself comfortable so sat herself down at the doctor's desk, enjoying the fact that this was clearly annoying him, so to piss him off further, she began opening the drawers one by one.

'Please don't do that,' he said stiffly.

'Why? Hiding some…oh wow,' her tone changed mid-sentence from taunt to one of surprise and not a pleasant one at that, as inside the latest drawer she had opened was a knife covered in blood, looking up quickly she managed to fend off the brutal attack that the doctor launched at her.

'Sylas is controlling you,' she choked as he grabbed her around the throat.

'Is that what you think?' He laughed as she thrust her arms up between his and removed his hands from her, punching him to the ground. 'Well I did until you just said that,' she rubbed her throat, then her eyes widened as the man on the floor stood up in front of her changing from Dr Nichols to Silas, 'you can shapeshift, that is so cool,' she admired as she kicked out sending him flying backwards into the filing cabinet, 'that must take so much of your power, I couldn't sense you.'

Down in holding, the three men waited as the guard opened the door to Silas' cell, he was lying on his bed with his back to them covered by his blanket. Jack walked over and pulled the cover off roughly. The dead eyes of Dr Nichols stared back at him, 'He's after Tannis,' Jack ran out of the room closely followed by Ben and the Admiral.

They heard the fight before they reached the office. Jack and Ben were armed and positioned themselves either side of the door; Jack nodded to Ben who then swiftly moved in front of the door and kicked it open; they both rushed into the room weapons raised, but not sure who to shoot. Hennessey joined them now curious as to why a shot hadn't been fired and blinked at the sight he now beheld, there a little bruised and battered stood two Tannis'.

'Sylas is a shapeshifter, he can use his powers to project the image of any person he wants to be,' one Tannis said as the men turned their weapons on the other, 'Ben it's me don't shoot,' the Tannis in their sights pleaded.

It was a dilemma, and they didn't have much time to react as Hennessey dropped to his knees writhing in agony, Silas was killing him slowly as the bulk of his powers were being used to generate his new persona.

'Shoot him, Jack, he's killing the Admiral,' one Tannis yelled now.

'No Jack kill me, and Silas wins, he'll finish you both straight away,' the other one cried.

'Which one?' Jack looked at Ben who just shook his head, 'I don't know.'

'You're married to her,' Jack looked at his friend again and saw a look of realisation wash over him. Ben looked at both Tannis' 'Before we moved in together where did you live?' he asked.

'On The Eldridge,' one Tannis replied, a well-known answer anyway.

Ben looked from one to the other 'What is it, what's The Eldridge?'

A Tannis wrinkled her nose, 'A boat.'

The other Tannis sneered, 'Ship,' she corrected.

That was all they needed to hear both men opened fire on the last Tannis to speak, two each in the chest and one in the head. As she fell dead to the floor her image changed back to that of Silas 'Whatever,' her teammates replied as Tannis always did when she had been corrected. Jack helped the Admiral to stand. He was a little shaken and his head was pounding, but he would be ok.

Ben holstered his weapon and held his hand out to his wife, Tannis took it as he helped her step over the blood that seeped from the agent's wounds. They all looked at the body on the floor as once more it changed from Silas to that of a faceless corpse, which proceeded to shrink and shrivel up like a mummified body, long since dead.

A short while later when the Admiral was feeling himself again, they made the leap back to The Eldridge, as the four of them stood in the hold Tannis looked around the room and groaned, 'Back on a boat.'

'Ship,' her team corrected her.

'Fine ship then,' she rolled her eyes.

'No boat!' Hennessey said as he walked away.

Tannis gave Jack and Ben a puzzled look, and Jack put an arm around her shoulder, 'It's what makes you-you!'

Chapter Three

It was a beautiful warm summer's evening on Atlantis, Caroline and Jack had invited Ben and Tannis over for dinner. It had been a relaxed family affair, Tannis helped Caroline in the kitchen to prepare the food while Jack and Ben played football in the garden with Katie and James.

'The ball's the wrong shape,' Ben teased the children as he picked it up, James laughed he was only five, but he knew what Ben meant 'No Uncle Ben this is a football, not a rugby ball, you're supposed to kick it not pick it up.'

Katie folded her arms, she was nine going on thirty and thought she was wiser than her years, 'Uncle Ben means American football James, they call our football soccer.' James didn't like being told what was what by his older sister, so he threw the ball at her, hitting her on the head with it. She launched herself at her brother, 'You little brat,' she yelled as she waded in fists flying, landing a punch before her father and Ben could break it up. Just like his dad Ben thought as he held a wriggling James. His nose was bleeding, and it obviously would've hurt, but he wouldn't let her see that; instead, he was trying to get at her for another go as was Katie who Jack held back. 'Give it up you two,' their father was firm but not harsh, 'now both of you say sorry,' the two men still held on to the children as they allowed them to move a little closer to one another. 'Sorry,' they both muttered.

'Now, James, you go inside and get cleaned up,' his son's shoulders drooped as he walked away. 'And when you get back, I'll show you how to block some of those punches,' James picked up his pace happily now and ran inside, 'and you, young lady. Remember you're bigger than your brother, you should be taking care of him, not trying to knock seven bells out of him,' Jack released his hold on her.

'Sorry Daddy,' she hugged her father. 'Will you teach me how to fight too?' She jumped up and down excitedly.

'Oh, maybe your Uncle Ben will teach you a bit of self-defence if you ask him nicely,' Jack winked at his teammate. Katie followed the two men as they went and sat on some wooden garden chairs near to the table. 'Uncle Ben will you please teach me, Semper Fu?'

Ben laughed, 'And where have you heard that?'

'I read about it in one of Uncle Ned's books,' she said innocently, 'so will you please?' She gave him the benefit of her sweetest smile.

'I think self-defence were the words your dad used Katie,' Ben looked to Jack to back him up.

'Ben's right love, I don't mind you learning to defend yourself, but there's no need for anything more.'

'But Tannis does,' she protested.

'Tannis does what?' Tannis asked as she walked towards them carrying a tray full of things to lay the table with.

'You fight and all of the women in the coalition do too,' she turned to her father, 'but Tannis is the best,' she told him, 'When I'm old enough I'm going to join up, so is James.'

'I thought your brother wanted to be a train driver?' Tannis put the last plate in its place.

'Well, he does, but I'll bring him round.'

'Don't you think that should be his choice?' Tannis smiled at Katie.

'I suppose so, but I'm going to do it, I'm going to be an independent woman like you,' Katie said confidently.

Tannis poured water into the children's beakers. 'I'm not independent Katie, I've always had to follow orders.'

'Then I'll join as an officer like Daddy and Uncle Ben.'

Tannis looked thoughtful, 'Good idea, but then being a woman in the past you won't be able to use your rank, you'll still have to follow their orders, and float about like a spare part not being much use to anyone.'

'I wouldn't like that at all, was your last mission very dull?' Katie knew better than to ask but tried her luck.

Alpha team looked at one another. *The Gustloff* mission had not been a pleasant one.

'I just sat around getting bored, not very challenging for someone as clever as you are,' Tannis told the young girl.

'Hmm, I would like to do something that makes me use my brain,' Katie frowned.

'Well, knowledge is our best tool,' Tannis planted the seed.

'I know,' Katie jumped up. 'I'm going to work with Uncle Ned that way I don't have to join up, and I can use my brain to help you all.'

'That's a fantastic idea,' Tannis smiled, 'Ned's always saying he needs an assistant with a sharp mind who's not afraid to speak up.'

'Hmm I'm going to tell mummy what I'm going to do with my life,' Katie skipped away to the kitchen door, and Tannis turned to follow her. 'Thanks love,' Jack called after her, she raised her hand in acknowledgement. He relaxed back in his chair, 'Now I just have to convince the coalition to build a railway and James will be sorted.'

They all sat and had a pleasant meal together. It was nice to relax in good company, and shortly after they had all finished eating, Ned called around to collect the children. They were sleeping over at his house tonight. Katie was keen to tell him all about her career plans, and as an experienced parent, he listened attentively. 'See you in the morning,' the three of them called back as they walked along the path towards Ned's. Katie's voice could be heard in the distance asking him when she could start working with him and what position she would hold.

Caroline looked at Tannis, 'Thanks for not encouraging Katie to join the coalition.'

'Oh, you don't have to thank her,' Jack grinned, 'she didn't even encourage us, did she?' He looked at Ben who just smiled and shook his head.

'And you can see what I have to put up with?' Tannis gave Caroline a woeful look.

The four adults sat and drank wine now as the sun went down all lost in their own thoughts for the moment until Caroline broke the silence, 'So when are you two going to have kids?' She looked from Tannis to Ben.

'Caroline!' Jack laughed, 'couldn't you think of something more personal to ask them?'

'I'm sorry,' she apologised, 'but you two are soul mates and our closest friends, I think you'd make great parents.'

'Err I'll let you answer that one Babe,' Ben deferred.

Tannis narrowed her eyes in jest at him, 'It would clash with work.'

'You can always stop work,' Caroline was not to be swayed. 'That's not an option at the moment,' Tannis was careful not to say too much as she looked at her teammates, 'there are still a few things I need to finish off.'

Caroline raised her hands in surrender, 'Ok I give up, I know not to ask, but I'd love to hear what you lot get up to out there.'

'Nothing terribly exciting, observation mostly, after all, what more can you do?' Jack said as he stood and went inside for another bottle of wine.

'Caroline darlin, where's the corkscrew?' he called.

Caroline smiled at her guests, 'Excuse me a sec if he doesn't have a grid reference he can't find a thing,' she left them alone and went back into the house.

Ben leaned over to Tannis, 'You'd look great with my baby in there,' he reached over and touched her stomach. She smiled 'Well we'll just have to keep practising until I've finished off those little niggles.'

He knew what she meant, so long as Phoenix and Kira and Nyra were still out there, she couldn't stop, and she certainly wouldn't leave her team. He kissed her softly but pulled away quickly as they heard a crash from inside the house followed by Jack yelling, 'Tannis get in here!'

They both raced into the kitchen, Caroline had collapsed, and Jack was on his knees checking her over, his teammates had never seen him so worried as he picked his wife up in his arms, 'She's sick, get us to the infirmary!'

Tannis nodded and grabbed Caroline's wrist, but as quickly as she did so she flinched and let go, 'What is it?' Jack stared at her. 'Nothing,' she lied and grabbed Caroline again, then Ben with the other hand and not wanting to take any chances he held onto Jack's arm too. A blink later they were in the infirmary, Dr O'Brian seemed to take it in his stride, them appearing in his workplace unannounced as he motioned to Jack to lay her on the nearest bed.

'What happened Colonel?' The Dr's voice was calm as ever.

'I dunno, she was fine one minute then she just collapsed,' Jack gabbled as he took his wife's hand.

'I need you all to wait outside while I conduct my examination,' O'Brian addressed them all, and Ben, and Tannis moved away from the bed, but Jack remained. 'Tannis,' O'Brian motioned toward her CO, she walked back and took his hand in hers and silently led him away.

They waited outside in the passage; no one spoke as Jack paced up and down; they left him to it, no point telling him to take a seat. After what seemed like an age but was only a few minutes, Jack stopped suddenly and turned to Tannis, 'Why did you flinch when you touched Caroline back at the house, you felt something didn't you, like with me on the Walpole mission?' He put his hands on her shoulders, 'I need to know love.'

Tannis shook her head, 'It wasn't like that Jack, I felt your pain, but with Caroline, I can't explain what I felt.'

'Try,' he was forcing himself to be calm, and it showed.

Ben stood by Tannis, Jack was ok now, but he'd never seen him like this before.

'It felt like there was more than her there,' she thought for a moment, 'when I touched Ben before we made the leap I felt him, then when he touched you, I felt you, but with Caroline, it felt like there was someone else there too.'

'I think I can explain that if you'd come with me Colonel,' O'Brian's soft Irish accent seemed to bring calm and Jack followed him into the examination room, where to his relief he saw Caroline sitting up in bed fully conscious. He sat next to her and pulled her into his arms, 'You ok darlin?'

She nodded and smiled 'More than alright actually.'

'What?' He pulled away and looked at the doctor who laughed 'Congratulations Colonel, Caroline is around three months pregnant, and apart from a little blood pressure, mother and baby are doing fine.' Jack couldn't believe his ears, it took a moment for the doctor's words to sink in but when they did, he grinned, hugged his wife and kissed her.

'I'll tell Major Rhodes and Tannis they can go home then, shall I?' The doctor asked.

'Oh Christ!' he'd forgotten about them, 'I'll be right back darlin, just give me a minute.' Jack jumped off the bed and hurried out of the door, he reached Tannis first and grabbed her hugging her tightly 'You knew, didn't you?' He kissed her on the cheek.

'I guessed, but I wasn't sure,' she smiled.

He let her go and grinned at Ben, 'Three months pregnant.' Ben shook his CO's hand, 'Congratulations sir.'

'Oh, the Doc says she can go home in a bit, I don't want her walking all that way, would you mind Tannis love? I'll walk back with the Major if you're tired after all Caroline is leaping for two these days.'

'I'm fine don't worry I'll get us all back,' she waved him away and laughed.

'Wanna share?' Ben leaned back against the wall in front of her, Tannis bit her lip as she looked at him, 'Oh she's leaping for more than two.'

'Really?' Ben straightened up and grinned. 'Should we tell them?' his wife looked up at him.

'Nah, let's leave that for the first scan, they've had enough surprises for one night.'

A few days later they were called into the briefing room, they took their usual seats and waited for Ned and Hennessey to arrive, which they did moments later. Hennessey was first, 'As you were,' he always said that in order for them to remain seated, 'and before you ask, I've no idea what Ned has for us.'

The screen flicked on as Ned walked in, 'Have I got news for you!' He showed them an old black and white photograph, 'San Francisco 19th April 1906.'

'The day before the quake?' Jack guessed.

'Actually, that's the day after,' Ben frowned as he looked at the image of the city still intact.

'Well done Major,' Ned gave a file to everyone. 'So, the quake never happened and as you can see from your data, world history has changed beyond recognition.'

'How the hell do you stop an earthquake from happening?' Tannis looked at them all.

'Might have something to do with this chap,' Ned changed the picture on the screen, it was a newspaper cutting from the same day telling of the finding of the body of Nicola Tesla in a San Francisco hotel room.

'He did die in a hotel room,' Ned looked to his sister like a teacher testing a pupil, and once again she didn't let him down, 'Yes on the other side of the country in January 1943.'

Ned sniffed his approval and continued, 'So basically, in theory, you just leap back, save Tesla, let the quake happen and get out of there fast.'

'Yeah, we said that about Seneffe and we all know how that one went,' Tannis slouched in her seat as her teammates nodded.

Ned sighed, 'Well anyway, study your mark,' he looked at the picture of the man on the screen. 'Tesla will be forty-nine years old; he was born in Serbia and still carried the accent; he was best known for his revolutionary work in the field of electricity and magnetism. He patented the A/C alternating current power, so he knew his stuff. His fame rivalled that of any scientist and inventor in history, but his downfall was his eccentric personality; he would make what was believed to be strange and bizarre claims about scientific and technological developments.' Ned looked at the people around the table, 'And rumour has it time travel too. He was ostracised and regarded as a mad scientist, but apparently, someone believed in him.'

'What have Phoenix gained from this?' Hennessey closed the file in front of him.

'I'm still trying to work that out, from 1906 world history is a mess Phoenix have hidden themselves well, that or their plan hasn't come to fruition yet.' Ned chewed his lip; he hated not knowing what they were up to.

Tannis read more of her file in silence then rested her chin on her hands and closed her eyes. Ned knew what she was thinking, 'History dictated their deaths already, you know that Tannis.'

'It doesn't sit right though does it, big brother, once again our success means over three thousand dead,' she sighed.

'No, it doesn't,' he too had a memory stirring inside him. Hennessey looked directly at Jack, 'Do you see this as a problem Colonel?'

'No sir,' he replied, 'we'll remain detached.'

'So, we go back three days before the quake is due and stake out Tesla's hotel,' Ben read aloud. Jack pulled a photo from his file now and tut tutted at Tannis as he showed her what she would be wearing.

'Great more armour plating,' she groaned then sat up and took the picture from Jack, 'a chambermaid!'

Ned nodded 'You must try and get a job at either Tesla's hotel or the one opposite where the rest of your team will be staying, but preferably Tesla's, if not though you'll have to get in with the girls that work there for any info on him.' He looked at Ben and Jack 'You two can pass as travelling gentlemen seeing the sights and sounds, it was a common occurrence.'

'Very well team, requisition your gear and meet in the hold at 17.30 hrs,' Hennessey stood and left.

Ned looked at them all, 'You have until 05.12 hrs on April 18th, that's when the quake hit, and this isn't defending yourselves in battle. This is mother nature at her most vicious, I'll see you downstairs.' He walked to the door, then turned as he remembered something, 'Jack, Caroline and the kids can stay with us while you're away.' Jack nodded to his friend, 'Appreciate it,' then he turned to his team and opened his file again, 'so what do we know?'

Down in the hold, Jack and Ben were dressed in their black cutaway morning coats with high button waistcoats, creased fly front trousers, high collar shirt and tie, they held their top hats and gloves in their hands. Tannis was dressed more conservatively as a servant; she wore a shirtwaist which was a costume with a bodice, tailored to look like a man's shirt with a high collar and an ankle length skirt with black button boots. She looked at her teammates and pulled a face, 'Toffs,' she teased.

Ned hugged her as always before she left on a mission, 'And you watch out for the real bloody toffs trying to take advantage of the servants,' he warned her.

'Oh, I think we both know how that will turn out, don't we big brother?' she raised an eyebrow. He squeezed her hand and stepped back to stand with Hennessey who addressed his people, 'Alpha team, good luck!'

It was April 15th, three days before the quake was due. Tannis had managed to find a position in the very hotel Tesla would be staying at; this was because Jack had paid one of the chambermaids handsomely to go and find work somewhere else. Tesla hadn't checked in yet though.

Her teammates had found rooms in the boarding house opposite which gave them an excellent view of the room Tesla would be occupying, and the two men took it in turns to sit at the window and keep watch, nothing was happening though, and they soon became bored. So, Jack decided to go for a walk and take in the sights until it was his turn to take over from Ben.

Tannis, on the other hand, worked like a dog, she was up at 0500 hrs and expected to work until 2100 hrs when the hotel then turned over to the night porter. She was told that she was entitled to one Sunday off a month and an afternoon off once a week at the manager's discretion. She was allocated a bed in the attic in a room that she shared with five other girls, fortunately for her they all had 'gentlemen' friends as they called them and covered for each other at night, when they slipped out through their dormitory window and down a trellis at the back of the hotel. It was a precarious way of escape at the best of times, but even more challenging in the clothes of the day; Tannis was amazed none of them had been killed or seriously injured. But no matter what, it was the only way out, and it was the route she took that night as she made her way to the park where she would meet with one of her team. She had no idea which one it would be as she rounded the corner and sat on the first bench she came to and waited.

She smiled and stood up as she saw Jack walking towards her, he was wearing working class clothes so as not to look out of place, she took his arm and they walked on together. 'Nothing yet,' she reported making sure they were out of earshot of the other strolling couples, 'I've looked in the guest book, and I don't see him booked in.'

'Well, it must be soon whatever Phoenix has got planned for him will surely take time to set up,' Jack replied quietly.

'The sooner, the better, they've got me knackered in there,' she yawned.

'Listen,' Jack stopped walking and turned to her, 'you're probably going to be the one who spots Phoenix first...'

'Jack, I've been doing this a long time, don't worry I won't engage unless it's my only option,' her tone told him she meant it.

'I know you won't love, just be careful there's no one to watch your back over there,' he whispered.

She smiled now, 'I was alone before you lot showed up, you know.'

'Yeah, and that was then, you're with us now, we're family,' he shrugged, 'besides, couldn't be bothered getting used to a new teammate,' he joked.

Tannis opened her mouth in mock horror, 'You'd struggle to find someone who'd put up with the pair of you!' She took his arm again, and he walked her back to the hotel. It was dark in the backyard, but it didn't take long for their eyes to adjust, 'You lot climb up and down that?' Jack looked at the shoddy trellis and the pitch of the roof that led to it.

'I can manage,' she followed his gaze.

'In that getup?' He looked at her outfit, 'And those lot aren't trained like you, what if one of them fell?'

'They've got a worse fate than that coming Jack,' she sighed.

He was silent for a moment deep in thought which she picked up on quickly, 'Don't think about it; it'll drive you crazy.'

He smiled now trying to shrug it off and looked up as he noticed someone looking down from the attic window, 'It would seem we have an audience.'

'No privacy when you share with five other girls,' Tannis rolled her eyes.

'I should go,' he whispered.

'So, Rose, is this your gentleman?' A voice came from behind them.

Tannis spun around, 'Charlotte, yes this is Jack.'

'And this is Herbert,' her roommate introduced, 'we should be getting in Rose,' Charlotte warned as she led her beau towards the trellis where she pulled him into a passionate embrace, only releasing him to climb back to the attic room. Herbert walked off into the night as Charlotte reached the summit and was pulled in through the open window by a roommate. Then the two of them then leaned out of the window as Charlotte called down in a loud whisper, 'Come on Rose, no need to be shy.'

They had no choice, Jack pulled her towards him and held her in his arms as she nuzzled his neck, it wasn't enough, Charlotte still stared down at them. Tannis looked up at him as she wrapped her arms around his neck. 'It's not real Jack,' he nodded, and his lips were on hers. Tannis was trying desperately to think of anything other than what was happening at that moment; her mind flashed back to as many of her previous missions as she could think of. Remembering all the fear, pain, tastes and smells; she was fighting the Romans, being shot down over Germany in World War Two, in the trenches of Belgium 1915, in a firefight in Vietnam and finally clinging to the Titanic as it sank into the freezing water.

Satisfied, Charlotte and her companion left them to it, which was fortunate as when Jack pulled back, he gasped and looked at Tannis in shock, he'd seen her thoughts too.

'Oh, my God Jack, I'm so sorry, I was trying to think of something else, I didn't realise,' she looked at him in wide-eyed fear trying to remember what she had thought of.

'That was incredible,' he whispered, then clarified, 'I mean the experience, not the kiss, I mean, you know what I'm saying, is that what happened to you that night in 1733?'

She nodded, 'I'm sorry Jack, I...'

'Do you do this to Ben, I know it's none of my business but...?'

'No,' she blushed, 'it's different.'

'What do you mean?' He pushed.

'Well, when you kiss Caroline, I doubt you have past missions on your mind.'

'Ahh yeah, I see what you mean,' it was his turn to be a little embarrassed now.

'Are you ok, I mean it was a bit of a crash course?' She looked up at him again.

'It certainly was a rush,' he grinned.

She kissed him on the cheek now as she always did, 'Night Jack,' and she walked over to the trellis to begin her ascent, unlike Charlotte's good time guy Jack waited in the shadows until he saw her safely inside.

As he walked back to his own rooms he wondered if he should mention it to Ben, he knew that he and Tannis had no secrets from each other, and it was only a mission after all. He opened the door to their suite and went inside; Ben was sitting by the window keeping a watch on a still unoccupied room. Jack walked over and sat with his friend, he retold the uneventful, yet hard day Tannis had endured, then told him about the moment back at the hotel. Ben's reaction surprised him, 'Better you than Harmon, I can trust you, she's had to kiss Will and Cole before on missions before too,' he told his friend.

Then the two men went on to discuss what Jack had seen of her memories. Tannis had told Ben about all of the missions she could remember, so none of them came as a surprise to him. But the fact that Jack felt her emotions as if he were there was a shock, especially when Jack told him that during all of what he saw she was terrified, but still carried on with the mission regardless, and not only protected her mark, but defended her brothers and sisters with no regard for her own safety.

Ben looked across to the hotel where his wife slept, 'Lionheart,' he said quietly.

'That's what I can never get across, no matter how many mission reports I write, I suppose Will summed it up, she's the best of us,' Jack too looked over the street and gave a small smile.

The morning of the 16th dawned early for Tannis, she was up and dressed at 05.00 hrs and having a meagre breakfast with her roommates, then it was off to work, cleaning the rooms downstairs, laying the dining tables and helping in the kitchen, basically anything she was told to.

It was hard work, but the time certainly flew by. It was 1000 hrs when Mr Smith, the man in charge of housekeeping, told Tannis to make sure room 37 was clean and ready for a guest who would be arriving at lunch time. She bobbed a half curtsey as was required to respect his authority over her and went to do her job.

'So, it's today,' she thought to herself as she unlocked the door to room 37 and stepped inside, locking it behind her she walked over to the window and opened it taking a breath of cool but maybe not so fresh air, the first she'd had all day. She looked across the street, it wasn't hard to find Jack and Ben, she knew they would be watching the room, and as soon as she opened the window, Ben had stood and opened theirs.

Aware that other guests occupied the room opposite Tannis used sign language to tell him 1200 hrs, then she got on with her work. In their suite, Ben didn't take his eyes off her as he spoke to Jack 'Tannis is making up the room, he's checking in at 1200 hrs.'

Jack nodded, 'Tell her to observe only not to interact; she's to stay out of sight.'

Ben waited for her to look over again, when she did, he signed the message, she nodded her understanding.

'And tell her I'll meet her at the same time and place tonight.'

Ben signed the new message and tacked on I love you and be careful at the end of it. She smiled and replied with her own words of affection then she was gone.

That afternoon, as Jack watched for Tesla Ben, went into town and made discreet enquiries to find out if anyone had been placing orders for any unusual amounts of electrical equipment. He thought he had struck out until the last store he called at told him they had an unusually large order placed just last week. Ben showed his fake ID, so the manager was more than happy to help the police and supply him with the delivery address. Out in the street, Ben read the address again and shoved the paper in his pocket and hurried back to their rooms.

He rushed into their suite, 'A large order was placed last week for generators and power cables. It was delivered two days before we got here.'

'Good work Major,' Jack stood up and put his jacket on, 'we'll check it out,' he motioned to the window, 'Tesla checked in, he's sleeping now.'

Ben walked over and looked out of the window and saw the man lying on his bed, 'That's the problem, sir, he had it delivered to the hotel, whatever Phoenix are up to it's all over there.'

Jack thought, 'Well there's nothing around the back, it must be in the cellar.' He looked again at the sleeping man. 'He's not up to much now, can you see Tannis anywhere?'

Ben scoured the windows, 'She'll be along to one of the rooms soon, the guests will be ringing for afternoon tea.' They waited, and sure enough fifteen minutes later she walked into one of the rooms carrying a huge tray full of tea, cakes and sandwiches. She placed it on a table and saw Ben signalling that they needed to talk, she nodded and left the room walking to the window in the hall. He gave her a brief outline of what he'd found out and told her to check out the cellar, but for God's sake be careful. She acknowledged her orders and left.

That night Jack waited at the prearranged meeting place for Tannis, she was ten minutes late, not like her, he thought, but maybe she'd been held up at work, as twenty minutes passed, he began to worry.

'Reckon Rose has found someone else Jack,' it was Charlotte with a different beau tonight.

'How so?' He asked her.

'She's gone, cleared out during afternoon tea,' she called over her shoulder.

Jack went quickly back to their suite; he startled Ben as he burst in. 'She didn't show and one of the girls told me she's cleared out and gone.' Ben was on his feet in an instant, he moved over to the nearby chest and opened it, arming himself with the weapons inside, Jack did the same. They went around the back of the hotel Tannis had been working in, it was deserted but, in the darkness, they could see that the cellar doors had been left open, they went cautiously inside; it was empty, but there were signs that something heavy had been dragged along the dirt floor. 'God, damn it she could be anywhere,' Ben cursed as he looked around for any sign as to where they could've gone.

Jack turned quickly as the door near to him began to open, he put an arm around the half open door and grabbed the person on the other side of it and pulled them into the room. It was Mr Smith, head of housekeeping, he raised his hands and trembled, 'Please don't hurt me, there's nothing down here worth stealing,' he babbled.

'What was down here?' Jack's tone was harsh.

'I've no idea; it was all arranged by telegraph before the guest arrived, just equipment to be stored here until he arrived and would move it to another location,' Smith still had his hands raised.

'Where?' Ben snapped.

'I don't know it was all taken away by cart this afternoon, I was just coming down to see how much mud needed cleaning up, they made two trips you see and brought it back in with them,' he pointed to muddy footprints on the steps. 'It's from the old mines, and if it isn't cleaned quickly it stains.'

Jack nodded to Ben, and they were gone, leaving Smith thinking he was lucky to be alive, but for how much longer was anybody's guess.

They ran to the stables and hired the two fastest horses available, then after getting directions to the mining area, they set off. They had been told it would take them until morning to get there; it was difficult terrain at the best of times, never mind in the dark. They rode hard through the night, minds racing as to what they might find, which Phoenix agents it might be, Ben hoped it would be Rafe for two reasons, the first being Rafe wouldn't kill Tannis, and secondly, he would like to finish Rafe himself. Jack too was wondering who they were up against and was Tannis still alive, if she were surely there would've been more of a mess in the cellar, blood for a start, when her back was to the wall Tannis would fight like a lion, so what the hell had happened. Both men rode on in silence pushing their thoughts to the backs of their minds, they had a job to do and thinking of the what ifs would only screw up their straight thinking, and they were no good to her that way.

The sun was rising on the morning of the 17th as they reached the abandoned mining area. The horses were exhausted as the two men dismounted and led them to a water trough to let them drink and pumped some fresh for themselves too. It was a vast area, and it took them a good few hours of searching to find a mine entrance with fresh tracks leading to it and horses tethered outside. Ben took out his map, 'This whole area will be devastated by the quake,' he said in a hushed tone.

'But why stop the whole thing, why don't Phoenix just save their mark and change history that way?' Jack couldn't see the reasoning behind it. Ben shrugged and took out his sidearm, 'Why don't we ask them?'

Jack nodded as he too armed himself and they slowly and silently went inside. Their eyes didn't need to adjust to the darkness because there was none, a string of light bulbs hung above their heads. The tunnel was a long one with a couple of off shoots along the way which took time to check out, but finally, the end was in sight as the tunnel opened out to reveal a more cavernous chamber. It was clear to see all the equipment had arrived, inside stood a huge generator, cables ran all over and joined with more equipment which neither man had any idea of their uses.

From their vantage point still hidden in the tunnel, Jack and Ben could see Tesla busying himself with the machinery. He must've left the hotel while they were checking out the cellar; there were others there too with him standing in the shadows still they were able to count just two of them, a typical Phoenix unit.

'Step into the light, c'mon let's see which of you bastards we're up against,' Jack muttered as Ben searched the shadows for any sign of his wife but found none.

One of the figures stepped forward now closely followed by the other, well that explained how Tannis had been taken; she wouldn't sense them sneaking up on her. The two perps were Dr Richardson and Sgt Hicks, if Kira or Nyra had gone into the body of anyone in the hotel Tannis wouldn't know there was an attack coming. The two men both looked at one another knowing they had just thought the same thing. A faint breeze blew over them as a small light passed by and rushed into Richardson's body, after which she looked up and called out, 'Why don't you come down and join us Colonel Marsters, Major Rhodes!'

'Bugger,' Jack frowned.

'Tannis is still alive, so let's talk shop shall we, unarmed of course, throw your weapons out in front of you,' as she spoke Hicks raised his own handgun.

With little choice, the two men threw their side-arms out and walked into the cavernous chamber.

'Well, I guess Tesla here is playing unwilling host to Nyra,' Jack looked at the scientist, 'and you're playing host to Kira,' he glared at Richardson before looking over to Hicks, 'So that just makes you a treasonous bastard.'

'You should mind your manners Colonel under the circumstances don't you think,' Hicks snarled then turned his attention to Ben pouting his bottom lip, 'What's the matter Major, lost something?' he taunted.

'Where is she?' Ben snarled.

'Oh, she's shall we say...resting,' Kira spoke from Richardson now, 'waiting to take her place with us.'

'Like that's gonna be an option,' Ben sneered.

'Oh, you will all be joining us soon Major, in fact, this has worked out better than we could've expected, not only will the future be ours, but Atlantis too,' she laughed maliciously.

'Atlantis doesn't take kindly to riff raff, you'll never get in,' Jack raised his head defiantly.

'It is ready,' Nyra spoke through Tesla.

'Excellent,' Kira's voice echoed as she looked from Ben to Jack, 'I suppose you want to know why we're saving three thousand lives gentlemen?'

'Well, I guess you want hosts,' Ben frowned.

'Very good Major, yes this is a natural weak spot between our dimensions and the two will merge at precisely 05.15 hrs tomorrow so long as there are no disturbances in the electromagnetic field.' Richardson waved her hand toward the machinery, 'And this will take care of all of that for us, it will create a field so strong the fault will be held together, our dimensions will merge, and we will be unstoppable.'

'You know Tannis is right, why does this kind always want to rule the world? What's wrong with a little coexistence?' Jack turned to Ben who just nodded and folded his arms across his chest.

Nyra leapt from Tesla and into Hicks as the scientist's body fell unconscious to the ground.

'Now this won't hurt, you just need to be contained until we're ready for you,' Richardson pulled two syringes from her pocket and mocked them as Jack and Ben both backed away, 'C'mon big heroes like you, afraid of a little needle, granted the medication is a little primitive, but I tested it on Tannis, and she survived, and her dose was much stronger than this.'

'You Bitch!' Jack spat.

Hicks aimed his gun at Ben's head; Jack had no choice; the needle jabbed in his arm, and he knew no more. It was Ben's turn next, his gun barrel still pushing into Ben's temple Hicks sneered, 'She's a feisty one Tannis, I like them with a bit of fight.'

'You're so full of shit Sergeant,' Ben knew he was lying.

'You think so, how can you tell I didn't have her?' Hicks' voice shook with anger.

'Cos you're still breathing.'

'Yeah well, when she's got a host, she's mine for the taking,' Hicks thought he had the high ground now.

'Where is she?' Ben struggled as the needle went into his arm. 'Waiting for me...'

He didn't hear any more of Hicks' threats; he was out of it.

Jack's head felt like it was made of marshmallow as he began to wake up, he could hear Richardson and Hicks talking close by. He opened his eyes a little; they had their backs to him, looking to his left now he saw Ben was beginning to stir he looked toward their captors first too then Jack who tapped his watch, it was almost 2200 hrs seven hours and twelve minutes to the quake.

Jack signalled for Ben to fake unconsciousness, he nodded and closed his eyes as Jack began to groan and stir. Richardson and Hicks moved over to him, she took another syringe from her pocket and flipped the cap off as Nyra questioned her, 'I thought you said they would remain sedated until it was time?'

'Richardson had not the exact measures to make certain, she had to be cautious or risk killing them, then Atlantis would remain,' Kira told her partner as the body she cohabitated knelt to administer another dose. 'We still don't know if Atlantis will let us in,' Nyra added.

Hicks made to kick Ben in the ribs to make sure he wasn't faking, but Ben grabbed his leg and pulled. Hicks fell flat on his back, his gun fired as he went down, but he didn't recover. Ben was on him in a second, he punched him hard and grabbed the gun shoving it hard in his temple this time, 'Where is she?' he shouted. Richardson had been a walk over for Jack, he threw her to the ground and dropped the syringe stamping on it.

'I believe Major Rhodes asked you a question,' Jack kicked Hicks as he lay prostrate.

'You can't kill me, it's against regulations I have to be taken back for trial,' he squirmed.

Jack laughed, 'Do you think this kind of mission is covered by regulations? And even if it was, Major Rhodes gets annoyed when someone threatens his wife, I doubt I could stop him even if I wanted to,' he leaned a little closer, 'and I don't want to.'

Hicks looked at Richardson; Jack knew exactly what they were thinking, 'Major the moment one of them tries to get their spooky arse near us kill the host.' Ben nodded and cocked his weapon, 'I'm not going to ask again,' he looked at Hicks his face full of hatred.

'She's in Tesla's room back at the hotel,' he cracked.

Richardson taunted them, 'What are you going to do Colonel, if you let the quake happen, you'll never get back in time to save her.'

Jack looked at his watch, it would be cutting it fine but what choice did they have, if they let history change, they'd be dead anyway or as good as. Ben kept watch on them as Jack tried to wake Tesla, the Serb began to stir, and Jack helped him to stand. 'What is happening, where am I?' His accent was still strong. Jack knew they had very little time, so he made it up as he went along. He showed Tesla his fake ID and told him it was a matter of national security. 'These people are from a government enemy to ours and are plotting to overthrow the west, can you fix the equipment to destroy itself?'

Tesla looked at the generator and all that surrounded it, 'Yes sir I can,' he nodded as he walked over to the power cables and began rerouting them and after a few moments he returned, 'you have ten minutes.'

'Very good Mr Tesla, now leave the mine, there are horses outside take one and head east, do you understand, ride hard and do not stop, and you must never mention this to a living soul, the security of the nation depends on it.' Jack told him.

'I understand sir and thank you,' Tesla nodded, and half bowed to them then hurried away.

Jack crouched down and ripped the timepieces off the traitor's wrists. 'Get up,' he motioned to the generator that was now humming louder and louder, 'that's rigged to blow, feel free to mess with it, it won't help you, but it will do us a favour if you die in the blast.'

'So, you're going to murder three thousand people, Colonel?' Richardson shouted, 'you're starting a quake that will kill them all, your precious Tannis included.'

Ben punched Hicks and left him where he fell, Richardson screamed and lunged at Jack, 'You can't leave us here to die,' she wailed as he pushed her away. 'Like you were going to kill us on the beach if Tannis hadn't stopped you, what goes around comes around Doctor!'

The two men hurried out of the mine; it was dark outside; Tesla had done as he was told and was long gone.

'This is going to be close sir,' Ben looked at his CO as they released the spare horses and mounted their own, 'maybe you should get back to The Eldridge the mission's over.'

'Nobody gets left behind Major, you know the rules.'

'You've got family to get back to, I've got nothing without her,' Ben told him.

'We are family Ben, and besides, I wouldn't have a family if she hadn't gone back for them, would I?' His tone indicated the conversation was over.

They spurred the horses on and rode as hard as they could, not even looking back when the mine exploded, they didn't care about Richardson and Hicks, Tannis was their priority.

God if it must end badly, please don't let her wake up Jack thought to himself as they rode into San Francisco with minutes to spare, the city was stirring, unaware of the fate that awaited them.

They ran into the hotel dirty from their ride, the night porter tried to stop them, they didn't have time to argue so Ben punched him out as they headed for the stairs. Room thirty-seven was easily found, the door was locked, Ben kicked it open, and they raced inside, Jack pushed the door into the splintered frame as best he could to close it. Ben hurried over to the bed and pulled the covers back, there she was bound and gagged but only sleeping. 'Tannis, wake up Babe we gotta get out of here,' he untied the ropes and took the gag off as she began to come around, slowly at first then she remembered herself, 'Ben, it's Richardson and Hicks we have to…'

'It's taken care of,' he smiled 'you've been out of it for a while, we have to go now,' he told her as she looked at the clock. 'Oh my God, two minutes,' her hand went to her head as she sat up, she was still groggy.

Jack joined them, 'Make the leap with Ben, you're too weak,' he began to adjust his timepiece Ben likewise.

'They're not working,' they both said at the same time.

'It's the quake, the Earth's electromagnetic field is temporarily shifting,' Tannis groaned then there was a deafening rumble, 'It's started,' she shouted.

'Move!' Jack yelled.

Ben took Tannis by the hand, and they all ran out of the room as the whole building began to shake so violently that they were thrown to the ground several times, finally they were almost hurled down the stairs and showered with chunks of plaster that fell from the ceiling. They picked themselves up and ran outside, but it was no safer in the street as huge chunks of masonry from the buildings surrounding them began to rain down, and terrified horses stampeded through the streets.

People now poured outside covered in blood and screaming, that was when the buildings began to fall like dominoes. There was another deafening roar followed by a massive explosion. The gas mains had ruptured; Jack was thrown across the street as the ground writhed and burst apart; the road beneath Ben's feet fell away. Tannis quickly grabbed his hand as he dropped into the chasm below, she landed on her stomach and looking over the edge she could see he was hanging in mid-air with a fire raging below him. She had nothing to hold on to, and his weight was slowly pulling her in with him. 'Let go,' he gasped with the heat. 'Never,' she leaned closer and grabbed his other hand then felt herself being pulled backwards by the ankles. Tannis was out of the hole now still hanging on to Ben as Jack leaned over and helped pull him out. The ground was still shaking, and all three of them looked up to see the huge brick building above them begin to buckle and collapse, it was going to fall on them. The team had nowhere to go, they huddled together and awaited their fate.

But fate had other plans; they were safe above the city in the hills. Tannis had managed a small leap, it was twelve hours later. The two men lay her down, and Jack covered her with his coat then left Ben to watch over her as he walked a few steps away and looked down on the devastation, the quake was over, but the suffering down there was just starting.

Tannis' eyes fluttered open, and she smiled up at her husband, he touched her face gently and helped her to sit up, she leaned into him as he put an arm around her. Jack returned and sat next to her too, 'It'll burn for four days down there,' he sighed. No one spoke for a long time; they were all trying to get their emotions in order.

The beeping of the timepieces brought them all back to reality, and they stood up ready to leap, Tannis tried to wipe her dirty face then realised her hands and clothes were just as filthy, 'I must look like…'

'Shit,' Jack cut in.

'Bit rude,' Tannis frowned as she undid her top button.

'Not you,' Jack sighed, 'these are bloody fake,' he held out the timepieces he had taken from Richardson and Hicks.

'Shit,' Ben and Tannis chorused.

Chapter Four

'Well Caroline, everything looks fine ready for your C-section tomorrow,' Dr O'Brian smiled as he looked at the screen in front of him, he then turned it a little so that Jack and Caroline could see the ultrasound images of their unborn twins. The proud soon-to-be parents both smiled at one another as Jack gently squeezed his wife's hand. But their peace was shattered as the ship's tannoy echoed 'Alpha team to the briefing room, Alpha team to the briefing room.' Jack tutted then kissed his wife's hand, 'I'll see you at home later love,' then he turned to the doctor, 'see to it Caroline gets an escort home would you Doc?'

'My pleasure Colonel, in fact, I'll take care of it personally, it's my afternoon off.'

Jack hurried to the briefing room, hoping it was nothing serious, as of tomorrow he was on a month's paternity leave, bloody hell, Phoenix had better be behaving themselves, he didn't like the thought of his team away on a mission with a stand in. Sure, he knew without doubt Ben could take command, but that wasn't the point, they were more than a team, they were family. Ben had even passed up on promotion in the past to stay part of Alpha team; he had been offered his own command with a new team. But the three of them knew they were a winning combination; besides, the chain of command within wasn't so strict. Even when he had put it to Ben that he was holding back his career and rank by staying with Alpha team, Ben had looked at his CO as if he were a madman, 'Sir; this isn't about career or rank, it's our life now, what more could I want?'

Never a truer word was spoken, Jack too had been offered a promotion and a safer desk job within the coalition, an offer he turned down in a blink. Although on the bad days, they all had to agree, retirement sounded appealing, but they soon rallied and got on with things.

Ben and Tannis were already in the briefing room when Jack got there, he gave them a questioning look as he took his seat, but both of them just shrugged, they had no idea either. Hennessey walked in with Ned and looked directly at Jack. 'Don't worry Colonel, this is just a quick job, Lieutenant Jenkins is to be returned to the real world to face her court martial and requires an escort. I would like Alpha team to take care of it, just in case Phoenix tries anything.'

'Not a problem sir, be glad to get her off the island,' Jack relaxed, just got to put the rubbish out, then a month off.

'There are a few minor details; Barbara is printing off the transfer papers now,' the Admiral explained.

'Prisoner, step away,' the burley MP called through the grill in the cell door. Inside Lt Jenkins moved across to the far wall, she was in plain green fatigues, her hair tied loosely behind her head. She looked tired and drawn, too many months in solitary contemplating her fate no doubt her guard thought as he opened the door and allowed another MP to enter and put her in cuffs. 'Time for your last leap,' he said with no emotion as he made sure the restraints on her wrists were tight, but not too tight.

Jenkins never spoke as they led her out of the brig and down the passageway toward the hold, she swayed a little and both men held her up until she regained her balance. 'Told you to eat your breakfast,' the senior MP grumbled, he didn't need this, he had been babysitting this treacherous waste of space for months now, finally he was going to be rid of her, the last thing he needed was for her to be deemed unfit to travel. After a brief pause, she seemed fine, and they carried on their way.

Inside the infirmary, Dr O'Brian was just about ready to leave, ever the gentleman he picked up Caroline's bag and offered her his arm, 'Shall we Mrs Marsters?'

Caroline smiled and accepted his gesture; they were almost at the door when a commotion outside soon made its way inside. The two MP's escorting Jenkins to the hold carried her unconscious body into the room.

'She just collapsed Doc,' the senior MP explained.

'Get her on the bed,' O'Brian sighed. 'I'm sorry Mrs Marsters, I'll have someone else escort you home.'

The MP's moved to lay Jenkins on the bed; no one could've prepared them for what happened next, as she slipped from her cuffs and grabbed one of their sidearms and without hesitation, she shot the man on her left, then turned the gun on the man to her right and fired.

It all happened so fast, then she turned the weapon on Caroline 'You, over here now!' she yelled.

'If you want a hostage, a pregnant woman will only slow you down, take me instead,' O'Brian said in a calm voice.

'Very noble of you Doc, but Mrs Marsters here is a priceless bargaining chip,' she positioned herself behind Caroline, and with one arm around her neck, she used the other hand to aim the gun at her belly, then nodded to the doctor, 'now, put a call through to the Admiral.'

Barbara had just returned to her desk after delivering the letters of transfer to the briefing room when the phone rang, she put the doctor's call through and got back to her work.

'Yes, Doctor?' Hennessey spoke into the receiver, then covered the mouthpiece, 'Ned, bring up the infirmary security camera.'

Ned did so, as Hennessey placed the receiver down and pressed the speakerphone button, everyone gaped in horror at the sight they were seeing.

'I want a timepiece now, or you can guess the rest,' Jenkins yelled at the camera, then motioned with her weapon for O'Brian to hang up.

In the briefing room, Hennessey also pressed the button cancelling the speaker phone.

'I could leap in behind her and put a bullet in her head,' Tannis offered, but Jack shook his head, 'Too risky if she twitches, she could pull the trigger,' his mind was racing now, trying to stay calm and figure out a way to save his wife.

Hennessey looked at his people, it was his call, no one else's 'Tannis, leap to the hold and return here with a timepiece,' he ordered.

With a nod, she was there and back in a flash, standing by the Admiral's side, her hand outstretched offering him the timepiece.

'And now, please leap us all to the passage outside the infirmary,' Hennessey stood and took her arm as did the other three men in the room, and once again in a flash she had done as she was asked. The Admiral walked toward the infirmary door, but Jack put a hand on his arm, 'No sir, you'd just be another valuable hostage, this is my problem,' he held out his hand for the timepiece. 'Very well,' the Admiral agreed, 'give her what she wants and get your wife back safely, take no risks,' he ordered.

'I'm coming in,' Jack called as he walked slowly inside, his hands in full view, the timepiece held in his fingertips.

'Give it to her,' Jenkins motioned her head towards Caroline. Jack passed his wife the timepiece, 'Be alright love,' his voice was full of concern, Caroline just nodded, she didn't trust herself to speak. 'Put it on my wrist,' Jenkins ordered.

Caroline did as she was told, her hands trembling. Jack felt sick to his stomach, this wasn't part of the job, families were never supposed to be put at risk. 'You've got what you wanted, now let her go,' he watched Jenkins setting the timepiece. But then she just smiled an evil smile and hit the button, they were both gone.

'No!' yelled Jack, but it was too late.

Hennessey and the others rushed in; Jack almost looked through Tannis as he said, 'You were right, I should've let you kill her at Seneffe.' She took her CO's arm, 'Jack I gave her Cole's old one, it still leaks, we can track it.'

Jack snapped back to his usual self as he winked proudly at Tannis, then looked at the Admiral, 'With your permission, sir?'

'Take Foxtrot team with you Colonel; you may need backup on this one,' Hennessey agreed to Jack's request, then turned to Ned 'Track that timepiece, and both teams to the briefing room in fifteen minutes.'

'Grand Canyon, 1162,' Ned told them all when both teams plus the Admiral were seated in the briefing room. 'You'll have to move quickly, Jenkins will have no idea she's being tracked, but that old timepiece as we all know is a wee bit unstable.'

'At least it will give us a chance to get the Colonel's wife back,' Hennessey was still fuming that a civilian had been taken hostage on his ship.

They would make their plan when they got there, and with it being a largely unpopulated area, they would be travelling back in full combat gear and fully armed. Ned gave them the exact coordinates, and they all made their way down to the hold. Ned followed Foxtrot team through the hatch, but Hennessey held Alpha team back for a moment and lowered his voice. 'Colonel, your wife is the priority of this mission make no mistake, but if you get the chance, you are authorised to take care of business, once and for all, the Joint Chiefs would prefer there be no court martial.'

Alpha team nodded their understanding and followed the Admiral through the hatch. Ben and Tannis exchanged glances but said nothing.

The two teams made the leap close to the location Ned had given them, then split up and searched silently for Caroline. It didn't take them long; they could hear Jenkins shouting and yelling at her. 'Sit down, and don't move, you won't have to wait too long.'

Jack lined his sights and took aim at Jenkins' head, but he couldn't take the shot, she'd moved too close to Caroline and held the gun on her again.

'Phoenix have arrived,' Tannis whispered.

Her words were confirmed as Gunther, or one of his clones at least, walked over to the two women, he knelt in front of them where they now sat and engaged Jenkins in conversation; they saw her nodding her agreement to something, and the three of them stood, Caroline albeit dragged to her feet. Then Gunther turned to where Alpha team were in position, 'Come out and show yourselves, Alpha team,' he called as he put his hand on Caroline's belly, 'I'm sure you've heard of my talents with the unborn,' he looked to his left now, 'Foxtrot team, you too if you please.'

'Do it,' Jack spoke to them through their earpieces.

Slowly the two teams walked out into the open. 'What do you want?' Jack knew this was going to cost them heavily.

'Why I would've thought that was obvious Colonel, I want Tannis, so many tests, so little time. You know how it goes.' Gunther sneered.

It was an impossible situation; Jack sighed heavily, what could he do.

'No,' Ben put a hand on Tannis to stop her as she began to move, she turned and touched his face gently, 'It's the only way, none of us could live with the alternative,' she kissed him softly on the lips. 'I love you and I trust you; I know you'll find me.' He pulled her to him and kissed her hard on the mouth, then choked as he whispered in her ear 'I love you,' then he let her go. Jack just watched numbly as his teammate walked past him, ready to make the ultimate sacrifice to save his wife and unborn children.

'Send Caroline over, we both start walking together!' Tannis yelled.

So far, Jenkins and Gunther kept their part of the bargain and let Caroline begin walking when Tannis did. The two women met halfway, 'Hands behind your back, Tannis,' Gunther called out, 'we don't want any cheeky leaps with Mrs Marsters now do we?' Tannis glared but did as he said. It turns out he did her a favour, as behind her Tannis dropped her timepiece into the dust. 'It'll be alright,' she smiled at Caroline, 'when I pass, stumble and pick up my timepiece, just press the button on the side, and you'll be back on The Eldridge before you know it.'

'You shouldn't have done this,' Caroline said tearfully, 'they'll kill you.'

'Oh, I wouldn't worry too much, they've been trying to do that for years,' Tannis bluffed, 'they're not very good at it.'

Jack and Ben watched as the two women passed each other, Caroline made her fake stumble, grabbed the timepiece and she was gone. 'Clever girl,' Jack smiled. 'Now let's get her back.'

Jenkins aimed her weapon at Tannis now as she picked up the pace on her path toward them. Tannis frowned at Gunther, who just shrugged, 'What can I say, she's not one of mine,' he apologised. Jenkins gave him a confused look, then looked back at Tannis and pulled the trigger. Instantly Tannis thrust her hand out, palm forward and stopped the bullets in mid-air. They dropped helplessly into the dirt as Tannis continued her march on the now unarmed woman. 'You can't touch me,' Jenkins backed away. 'I have to be sent back for trial,' she stammered. Then she noticed the red dot making its way up her chest toward her head. 'No trial,' Tannis sneered as the bullet spat past her and into Jenkins' skull.

Some way behind her Jack lowered his weapon; she then turned her attention to Gunther, 'Mine I think,' she spoke to the two teams. But before she could even make a move on him, all hell let loose, explosions detonated all around, Tannis was knocked to the ground by the first, and a short while later both Jack and Ben were out of the fight as an explosion close by sent debris flying in their direction.

Sgt Williams of Foxtrot team managed to run to Tannis and tried to drag her to cover while his teammates were being pinned down by heavy bombardment and could see nothing until the smoke cleared. When it did, Sgt Williams lay dead, and Tannis was nowhere to be seen.

By the time, Jack and Ben regained consciousness; they were already back on The Eldridge in the infirmary with Caroline hovering nervously between the two of them. 'Mrs Marsters, you really should sit down,' Dr O'Brian said firmly as he brought her a chair.

'Caroline?' Jack croaked, both he and Ben had had their throats suctioned to remove debris. He sat up, and his wife was in his arms sobbing her heart out. 'Calm down love; this isn't going to do you or the babies any good.'

Ben began to stir now in the next bed, he opened his eyes and saw Caroline with Jack as he sat up, 'Where's Tannis?' he croaked.

'She's missing,' Ned stood at the foot of his brother-in-law's bed.

After washing and dressing their bruised and battered bodies, and making their way to the briefing room, Ned and Hennessey filled them in on the events leading up to Tannis' disappearance.

'So, no one saw anything, and we've no idea who took her, or where she went?' Ben fumed.

There was a knock at the door, and Major Watson of Foxtrot team hurried into the room, 'Sorry to interrupt sirs, but I had an idea, with my Sgt being the only one to reach Tannis and drag her out of the shelling. 'Well, I checked his helmet camera and found this,' he handed a small memory chip to Ned, who loaded it into his laptop. The screen on the wall came to life, showing the Sgt's view as he was dragging an unconscious Tannis out of harm's way, but suddenly he let go of her and fell to his knees and looked down at his chest, his hands were covered in blood, he had been hit by something. Then he fell on his side, presumably dead, but the camera kept running, focused on Tannis. Seconds later as she lay motionless, a man knelt by her side to check for signs of life, they all recognised Rafe.

Ned paused the film, 'Well at least we know who, but where?' 'Keep rolling,' the Major gestured.

The film continued, and they watched as Rafe injected her with something, then clearly not noticing the camera he set his timepiece and reached down to pick Tannis up. 'Freeze it there, and zoom in,' Ned did as he was asked, and there right in front of them on Rafe's timepiece were the coordinates.

'Excellent work Major Watson,' Hennessey said proudly.

'Fine Marine,' Ben grinned.

Jack winked at Watson, then turned to Ned, 'Right, where are we off to then?'

As Ned brought up the location on the laptop and relayed it to the main screen, Hennessey turned to Jack, 'Colonel; your leave begins in less than two hours, Major Rhodes will have to lead another team on this mission.'

'With respect sir, this shouldn't take too long, I'll be back before the twins are born and besides, she's my teammate, and it was my wife and children that she risked her life to save... again.' Jack objected.

'Knew you'd say that Colonel, but I had to put it to you,' Hennessey shrugged.

'Err Ned; you wanna run those coordinates, one more time?' Ben frowned at the screen.

'50 degrees 03 degrees North, 6 degrees 04 degrees West, 8th November 1099,' Ned confirmed without looking up.

'Well, that doesn't make sense, there's no land there, just a reef off the south-west coast of England.'

'Oh God, not seven stones reef,' Ned groaned. Ben just nodded.

'Crazy bastard, he's taken her back to the lost land of Lyonesse,' Ned slumped back in his chair, 'what bloody reason could he have for taking her there?'

'Let's back it up here, why did it become known as the lost land of Lyonesse?' Ben knew it wasn't going to be a pleasant explanation.

'Oh right, yes,' Ned gathered himself 'In 1099, Lyonesse was an exceptional country located beyond Land's End, it boasted fine cities, 140 churches, enormous wealth, however on 11th, November 1099, a huge storm hit, and the whole country was lost, submerged beneath the sea. The only part that remained above the water were the mountain peaks, now known as the Scilly Isles. It's only a legend, but sailors say on a stormy night, they can still hear the church bells ringing.'

'Some kind of Tsunami?' Jack mused.

'Wrath of God, call it what you like, some say it was a punishment for the inhabitant's Godless ways. But it doesn't explain why he's taken her there and more importantly then,' Ned puzzled.

Hennessey nodded slowly, 'Yes, there's more to this.'

It was a beautiful cold winter's morning when the two men made their leap to Lyonesse; they arrived a short distance from the coordinates that Rafe had plotted and from their cover in the trees they looked ahead and saw a huge castle sprawling on the hillside 'Typical Rafe, all show,' Ben sighed.

'I was thinking along the lines of Gunther, and the whole mad scientist's lair,' Jack muttered.

'Yeah, that too,' his friend agreed.

They were dressed in woollen shirts, trousers and leather boots, all covered by long cloaks, the hoods of which they now pulled over their heads as they made their way to the rear of the castle.

A wooden door in the wall was open, and from inside they could hear swords clashing, peering cautiously around the entrance they rushed in, as they heard a woman calling for help. 'That's Tannis,' Ben would know her voice anywhere, they raced into what looked like the kitchen garden, two men lay dead on the ground, they were well-dressed men at arms. Meanwhile, two hooded assailants now chased Tannis.

'Why is she running?' Jack looked across at his teammate as they gave chase, they both knew she could take these guys. In her haste, she tripped on her long skirt and fell. Her attackers were close and raised their weapons for the kill, but they hadn't counted on her teammates having her back, they quickly dispatched the two thugs, and Ben offered a hand up to his wife, 'Tannis, are you alright?'

'You know me?' She was still wary of the situation.

'Are you kidding, of course, I know you,' he laughed thinking she was joking.

'I'm sorry, I had an accident, and my memory is lost to me for the moment,' she showed them a stitched scar on her head, it was healing, but there had been no wound when they saw her on helmet cam footage. She thought carefully, 'I feel I should know you, and your friend,' she acknowledged Jack now.

'Tannis,' Rafe yelled as he and Gunther thundered across the lawn towards them and raised a handgun at Ben.

'No, you will not harm these men, they protected me when yours failed to do so, leaving the garden door open again when they slope off into town, this has to stop, thieves breaking in, raping the servants and stealing what they can.'

'You do not know these men,' he countered.

'I do, well I think I do,' she turned to her teammates, 'I thank you for your protection and am sure when my memory returns, I will know you because I trust you already and that does not happen. As my latest bodyguards are no longer with us, would you consider taking their place? We can give you food and shelter and pay you for your services.'

Jack bowed to her, 'Thank you, my lady, we accept.'

Ben meanwhile glared at the two Phoenix agents, who returned his stare in kind.

'Very well,' Rafe begrudged, 'but as your Doctor, Gunther should have a talk with them about your condition,' he led Tannis a short distance away.

Gunther was clearly condescending to speak with them. 'If her memory is to return, it is to be of her own free will, if you, or we for that matter try and force memories on her, she could lose her mind forever. Do not try a leap with her; you will have noticed the incision I have made in her skull. There is a small explosive device in there if a leap of any sort is tried, it's game over.'

'You bastard, you know fine well what's going to happen to this place in a few days,' Ben was held back by his CO.

'Oh, don't worry, it will dissolve, once her memory has been reconditioned and she is one of us.'

'I thought you said none of us could force a memory onto her?' Jack glowered.

'Oh, we can't, but there are other factors at work here, and if she is still reluctant, then the terror of what will happen here will make her more susceptible to the process.' Gunther turned and left.

'He's drugging her; there's no way Tannis would've run from those men back there, even if she had lost her memory, her instinct would've kicked in,' Jack sneered. 'We've got our work cut out for us Major.' Jack looked at his friend, but Ben was staring at Rafe and Tannis, he was trying to put his arm around her, but she kept shrugging him off, 'Something of her is still there,' he whispered.

That night at dinner Rafe took his position at the head of the table with Gunther to his right, opposite Jack, Ben took his seat next to Gunther. Tannis soon followed them in and sat next to Jack.

Rafe frowned 'Tannis, you're seated in the wrong place.'

She looked around the table as if struggling with a memory, 'No, you and Gunther are,' she said as a sharp pain shot through her head, her hand went to her temple as she gasped at the sensation. Then a drop of blood trickled from her nose which she quickly wiped away with her napkin.

'Did you remember something?' Rafe raised an eyebrow.

'I was trying to, but then the pain came again,' she touched her head once more.

'So, have you told our guests about our impending wedding?' Rafe sneered at Ben.

'Well, as I have no memory of you proposing and me accepting, all I have is your word for it taking place,' she shot back.

The room fell silent as the food arrived, but before anyone took a bite, Tannis leaned across the table and pulled Ben's plate toward her and made to eat from it.

'No!' Gunther glared at Tannis as he stood and took Ben and Jack's meals away.

Tannis returned his glare as she stood quickly, then told the maid servant to bring food enough for the three of them to her rooms. 'We will share the food between us,' she said to no one in particular, but it was a warning not to try anything like that again. As she passed by Rafe, he grabbed her by the wrist and tried to pull her down to him,

'Not even a goodnight kiss for your future husband?' he asked, a direct taunt at Ben.

Tannis just pulled free and walked away.

Once the three of them were inside her rooms, Tannis slammed the doors as hard as she could and paced up and down. 'This cannot be right, the feelings I have toward him, and we're not even married yet.'

Ben sat down heavily on a bench, 'You have feelings for Rafe?'

'Ben,' Jack shook his head, why was his friend going to put himself through this.

'What sort of feelings?' he pressed, ignoring Jack's warning.

'Well, like tonight at dinner, when he asked me to kiss him, I really had to control myself,' she confessed.

'You wanted to kiss him?' Ben was stunned.

'God, no,' she wrinkled her nose, 'I wanted to stab him, and that's got to be wrong hasn't it, I mean to feel that way about the man I'm supposed to be marrying?'

Ben grinned, 'Just follow your instincts and you'll be fine.'

The servants brought more food and left them in peace to share their meal. Tannis seemed to relax as it was just the three of them, but her mood changed once more when Gunther let himself into the outer chamber, 'I have your medication Tannis,' he snapped as he carried a syringe on a small metal tray.

'No,' she shook her head. 'I don't want it; it clouds my mind and makes my reactions slow.'

'You must take it; it will help with the pain in your head,' he commanded.

'The pain is the only thing that reminds me I am alive, I won't take it,' she held her head high in defiance.

'You will follow orders!' He snapped.

'I don't follow your orders,' Tannis threw back at him, then something in her subconscious made her turn and look at Jack, who just gave Gunther a sarcastic grin, 'The lady said no.'

'The ruler of time follows her own path,' Rafe hastily cut in from the doorway; he didn't want the conversation going any further, 'leave it for tonight,' he told Gunther.

'Oh, don't start that again,' Tannis went into her bedroom and slammed the door shut.

'Sleep well,' Rafe scowled as he and Gunther left the room.

'Ruler of time?' Jack gave his friend a knowing look, 'using drugs to suppress and alter her memory, same old Phoenix.'

'Yeah, well let's see how far they get now she's refusing her medication,' Ben stared after her.

An hour or so later, the two men were still awake when they heard Tannis open her bedroom door; she was in her long flowing nightgown, showing only her bare feet at the hem. She shivered and moved to sit by the fire. Ben wrapped a blanket around her shoulders and sat next to her, while Jack sat opposite.

'They tell me that we have fought to put time right for many years, firstly against a group called *DE-173*, then the coalition. Rafe says that we were to be married, but the coalition attacked us, that's when I lost my memory,' she looked from one man to the other for any expression that might give her some clue as to the truth, 'he says, that together we can rule time and put an end to the coalition, who are always changing the past and making innocent people suffer.'

'And what do you think?' *Bastards*, Jack thought, they couldn't tell her the truth, but Phoenix can fill her head full of lies and enforce them with memory-altering drugs.

Tannis stared into the flames, 'If I don't take the medication, at night I have the most terrible nightmares, I see people suffering and dying. Rafe tells me that this is the work of the coalition, and that is why we must stop them,' she didn't take her eyes from the flames 'but personally, I wouldn't trust Rafe as far as I could throw him,' she smiled a ruthless smile. 'Although there's a pretty high cliff on the other side of the castle, I wouldn't mind shoving him off.' She gave them both a serious look now, 'Why did you come here? Rafe said you were sent by the coalition to kill me, but I know that's not true,' she stood and walked to the window. 'Let's just say; we've got your back.' Jack replied.

Next morning Tannis sent her ladies away again when they came to help her get dressed, then, when she didn't come out of her room after they returned with breakfast, Jack sent Ben in to get her. He knocked on the door, when he got no reply, he opened it and went inside. The room was empty; he was about to turn and leave when he heard a sound outside on the balcony. He crossed the room to see

Tannis' hand reaching up over the rail; she was trying to climb back inside. He grabbed her wrist and pulled her safely over, 'What the hell do you think you're doing?' He whispered as they stood so close on the small balcony that their bodies were pushed together. He hadn't realised that he had automatically put his hands on her waist, she rested both of hers on his chest as she looked up at him. 'I'm feeling much better today,' she smiled breathlessly, 'so I decided to check out some of my prison, see if I could find out the truth, as none of you will tell me.'

'You know we can't,' his voice was stern, but he didn't release his hold on her, 'how can I protect you if you're gonna go solo?'

Tannis looked hurt at his chastisement, 'You know me,' she whispered, 'better than I know myself at the moment, I need to find out who I am Ben,' her eyes filled with tears of frustration as she rested her head on his chest. He slid his arms around her and held her to him, feeling her relax as he did so.

'Breakfast?' Jack was standing in the doorway; Ben nodded and led his wife from the balcony. They sat together, and Tannis removed the cover from one of the dishes to reveal a plate full of tripe, she almost gagged on the smell as she slammed the lid back down.

'Jesus, even Ned wouldn't eat that,' she muttered before she froze on the spot, her eyes glazed over as memories rushed into her mind.

'What do you see?' Ben touched her arm gently.

'A man, he's wearing a dress,' her voice was barely audible. 'Five graves with white crosses,' she narrowed her eyes as if looking into the distance, 'The USS Eldridge, it's a boat.'

'Ship,' Rafe's voice interrupted her thoughts.

'Whatever,' Tannis collapsed on Ben; she was only out of it for a second or two, then she sat up with her head in her hands.

'You have seen the coalition base, a place we have wanted to destroy for a long time,' the agent continued.

'Hang on a minute, how come you can tell me all this stuff, but they can't say a damned thing?' Tannis frowned.

'A drop at a time will do no harm, besides your memory seems to be returning of its own accord,' he inclined his head to her as he turned and left the room.

'I'm going out riding today.' She announced just before he was out of earshot.

'It is not wise, with so many rogues about, I forbid it.' He called over his shoulder.

And so straight after breakfast, Tannis led the way to the stables. 'I thought Rafe had forbidden this?' Jack mocked.

'I only promised to take orders from you Jack,' the words came out before she knew what she was saying, she spun around to face them both, 'what the hell did I mean by that, if I rule time, why do I take orders from you?' She backed away from them both. 'Someone is messing with my head, mixing up the truth with lies, so much so I don't know what to think anymore.' Then came the searing pain, it was like a white-hot poker had been shoved in her eye socket, the only blessing was that she passed out quickly.

It was dark when she woke up, but it wasn't the slow awakening of someone that had been in a deep sleep, she was writhing and tossing, bathed in sweat and calling out the names of her dead family. On hearing her cries from the next room, her teammates ran in. Ben sat down on the bed next to her, putting his hands on her shoulders. 'Tannis, wake up, it's me, Ben, you're safe, wake up.' Jack paced the floor at the bottom of her bed; he hated seeing her like this.

Her eyes flashed open, and she sat up, she was in his arms in a moment sobbing, 'I saw them again, all of the people, suffering and dying and it's all my fault, I made it hit the iceberg, I am evil, I must be one of them.'

'No, you're not,' Jack sat close by on the windowsill. 'You are nothing like them, you have one of the purest souls I've ever come across, just do as Ben says, trust your instincts.' A noise came from the outside chamber; it was one of the servants, who came to make up the fires for the night. Jack went out to stop her from coming into the bedroom.

Ben tilted Tannis' chin up and wiped away the tears as she clung to him, 'Trust my instincts?' She whispered, pulling away from him a little, so they faced one another now. Ben didn't trust himself to speak; he just nodded as she touched his face with her hand, and put her lips on his, he returned her kisses with gentle ones of his own, which gradually became more passionate as she wrapped her arms around his neck when he pulled her to him. Her mind filled with all the memories, the tastes, the feelings, the emotions, sensations and the passion of them making love. The memories were not just contained within Tannis' mind; she unknowingly allowed them into Ben's too.

They gasped as they pulled apart just as Rafe strode through the door, Jack close on his heels.

Tannis was holding her head again now, sitting a little away from Ben.

'What is it, another memory?' Rafe demanded.

'Oh, God I hope so,' she winced as the pain in her head began to subside.

'Tell me what you saw?' He pressed.

'I'm tired,' Tannis defied as she lay down and closed her eyes.

The three men stood in the outer chamber, as Rafe demanded to know what Tannis saw. 'She said nothing,' Ben hissed at his enemy, he could feel Rafe searching his mind, but he found nothing in either man's thoughts, as Tannis hadn't actually said anything about the memory that had just returned.

'She will turn,' Rafe threatened as he left the room.

The rest of the night passed without incident and Tannis slept well. The following morning after breakfast she allowed her ladies to draw a bath for her, on the condition that she would take it in one of the rooms downstairs; she would not stand for them carrying countless buckets of hot water all the way up to her rooms from the kitchen.

When it was ready one of the maidservants came to collect her mistress, and Tannis padded barefoot along the stone floored passageway in her nightgown. Jack and Ben decided to wait for her in her rooms, as there was no way the ladies in waiting were going to allow them anywhere near. So, it came as a surprise to them when a short while later, one of the maids returned to the rooms looking for her mistress, worried that the bath would go cold before she took it.

'I thought she went with you to take her bath?' Jack asked as he stood ready to go looking.

'She did sir, but then she saw Master Gunther and told me to go on ahead, and that she would be along as soon as she'd had a word with him.' The young girl shuffled nervously, 'When she didn't come for her bath; I thought that she had returned here sir.'

They dismissed the girl and hurried out of the room to Rafe's quarters, where they burst in without knocking. 'Where's Gunther?' Jack challenged.

'How dare you speak to me!' Rafe haughtily replied.

'I know, but just for Tannis' sake, I'll lower my standards,' Jack was always quick witted.

Ben, however, had no time for this, 'Tannis is missing, last seen following Gunther along the lower halls of the castle.'

Rafe clearly didn't trust Gunther either as he shoved his way past both men and hurried out of the door.

The stone steps they descended were dimly lit by a few burning torches, adding to the eerie feeling of dread. 'If that son of a bitch has laid a finger on her I'll …' Ben didn't finish his sentence, Rafe did it for him 'I will kill him myself.'

With the passage being so far below ground level, the stone walls were wet and slimy with damp, halfway along Rafe stopped outside a large wooden door and shoved it open. The room inside was empty, but for eight large cylindrical shapes, their contents if any covered with sheets. Rafe paid no attention to them as he marched on his way to another door on the far side of the room, this opened to reveal a brightly lit room with Tannis standing alone inside, shivering with cold, or was it rage as she turned to Rafe and threw the paperwork, she was holding at him. 'Is that what I am, a lab experiment?' She yelled as she pushed past them and back out into the next room, just as Gunther walked in from the passageway.

'You monster!' She screamed at him as she pulled at the cloths covering the fluid filled cylinders, but it wasn't just fluid that they contained. Each one held a half-formed body, some of them just babies, they were all disfigured, some looking like they had died in agony, and all bore a striking resemblance to Tannis. 'How could you?' She sobbed, then began to push the containers to the ground, smashing them, sending blood-stained fluid across the floor.

Even Rafe was disgusted, 'You animal; you know she cannot be cloned,' then he looked at some of the paperwork Tannis had thrown, 'you placed an explosive device in her head!' He raged.

Tannis stepped back as the blooded fluid ran toward her, she stopped suddenly, turning to see who she had backed into. It was Ben; he said nothing, just picked her up in his arms, she buried her head in his neck as he carried her out of the hell hole. Jack followed, closing the door on the two agents who stood yelling at each other.

Once back in her room, Ben lay Tannis on the bed and covered her with a blanket as she turned her back on them both and just stared at the wall. She didn't even flinch when moments later the door burst open and Rafe confronted her teammates, 'You two will leave now, you're not helping.'

'We're not going anywhere,' Jack folded his arms defensively, for this act of defiance Rafe turned his mind powers on both men, they groaned in pain and dropped to their knees. Tannis leapt off the bed and put herself between him and her team, then turning her power on Rafe, she blasted him back against the far wall. 'No,' she shouted, 'they will leave, but alive and unharmed.'

'See to it,' Rafe snapped as he picked himself up and stalked out of the room.

Her teammates had got to their feet when Tannis turned around, and with a voice drained of emotion, 'Go back to where you came from,' she sighed and turned to leave. Ben was having none of it, he put a hand on her shoulder and turned her back to face him, tears rolled down her cheeks as she choked, 'I am one of them, a lab experiment, just leave me and go, while you still can.'

'No,' Ben shook his head. 'I'm not leaving you.'

'We're not leaving you,' Jack put in.

It was her turn to shake her head now, 'Those files that I read in the lab, when Gunther put the device in my head, he also pumped my system full of mind controlling drugs. The stuff that he was giving me at night was just hurrying it along. It will start to take effect soon on its own, so you see, it doesn't matter who I was, I will be one of them by the end of tomorrow.'

Ben sat her on the bed and knelt in front of her, taking her hands in his, 'Whatever they gave you, there must be an antidote,' he looked at his CO, who followed his line of thought. 'I'll get what we need,' Jack said as he left the room.

'We'll take a blood sample back with us, the Doc will figure it out, and we'll be back before you know it. Trust me Tannis, you'll soon be back to yourself again,' her husband squeezed her hands gently.

'Promise me something Ben,' she whispered as she leaned closer to him.

'I'll try.'

She took a breath to steady her voice. 'If you come back, and it's too late, I've already turned, promise me you'll put a bullet in my head before I can do any harm.'

'Tannis, no,' he put a finger to her lips, she held it and kissed it, then his lips were on hers, their arms wrapped tightly around each other as more memories filled both their minds. The most prominent being their wedding day, they pulled away slowly smiling, 'Husband,' Tannis grinned.

'Wife,' Ben kissed her again. 'Do you remember anything else?'

She shook her head, 'I know the memories are there, but it's like they're being blocked.' A few moments later Jack returned from Gunther's lab, carrying the few items they would need to take a blood sample.

Before they left, Jack sat next to her, 'Now listen love, we'll be back as soon as the twenty-four-hour window will let us, but by then, there's going to be an almighty storm here. You must get as high as you can, right up into the mountains.'

'If the island is going to be destroyed, we should warn the people, save as many as we can,' then she stopped and looked at the floor, 'history is already written,' she remembered that much.

Jack stood her up and hugged her, 'Get to safety as soon as you can, that's an order.' Then it was Ben's turn to say goodbye; Jack tactfully turned away as his friend pulled his wife to him, he kissed her tenderly, 'You fight this and stay alive, I will come back for you, I promise,' he whispered. Then she stepped back, and they were gone.

Back on board The Eldridge, both men went straight to the infirmary to get the blood sample to Dr O'Brian as fast as possible.

They gave him a full briefing of what had happened, 'Unethical bastard,' O'Brian chuntered as he immediately got to work.

With that done Jack and Ben made their way to the briefing room where they then retold the same story to the Admiral and a stunned Ned. Hennessey listened and put up with Ned's outbursts as patiently as he could, and when his men finished their report, he nodded slowly. 'We will await Dr O'Brian's findings, then you may return and bring Tannis home,' he rose from his seat 'if you will excuse me, gentlemen, the Joint Chiefs have asked to be kept informed.'

It was like an eternity, waiting for the doctor to complete his work, but just as soon as he had, he went straight to the briefing room with his findings. He caught his breath as Ned pulled out a chair for him to sit on. 'It seems Gunther thinks he's a smart boy, inventing a serum that has no antidote,' the Irishman began.

'There's no cure,' Ben was horrified.

'Major, let a man finish,' the doctor chastised, 'from the sample of Tannis' blood that you gave me, it doesn't matter; her immune system is having none of it. I'd say if she isn't allowing any top ups, it should be out of her system by the time you get back, although her memory may be a little slower returning.'

'What about the device in her skull Doc, if we try and leap her out of there it'll kill her?' Jack worried she might try it anyway with what was going to happen to the island.

'Our Tannis is an amazing lady, as you know her metabolism works faster than ours for healing and such?' O'Brian saw them all nod, eager for him to continue, 'well, traces in her blood show that the device is already being broken down, her body has seen it as a foreign object and attacked it, judging from the data I have, I doubt it has completely dissolved. But as it was designed to deliver shocks to the head also when Tannis had a memory, and Major Rhodes, you said the last recall she had, there was no pain,' he didn't wait for Ben to concur. 'I would say it should soon be completely gone.'

'How're we supposed to know when that's happened Doc?' Jack held out his hands in a helpless gesture.

'Oh yes, sorry,' the medic reached into his pocket and pulled out a small handheld scanner. 'Pass this over the location of the object, if it reads anything at all, the device is still active,' he gave it to Ben who was closest to him.

Barbara entered the room now carrying a communication from the Joint Chiefs for the Admiral, she handed it to him and left.

His facial expression remained neutral, but those present could tell he was livid about something. He screwed up the piece of paper he held and drew a breath, 'Gentlemen; it seems that the Joint Chiefs have been ordered by their governments to issue a termination order for Tannis, it is considered too great a threat if she can be turned.'

'But the Doc's just proved she couldn't be, so the order can be rescinded right sir?' Jack didn't see why he was so pissed off, sure the order was harsh, but nothing that couldn't be changed.

Hennessey looked at them all, 'A team has already been dispatched from the real world.'

'Bastards!' Ned jumped up, 'that's my sister, all the things she's done for the real world, and they won't even give her a chance,' he shook with rage and turned his gaze to the Admiral, 'I take it you'll give Jack and Ben the chance to bring her home?'

'Of course,' Hennessey assured him.

Ned turned to his brother-in-law and Jack, 'I know you will do all that you can for her,' and with that, he headed out of the door.

'Ned, where are you going?' Ben called after him.

'To write my resignation,' he replied without breaking his stride. 'Anyone else?' Hennessey barked, if he lost Ned, he was losing their best brains in the defence against Phoenix, not to mention a good friend. He looked at Jack and Ben.

'I just wanna bring my wife home sir,' Ben said, struggling to keep his tone even.

Jack nodded; he could see his teammate was thinking the same thing, get her out safe, then tell them to shove it. 'Like the Major said, sir, I just want to bring my teammate home safely.'

O'Brian was not so polite, 'Stabbed in the back by your own side,' he mused 'do Phoenix even stoop that low?'

'Perhaps you should return to the infirmary Doctor,' Hennessey growled, 'Colonel Marsters, Major Rhodes, you leave when ready,' he dismissed and left the room, contemplating handing in his resignation too.

It was dark as they'd expected when the two of them made their leap back to Lyonesse, but they weren't prepared for the force of the storm that was raging around them; the wind howled and uprooted trees that had stood for centuries as the rain lashed down. This time they had been allowed to leap back in their black combat gear, fully armed. They had arrived within the castle grounds, although they had told Tannis to get to high ground, they had to check, she may have been compromised; if Rafe couldn't turn her, who knew what he might do. The castle appeared empty; there were no lights in any of the windows, they made their way inside only to find a handful of servants taking what they could, recognising one of the maids, Ben took her by the arm and led her to one side, 'Where's Tannis?' He yelled over the storm. 'My lady left with the master's a few moments ago, they took their horses and rode for the mountains sir, we tried to tell them it was folly to go riding in such weather, but my lady asked me to take what I could and go to the mountains too.' Ben thanked her, and as an after-thought, she told him, 'My Lady also asked that two horses should be ready in the stable for your return.' They left her to go about her business and hurried to the stables and were soon on their way up the mountain road.

It was a perilous journey, the road looked as though it was poor at the best of times, but now it was practically a stream of running water, the wind seemed to batter them from all sides and to try to dodge flying debris was a task in itself. They rode past others whom it seemed had the same idea of taking refuge on higher ground. With so many people on the road, it would make finding Tannis even more difficult. They both scoured the crowd ahead of them, 'Colonel look,' Ben pointed ahead and a little to the left, it wasn't the people he recognised, but in the darkness, he could see the tell-tale red dot of a laser sight. They moved as fast as they could, and as they drew closer, they could see Tannis and the agents had dismounted from their horses and were going to lead them, it was evident why; thunder and lightning had now joined the storm, and the horses shied away. Tannis was arguing with Rafe as usual as they walked on, then as if sensing she was being watched, she turned and looked behind her. Gunther stood by her side; he clearly sensed something as he turned too. Tannis looked down and saw the red dot moving up between her breasts toward her head. Her instincts and swift actions had obviously returned as in the split second between her seeing the red dot and the sniper pulling the trigger, Tannis grabbed Gunther with one hand by the collar and pulled him directly in front of her. The bullet hit him square in the forehead. She let him drop and ran into the crowd. Rafe, when realising what had happened, was right behind her. Jack and Ben were forced to dismount now too and tried to follow in the direction Tannis had taken off in; they looked across to the position from where the sniper had taken the shot but could see nothing, they would be on the move too.

'She'll take cover in the rocks,' Jack pointed to some outcrops ahead of them. Ben nodded, it was what they would do, make a stand rather than be picked off. They battled their way closer and once more began their search, following the laser sights, the snipers were close. 'You keep looking, and I'll go and belay the order,' Jack shouted to his subordinate. Jack's plan was never put into action though, Rafe too must've sensed the advancing snipers and used his powers as a few yards away, they fell dead from the cover of a tree, blood pouring from every orifice.

Then they saw her, Tannis stood now, thrashing the hell out of Rafe for what he had done, he fought back, they were both at the top of their game. As her teammates caught up with them, they heard Tannis yelling, 'You bastard, I told you not to kill them.'

'Little fool, can't you see the coalition want you dead, your own side has turned on you now…' he stopped short, realising what he had said.

'My own side?' She glared at him and launched another volley of punches, that was when Rafe saw Jack and Ben standing, watching.

'Have you come to neutralise the threat too?' He laughed.

'No, I've just come to take my wife home,' Ben yelled above the din of the storm.

Jack pulled out his side arm, aiming it quickly at Rafe's head, but Rafe was too fast, he touched his timepiece and was gone.

Tannis ran into her husband's arms, he pulled out the scanner and ran it over her head, his face fell 'It's still active,' he pulled her to him as people way down the mountain path began screaming.

'You should go too sir; I won't leave her,' Ben yelled to his CO as he held his wife tightly, 'Jack, you've got family, she's my life,' Ben practically ordered his friend.

Reluctantly Jack set his timepiece, this was all his fault, and now his two best friends were going to die. The roar of the giant wave coming behind them got louder and louder when Jack grabbed Tannis, her face in his hands. 'You're Tannis, you were born on the island of Atlantis, you fought Phoenix with your brothers and sisters, you were called *DE-173*, and now, you fight them with us we're…'

'Alpha team,' she yelled, remembering all that he told her, her hands went to her head as she half-collapsed in Ben's arms and blood poured from her nose. He scanned her again, 'It's gone, she's all clear,' he shouted as he set his timepiece. The three of them were on their knees as the wave rose above them, Ben pulled Tannis to him again and held her tight.

The noise stopped, it was gone, over with 911 years ago, Alpha team were on their knees in the hold, Tannis was still clinging to Ben as he held on to her, Jack too had grabbed her arm just in case. He let go now and heaved a huge sigh of relief.

'Welcome back, Alpha team,' Hennessey's voice broke the silence, then Ned ran over and fell to his knees as Ben released his hold on his wife and her brother hugged her tightly.

Tannis was sent to sick bay for a check-up, while her teammates wrote up their reports, O'Brian gave her a clean bill of health and told her it was good to have her back, then gave her a puzzled look as he told her that she had a visitor.

'My God, of all the people in the whole history of the whole history, you're the last person I expected a visit from,' Tannis told Barbara.

'Don't worry, I won't be making a habit of it, but I thought you should see these,' she rasped as she handed some paperwork to Tannis.

'Have you processed them yet?' Tannis frowned.

Barbara just shook her head, 'I have to get back, the Admiral wants us all in the briefing room,' and with that, she left.

Tannis looked open mouthed at Dr O'Brian who had heard everything 'Thank you for your help, Doctor, may I please be excused now?'

The doctor smiled and nodded, oh, he'd love to be a fly on the wall in the briefing room.

Tannis stormed in, paperwork in hand, everyone was in their usual position, with Barbara standing at the back of the room.

'What the hell is this?' She threw the papers on the table, Hennessey made to speak, but Tannis raised a finger and totally out of character, he fell silent.

'So, you had a reality check, and now you want to spit the dummy, do you? So, the arsehole politicians can put who they like in control here. Before they left, I asked Ben to put a bullet in my head if they managed to turn me, this was nothing different to what the snipers were told to do. But now you all want to quit,' she looked at Jack and Ben, who's going to stand up for the other teams and back them up when they need it if there's no Alpha team? You two are the ones the others look up to, if you're not afraid, neither are they, or me for that matter. And you,' she rounded on her brother, 'could you live with yourself knowing an A average history grad was prepping our teams for their missions?' Then it was the Admiral's turn, 'And who's going to stand up for us when we get a bit unorthodox on our mission plans, you're the one who holds us together. The three of you were the reason Ned, and I agreed to the coalition in the first place.' She looked at each one of them in turn, 'Do you know who has the ultimate right to be pissed off here? Who they used and were prepared to let die?' She didn't give them a chance to answer, 'those poor souls they sent to kill me, they were just following orders as we do on every mission and they paid for it with their lives, I suggest you rethink!'

Each man quietly took their letter of resignation and tore it up in silence, Barbara then walked around them all with the wastepaper basket, and they put their litter in it. Then she walked back over to the door, placing the bin back in its spot, just as Tannis was leaving the room, 'This doesn't change anything,' Barbara rasped.

'Wouldn't have it any other way,' Tannis muttered as she passed by.

The next morning, Jack and Caroline became the proud parents of a healthy set of twins, a boy Thomas and a Girl Emily.

Chapter Five

Not that Ned needed an excuse to throw a party, today however, was special, it was his wedding anniversary as usual most of the town were there. Jack and Caroline sat with Admiral Hennessey and the happy couple; they were watching as Ben danced with his wife on the crowded dance floor. Tannis wore a tight-fitting white silk dress decorated with hand sewn teardrop pearls. 'Have I told you how gorgeous you are?' he held her close, 'Yes, but I'll let you tell me again,' she smiled. The song ended, and Ned sprang to his feet taking Elea by the hand as he led her to the dance floor, 'their tune' had begun to play, *Everlasting Love* by *The Love Affair* and Ned serenaded her all the way there.

Ben and Tannis found themselves a quiet space near the garden archway that led down to the beach, he stood behind her his arms wrapped tightly around her waist, and she leaned back into him as they faced the dance floor.

It was Dr O'Brian who watched them all now; he had been talking with Major Charles, 'An appropriate song for all three couples I'd say,' he looked from one pair to the next, Jack and Caroline, Ned and Elea and Ben and Tannis.

'You're just an old romantic Doc,' Sam sighed nonchalantly.

'Not really Major, few of us will be lucky enough to have what they do.'

The song ended, and Ned kissed Elea then led her back to their seat, once she was sitting, he excused himself and hurried over to his sister and her husband looking a little shamefaced.

'You, ok?' Ben frowned.

'No,' he said awkwardly, 'I've bloody well gone and left Elea's anniversary present in my desk on The Eldridge,' he gave his sister an apologetic look, 'you wouldn't nip and get it, would you?'

'Good job, your heads attached,' she laughed as she stepped away from Ben. 'Be right back' she smiled.

'And tell Bravo and Echo team to get a move on,' he said as an afterthought, but she was gone.

It was eerily quiet on The Eldridge when she appeared in Ned's office. There was only a skeleton crew on board as there were no away missions at the moment so those that could be, were at the party, she walked over to the desk and opened the drawer taking out a beautifully wrapped box that sat easily in the palm of her hand. She admired it for a moment wondering what was inside, but her attention was soon turned to the door as she heard someone hurrying down the passage.

The footsteps came to a stop as Colonel Bradley U.S.A.F burst into the room. He was in temporary command while Jack and Hennessey were at the party, he was often given caretaking shifts as he hadn't been with them long and he was under strict instructions should anything arise Admiral Hennessey was to be informed immediately and if he was non-contactable the next in command was Jack.

'Colonel Bradly,' Tannis showed him the gift in her hand, 'Ned forgot it.'

'Briefing room now,' he said bluntly.

'What's wrong?' She had an uneasy feeling, but he had already hurried on his way, 'Miserable sod,' she glared after him then made a leap to the briefing room beating him there, she didn't gloat, she didn't have to.

'So, what's the problem?' She didn't sit, just placed Ned's package on the table and folded her arms.

'Four hours ago, a time threat was identified,' he began his proud boast, 'I was able to determine the problem myself and so sent Bravo team back to deal with it.'

Tannis' jaw dropped, 'You sent a team back, on whose authority?' She knew she was right to have had a bad feeling, neither Jack nor Hennessey had mentioned a mission.

'I have the Admiral's full confidence,' he snapped.

'What was the mission?' She sat down now.

'France 1794, somehow Phoenix had engineered things so that Citizen Robespierre wasn't executed but rose to power as a dictator, it was easily detected, so I sent Bravo team back to July 24th or as the French called it 24 Thermidor to set things straight.'

'And now they're overdue?' She raised an eyebrow.

'Yes, so I am ordering you to go back and complete their mission, we must assume Bravo team are lost,' his voice was a little too nervy for her liking.

'We should call the Admiral,' Tannis made to stand as Bradley brought his hand down hard on the table. 'I am in command, and you will follow my orders. I have spoken to Admiral Hennessey, and he has given me his full support, so if you choose to disobey me, you will be violating a direct order from the Admiral and will be suspended from your team,' he calmed himself, 'of course it's your decision, I can always have Major Rhodes report for the mission, he follows orders, but I thought you would be best as you've gone solo before, and this should easily be rectified.'

Tannis narrowed her eyes at him, 'I admire your courage from the safety of Atlantis.'

Bradley shrugged, 'Be ready in the hold in ten minutes,' he dismissed and left the room.

Tannis hurried down to the wardrobe store and chose her outfit and weapons then made her way to the locker room where she changed into men's clothing; a tri-horn hat, breeches, knee length black boots a white ruffle shirt and a long black cloak. She wasn't taking any chances, going back alone dressed as a woman would just be asking for trouble; she also checked out two purses of gold coins.

As she fixed her cape around her shoulders, Dr Kelsey crept into the room.

'Tannis what the hell is going on, why is Bradley sending teams on missions?' She whispered.

Tannis told her all she knew then said, 'Amanda, get to my brother's house, find Jack and Ben and tell them what's going on. I have a bad feeling about all this. There's something wrong about the dates of the mission; I'm sure the French buggered about with their calendar after the revolution.'

'So, don't go, leap to the Admiral and check it out.'

Tannis shook her head, 'No Hennessey has already cleared it and if I don't go,' she glared, 'well he'll just send someone else.'

Tannis waited and watched as Amanda left the locker room and headed up towards the deck, then she made her way to the hold where Bradley was waiting for her.

'Do we have a location I can use to look for Bravo team?' She
asked him.

'This is not a rescue mission, set history straight and get back
here, Bravo team knew the risk they are to be considered lost,' he
hissed, 'follow your orders.'

Tannis stepped a little closer; she could see the crew were looking
at them as she whispered, 'You and I are going to have a serious
falling out one day!' And with that, she made the leap.

Amanda ran all the way to Ned's house; she was exhausted when
she got there but breathlessly carried on her search for Jack and Ben.
It was Ben she saw first as he was standing talking with his brother-
in-law; both men wondering what the hell was taking Tannis so long.
She hurriedly explained the situation as Ned pulled a chair around
for her to sit on. Jack, ever on the alert, saw something was going on
and hurried over.

'He sent Tannis solo!' Ben raged.

Ned was furious too, 'Why wasn't I consulted?'

'The question is why wasn't I?' Hennessey's voice boomed
behind them.

Both Jack and Ben exchanged worried looks which soon turned to
anger, Hennessey quickly picked up on this, 'Colonel Bradley will
face his disciplinary charges through the correct channels gentlemen,
no other, now let's get back to The Eldridge.'

Back on board the Admiral pulled the CCTV, and they watched
the whole story unfold from the moment Bradley sent Bravo team
back, to when Tannis made the leap; they were all seated in the
briefing room Bradley too had been brought in under guard, more for
his protection than any other reason. The footage finished, and Ben
turned to look at Bradley, Jack had never seen such a look of hate in
a man's eyes, 'You used me against my wife you son of a bitch!'

'Major Rhodes that is enough!' Hennessey raised his voice as he
saw Ben make to stand, 'this will not help Tannis or Bravo team.'

Jack gave his teammate a small nod, and he sat back down as
Hennessey continued, 'The recovery of our team members is our
priority, and to bring them home safely we need to know what we're

up against, Ned you will go through Colonel Bradley's notes and see what you can find.'

Ned nodded and pulled the waiting file toward him. Then Hennessey turned to Jack and Ben, 'Gentlemen if you would join me in the infirmary Dr O'Brian is preparing the memory machine.'

Bradley who had remained silent until now suddenly found his voice, 'Sir I was only trying to show I could manage the situation.'

Ned's temper snapped, 'Manage, you couldn't manage a fart without shitting yourself!' He snarled as he threw the file he had briefly glanced over down on the table and glared at Bradley, 'Any harm comes to my sister, I'll come for you in your sleep.'

'Take a number,' Hennessey could see the same expression on Jack's face too, he turned to the MP's, 'escort the prisoner down to the infirmary.'

'I don't know which result I would've preferred,' Hennessey said later as he sat with Ned, Jack and Ben in the briefing room, 'for Bradley to be a traitor or the fact that the damn fool really was trying to show he was ready for command.'

'Or not,' Jack muttered.

Ben was trying to remain as calm as possible when really all he wanted was a date and a destination; this showed a little as he turned to Ned, 'What do you have?'

Ned sighed heavily and began, 'France 1794, the revolution had been a success for those in power as usual, as you probably know one of the most prominent figures of the time was Maximilian Robespierre. He was a keen enforcer of what was known post-revolution as *The Reign of Terror*; this was a period of violence that occurred around fifteen months after the beginning of the revolution. It was incited by the conflict between rival factions and marked by mass executions of the so-called enemies of the revolution.'

'Nasty piece of work,' Jack looked at the portrait of Robespierre on the main screen.

'Indeed,' Ned continued, 'Robespierre was an ambitious chap, he also wanted to change France's religion from that of mainly Catholic to *The Cult of the Supreme Being*, his belief was that someone was watching over France and that was *The Supreme Being*. Meanwhile, his adversaries wanted to have their form of religion called *The Cult of Reason*; these lot ransacked churches and defaced religious images, wanting to have martyrs of the revolution instead of martyrs of the church.'

'I remember studying *The French Revolution*, but not any of this,' Ben frowned as he scanned the notes in front of him.

'Well, it didn't really take off,' Ned wrinkled his nose. 'Robespierre was getting a little too big for his boots, in the end, both sides turned on him. It was called *The Thermidorian reaction*, on July 27th, 1794, there was a revolution against *The Reign of Terror*. It was triggered by a vote of the committee of public safety to execute Robespierre and other leading members of *The Terror*, he and others were arrested and the following day without trial executed.'

'Or not now,' Hennessey looked at the main screen which showed the time screens.

'Tannis mentioned something to Dr Kelsey about not being sure the dates were right, something to do with the French buggering about with the calendar?' Jack seemed confused by that remark.

'That's where we come to the serious problem.' Ned gave them all a concerned look, 'Tannis was right to have her doubts; she must've remembered me telling her about it on her missions during the Napoleonic wars,' he took a breath. 'The French changed their calendar after the revolution; their new one was entirely different from the Gregorian; there were twelve months in a year each divided into three ten-day weeks called decades. The tenth day Decadi replaced Sunday as the day of rest and festivity. Each day was divided into ten hours, each hour into 100 decimal minutes and each minute into 100 decimal seconds.'

His three companions exhaled slowly as they looked at the paperwork in their files and tried to fathom out the calendar.

Ben seemed to make order of it first, 'So in the Republican calendar Robespierre was executed on 10 Thermidor, 28th of July our calendar.'

Ned nodded, impressed and let his brother-in-law continue. 'According to Bradley's notes he sent Bravo team back on 24 Thermidor and Tannis back on 25 Thermidor, thinking that only the names of the months had changed, but wouldn't that be August 11th and 12th?'

'Exactly, and well done, by the way, you worked the mission out better than Colonel Bradley,' Ned dropped his file on the desk now. 'So, you also know what that means?' He looked at Ben again.

'They were all sent back into an altered timeline two weeks too late,' Ben rubbed his hands over his hair.

'Exactly and as, you can see its anarchy, *The Cult of the Supreme Being* has power with Robespierre at the helm while civil war is impending from *The Cult of Reason*. There are serial executions of strangers or anyone who opposes Robespierre; rape gangs patrol the outlying towns and villages trumping up charges against the men, executing them and then raping and killing the women. And that arsehole sent my sister back alone into that!' He snapped.

'I'm afraid there's worse news to come,' Dr O'Brian stood in the doorway.

'Come in please Doctor,' Hennessey wondered what could possibly be worse.

The doctor stood to the right of the Admiral and placed a file down in front of his CO. 'You left before Colonel Bradley's questioning had finished, it seems he went to your office Ned to double check he was right and found the discrepancies in the dates.' He looked around the table at them all, 'He sent Echo team back, to make time run as it should.'

'Jesus Christ if they make things right, time will change around Tannis and Bravo team and they will cease to exist!' Ned raged.

'How long do we have?' Jack looked at Ned.

'I could send you back with no more than eighteen-hours, but you wouldn't know where to look.'

Ben shook his head. 'No, Tannis wouldn't go without leaving a message,' he looked at the Admiral, 'we need to go to the locker room.'

Sure enough, sticking out of Ben's locker door was a note.

Ben,
There's something wrong with this mission I'm sure about it.
There is an Inn ten miles south of Paris; Ned knows where it is.
I shall wait by the nearby crossroads every night at midnight.
I Love You
Tannis xxx

Ben passed the note to Jack, Ned stood by his side and read it, 'I know where she means,' he acknowledged.

Jack folded the letter and handed it back to Ben, 'Let's bring them home then, shall we?'

Both Jack and Ben were changed and ready in the hold as Hennessey walked in with Ned, 'Gentlemen, you have eighteen-hours, good luck!'

'Well at least it's warm,' Jack commented as he folded his arms and leant against the wooden signpost at the crossroads. Ben smiled, 'Yeah she does hate being cold.' Both men were alerted to the sound of horses approaching in the darkness, so they took cover in the hedge by the roadside, but soon showed themselves as Tannis rode into view, leading two other horses behind her.

Jack took the reins of the two spare mounts as she jumped down and hugged her husband. He held her close, 'You, ok?'

She smiled and nodded then turned to Jack as he asked, 'You been alright love?' She didn't reply, there was an explosion and the sound of pistol shots in the distance then a red glow appeared on the horizon; 'Rape gangs,' she glared, 'I ran into a couple of them last night.'

'What did you do with the bodies?' Jack asked as he and Ben mounted their horses.

'Left them in a ditch,' she said coldly as the three of them rode away, 'I'm afraid we'll be sleeping under the stars tonight too, any strangers are taken away for questioning,' she called over her shoulder as she led the way, taking them deep into the woods to a clearing where they could see anyone approaching from all directions. 'I've set early warnings all around, but it's mostly wildlife that triggers them,' she referred to the makeshift traps and strategically placed branches around the clearing.

Jack sniffed the air, 'Roast pork?'

Ben tethered the horses as Tannis moved some branches and stones away from a pit she had dug, inside was a small wild boar roasted to perfection, Ben joined them now and licked his lips.

'Hardly a damsel in distress,' Jack gave her a sideways look. 'Maybe I should act like one sometimes then I wouldn't end up in these situations,' she grumbled as they all sat down. Ben grinned as he cut her some meat 'Well you know you could always work from Atlantis like your brother,' he would love that knowing she was always safe. She took the meat he offered her and gave him a knowing look, 'Not yet.'

As they ate their meal Jack filled Tannis in on the situation 'Another glory hunter,' she muttered under her breath referring to Bradley.

'Anyway, we've found you, and we've got plenty of time to get to Bravo team. I take it you've located them,' Jack looked at her in the firelight.

'God, am I that predictable?' She frowned.

'Dependable,' he corrected and made her smile.

'They were taken to the Bastille for questioning yesterday; I bribed my way in and took them food and clean water.'

'How're they doing?' Ben and Harmon had personal issues, but it didn't mean he wasn't concerned for his welfare.

'They've been tortured, I cleaned and dressed their wounds, but the conditions in that place are awful, the dead are still lying next to the living,' she shuddered.

'Can they expect more torture or are they for execution?' Jack knew the way of things.

'I gave the guards all the gold I had left so they won't be tortured anymore, but they told me all English spies face the guillotine.'

'I guess their timepieces were confiscated so they can't speak French anymore?' Ben stared into the flames. Tannis gave them both a worried look, 'Robespierre personally took their timepieces when they were arrested.'

'Bugger.' Jack cursed, 'do we know where to look for them?'

'He seems to be hold up at the old Notre Dame Cathedral, it belongs to *The Cult of the Supreme Being* now,' she looked apologetic, 'sorry Jack, I tried to get in, but it's too well guarded.'

'Don't you apologise,' Jack wouldn't have it, 'you did what you could under the circumstances.'

'Yes, but if I'd known it was an altered timeline, I could've just grabbed Bravo team and gone home yesterday, end of story,' she fumed.

'Too late for ifs and buts, you look knackered: I take it you didn't sleep last night?' She just shook her head as Jack continued, 'You two get some sleep, I'll take first watch.'

It didn't take Tannis long to fall asleep knowing she was safe in her husband's arms with Jack watching over them. Ben, it took a little longer though, his emotions were mixed. He was still furious at the situation but relieved to have his wife with him safe and well at the same time.

The sun rose early as it was the summer months and Tannis found herself sleeping next to Jack now; she must've been in a deep sleep not noticing Ben moving away from her, she thought as she sat up. Jack too woke, and Ben broke out the rations they had brought with them. 'Not as good as last night's meal, but better than nothing,' he smiled at his wife.

'What time is it?' She rubbed her eyes sleepily.

Jack looked at his timepiece, 'God knows I still haven't fathomed out the bloody Republican calendar,' he grumbled. 'They have a revolution for a better life and conditions for the masses, then change the working week, so they only get one day off in ten.'

'It's 0430 hrs,' Ben told her.

They readied themselves and made their way through the woods and got on to the road to Paris, as they did so they came upon the village that had been burned the previous night, not a soul had survived, neither man, woman nor child; the dead lay where they had fallen.

'It'll all be put right when Echo team puts the timeline back as it should be,' Ben whispered to her.

'I know this one will, but in the real world, I've seen this too often down through the centuries; so many times, my brothers and sisters risked themselves to put time right and for what, more wars and killing,' she said coldly, 'no training helps with this, my mother had her doubts before they left for Montauk, but Dad gave her one of his famous quotes and off they went.'

'Must've been a stirring speech,' Jack said, his eyes everywhere. 'But when a long train of abuses and usurpations, pursuing invariably the same object, evinces a design to reduce them under absolute despotism, it is their right, it is their duty, to throw off such government and to provide new guards for their future security,' she recited as if she'd been made to do so a thousand times.

Ben smiled proudly at her, 'Declaration of Independence, it means…'

But Jack jumped in and finished for him. 'If there's something wrong those that have the ability to take action have the responsibility to take action.'

'I'm impressed sir,' Ben was a little taken aback.

'Don't be Major,' Jack sighed, 'Caroline is a big Nicholas Cage fan, I've had to sit through *National Treasure* so many times I've lost count,' he admitted.

They rode on in silence for the rest of the way, as they drew closer to the city the last few miles were lined with gibbets from which dangled an array of corpses all in various states of decomposition; the stench was overwhelming. The three of them pulled their capes over their mouths and noses to try and filter it out a little.

The busy streets were made even more crowded this morning as people were gathering to witness the next lot of beheadings, market traders called out their wares as women bustled about buying food and other goods. Soldiers patrolled the streets, as too did what looked like the secret police.

They dismounted at the nearest stables and paid for the horses to be taken care of. Tannis remained at a distance as her teammates passed the time of day with the stable lads telling them they were on business for *The Cult of the Supreme Being*, this seemed to frighten the hands, and they asked no more questions now looking in a hurry for the travellers to be on their way.

Once back in the street, Tannis led them to the Bastille where Bravo team were imprisoned, both Jack and Ben had bought plenty of gold. Tannis showed them to the guardhouse near the gate, and Jack took over telling her to stay out of sight, just in case Ben stayed with her, it looked better two people talking than just one hanging around.

'Somethings wrong,' Ben whispered as Jack hurried back towards them but didn't stop, instead gesturing for them to follow him quickly, he put a good distance between them and the Bastille before coming to a halt and checking all around for prying eyes and ears. 'They were moved this morning under strict orders from Robespierre.'

In the background, they heard the crowd cheer as the guillotine dropped and another poor soul was beheaded. Tannis put her hand to her mouth and looked at Jack as she feared the worst, but Jack shook his head, 'No, they were taken to the cathedral; Robespierre wants them for further questioning.'

'You think Phoenix knows who they are?' Ben was thinking fast. 'That would be my guess,' his CO agreed.

Tannis chewed the inside of her mouth as she thought, 'We have a better chance of getting in during the day when the doors are open to the faithful.'

'That's bigger than I expected,' Jack frowned at the huge building in front of them, thinking that Bravo team could be anywhere inside. Fortunately, there was a large crowd of people making their way up the steps, more driven that led it appeared as men in robes shoved them towards the massive doors. Once inside and satisfied the place was full, the robed guards closed the doors and securely locked the nervous congregation inside.

The room fell silent as Robespierre himself walked onto the makeshift stage in front of them and raised his hands in a Godlike gesture. 'My flock do not fear, by welcoming *The Supreme Being* into your life your world will be enriched, you will never have a day's illness and everlasting life will be yours.' The nervous crowd rallied a little and cheered as he then gestured to the long tables that filled the wall to one side of the great room, laden with food. 'Please help yourselves, we have but a short time until *The Supreme Being* joins with us all.'

Ben puffed out his cheeks, 'Not Phoenix then.'

Jack knew exactly what his friend meant, 'Yeah and we're stuck in a room full of potential hosts, which can only mean one thing.'

'Kira and Nyra have found another weak spot between the two dimensions,' Tannis took her turn, 'and now they've got three more timepieces too.'

They watched Robespierre now as he made his way down some stone steps towards the crypt area, Jack motioned with his head, and his team followed him. People were milling about all over, eating and drinking, so it was easy for Alpha team to slip down the steps undetected. The scene that opened up ahead of them was not what they expected, the stone tombs had been smashed and shoved to one side, the far wall had been entirely obliterated, and a tunnel dug out of it. They made their way along the dimly candle lit tunnel in silence, the end of it was brightly lit, and Alpha team could hear voices as they drew nearer to the wide opening. How to get in the cave undetected was going to be the puzzler, but that was soon solved for them as footsteps behind them got closer; in the half‑light they could see the congregation had made their way downstairs in what appeared to be a drug-induced trance. Alpha team shoved themselves against the wall of the tunnel and allowed some of them to pass, then joined the crowd and walked inside.

Robespierre stood in a semi-trance now next to another short man 'Little shit,' Tannis glared at a twenty-four-year-old Napoleon Bonaparte, who too was in a trance. She had a lot of bitter history with him as her team were aware.

Then they stepped into view, 'Richardson and Hicks,' Ben sneered.

'No sign of Bravo team though,' Jack confirmed as he looked around the enormous cavern.

As if to contradict him, a battered and bruised Bravo team were dragged into view by robed thugs. Richardson stood in front of the three of them, she was speaking to them but was too far away to be heard, they looked on as Richardson lifted Harmon's head up and kissed him on the lips, he struggled to get her off his face and spat on the ground before she slapped him hard.

'Huh, what do you know the guy does have standards,' Ben muttered.

Tannis gasped, 'It's happening, the dimensions are almost touching.'

Jack looked around; there was no machinery, nothing, 'Where are they gonna get the power from to break through?'

This time Hicks gave them the answer; as he carried Bravo teams timepieces, they had been dismantled and rebuilt into something else, but the essential components showed what they used to be.

Jack had to think fast, 'Tannis, can you blast whatever comes through back to where it came from?'

'I'll try, but it depends on how many come through,' she replied honestly.

'Right do your best,' he touched her arm, 'give me your timepiece.' She handed it to him as he looked at Ben now, 'When the dimensions open, we're just gonna have to fight our way to Bravo team, slap our timepieces on them, send them home, job done, get to Tannis and she can leap us out of here.'

Ben acknowledged his orders but didn't have time to speak to Tannis, the whole place trembled, at one point they thought it was going to collapse on them then the ground below split in two and a blinding white light burst out and hit the ceiling. Out of it came hundreds of white floating little lights, screaming and darting towards their waiting hosts knocking the drugged victims off their feet as they entered their bodies.

One of them headed straight for Alpha team, Jack and Ben split from Tannis as she went one way and they went the other, all dodging the attack on their freedom. The portal had closed now, but the cave was still full of the floating, bodiless spirits still choosing their hosts. Tannis was trying to distance herself from the crowd to get ready to send the aliens packing. She looked across to the other side of the cave where her teammates had made it to Bravo team. Richardson and Hicks had left them alone for the moment as they walked around enjoying the sight of their fellow beings taking control of the bodies in front of them.

The two men programmed the timepieces and strapped them on their wounded colleagues, 'Sorry Major; you get the girly one,' Jack winked at Harmon as he gave him Tannis' to hold on to. 'Thank you, sir,' was all he could manage, Jack stepped back with Ben and watched as Bravo team made the leap back to safety. Then they hurried over to Tannis, she was busy knocking seven bell's out of the young Napoleon, Jack looked at Ben, who just shrugged 'Altered timeline, I guess anything goes.'

'You're on love,' Jack said as the two men quickly stood behind her, she dropped the battered corpse of her opponent to the floor, took a deep breath and summoned all her energy just as the ground opened again to allow more beings through, but Tannis gave it all she could, then everything went dark.

Jack's eyes flickered open. He was flat on his back looking up at the roof of the cave, he looked to his right and saw Tannis still unconscious, but Ben was sitting up rubbing the back of his neck, 'She's ok,' he told his CO, 'She'll come round soon.'

After a few minutes, Tannis began to stir, and her teammates helped her to stand, they stood either side of her holding an arm each. Jack looked around the empty cave, 'That was one hell of a blast, you outdid yourself this time, you up to a leap yet?' Jack could see she was still drained.

Tannis laughed, 'Just give me a minute I'll be fine I …' her sentence was cut short as something hit her in the chest spraying her teammates with her blood. Tannis had been shot. Across the cave, Richardson stood with Hicks, who threw the pistol at them just before they both made a leap.

Ben lowered his wife slowly to the ground and cradled her in his arms. Both men knew this wound was too much for her to heal from 'I'm sorry, I let you down,' she coughed.

'Don't talk, just lay still,' Ben could barely speak for the tears that stuck in his throat and ran down his face.

'I love you Ben,' she was crying now too. She made to speak again but fell limp in her husband's arms.

Jack couldn't speak, just held his hand to his mouth.

'Come back to me,' Ben held her to him, but he knew it was no good.

They didn't notice him walking toward them, an immaculately dressed gentleman, powdered wig and all. Later they both agreed they weren't sure if they just didn't care or if they somehow knew he wasn't a threat to them. His voice was soft with a French accent, he spoke as he picked up the discarded pistol from the ground. 'Was this the weapon that caused the wound?'

Jack just nodded.

'Bon, then we shall see what we can do,' he aimed the pistol at Tannis, and the two men couldn't believe what they were seeing, the bullet burst out of her chest and back into the gun. Tannis, still unconscious, gasped a breath of air. Ben laid her down gently and ripped open her shirt; the wound was gone; it was as if it had never happened.

'Who are you?' Jack stood now.

The man gave a little smile, 'A friend,' he looked down to where Tannis lay, 'I have not seen her in many years, her soul is still as pure as the day she was born,' he looked at Ben and Jack now as the cave began to collapse around them. 'It would seem your Echo team have been successful in their mission; this altered timeline will now cease to exist.'

'How do you know so much?' Ben looked up at the stranger.

'Sadly, we have little time for chit-chat, I cannot take you to Atlantis, but I am able to leap you to safety, and when Tannis is recovered you may continue your journey home.'

'At least tell us your name?' Ben asked.

'I am The Comte de Saint Germain,' he bowed quickly, and they were gone.

Tannis sat bolt upright as soon as she regained consciousness and pulled open her shirt touching her chest. Her team were with her in a second, her shirt was covered in blood, and she could see they had been sprayed with it too. 'I was shot, what happened?' She began to panic as she looked from one man to the other.

'It's ok Babe, take it easy,' Ben closed her shirt, she was trembling. 'I was shot, I was dying in a cave in an altered timeline and now,' she looked around her, 'where the hell are we?'

'Not really sure,' Jack looked around the tropical island, 'but it's safe.'

Ben calmed her and explained what had happened right up until the moment she just woke up.

'He knew me?' She was puzzled, 'I don't know anyone with powers like that.'

'Well, we can talk more back on Atlantis,' Jack offered her a hand up, 'you ready to go?'

'Oh bugger, the anniversary present,' Tannis had forgotten all about it.

They made their way back to The Eldridge not long after Echo team had returned. Ned was pacing the floor frantic with worry; Hennessey too was full of concern but was a good poker player and showed no signs.

Major Harmon had managed to tell them what he could when Bravo Team returned, and before they were taken to the infirmary had given Ned his sister's timepiece then passed out.

Ned almost jumped out of his skin when Alpha team appeared, and his nervous state wasn't helped by the fact that Tannis' shirt was red with blood and her teammates spattered too. She threw herself into his arms and hugged him tightly, 'I'm sorry I forgot all about Elea's gift, can we still make it to the party?'

'I think a debrief is in order,' Hennessey spoke up now.

So reluctantly they all went to change and debrief, they did manage to make the party later than expected and Elea loved her gift. Caroline gave Jack a curious look when he returned and sat next to her hugging her tightly, 'Problems?' She asked, it was worth a try.

Jack looked at Tannis and Ben as they slow danced in each other's arms, 'Nah, usual day at the office,' he grinned and kissed his wife glad to be back safe, although this time it was thanks to a stranger and one, he really would like to meet again.

The song ended, and Ben pulled Tannis closer and kissed her, then he whispered something in her ear and flash they were gone. Back in their apartment, their lovemaking was passionate and forceful, he knew she would never stop going on missions and until she stopped neither would he, but now it seemed like she had a guardian angel out there and yeah that made him feel a lot better. They lay holding one another, and as Ben slept Tannis' mind raced, who was it that brought her back from the brink of death, he knew her, but she was sure she had never met anyone like that before.

And one thing was for certain now, the coalition would want to go looking for him, they needed all the allies they could get, and that would be one mission she was looking forward to.

Chapter Six

They all knew why they had been called into the briefing room, having recently returned from the altered timeline they had been sent to and subsequently submitted their reports on the mission. It didn't take a genius to work out that the coalition would show a keen interest in The Comte de Saint Germain, perhaps another possible ally.

Admiral Hennessey dropped the file containing their mission reports onto the table. 'People as you must have already surmised the coalition would like to find out more about the Comte; it could prove a huge help in our fight against Phoenix. But first we need to ascertain his intentions,' he looked at Tannis now, 'saving your life could merely be a ploy, Silas tried to lull us into a false sense of security.'

Tannis raised an eyebrow; she didn't need to say it, everyone present knew she had wanted to kill him from the start.

Ned changed the unspoken subject by adding, 'Kira and Nyra spring to mind too, we don't even know if the Comte is Phoenix,' he sighed with frustration as he looked at his sister, 'are you sure you don't remember anything, any hint he was Phoenix?'

Tannis frowned how many times would he ask her this 'I told you no, I was out of it.'

'So, none of you ever ran into this guy before?' Ben asked Ned, trying to expunge the thought of his wife dying in his arms.

Ned shook his head, 'No, but I've heard of him.'

'How so?' Hennessey raised an eyebrow in reserved interest. 'Well during the eighteenth century, the Comte was best known in the stories of occultism where he was accredited with almost Godlike powers and longevity. It was also rumoured that back in Tudor times he was Francis Bacon who in turn was the secret love child of Robert Dudley and Queen Elizabeth the First, raised by the Bacon family and faking his own death, to drop off the radar until we pick him up again in the eighteenth century. There have also been documented reports that he was Plato.' Ned concluded as he flicked on the main screen to show images of the man in question, he scrolled through them until he reached the most recent one, a portrait from the 1700's.

Tannis stood up slowly, not taking her eyes off the screen and moved closer.

'You know him,' Ben said, it wasn't a question.

'Louis,' she whispered as if drawing on an oh so distant memory. 'You've never mentioned a Louis before,' Ned frowned.

'Oh, I have, but no one ever believed me,' she turned to her brother.

The penny dropped, and Ned gaped at her, 'Your imaginary friend Louis?'

'Not so imaginary now,' she glared at her brother as she sat back down.

Ned didn't wait to be asked; he just brought the others up to speed 'As you know Aunt Catherine started Tannis' training very early,' he sneered at the memory, 'well it turned out as with a lot of children that Tannis was afraid of the dark, instead of a night light like most parents, Catherine decided that Tannis should face her fears, so when James was out of an evening, she would lock their little three-year-old in the dark cellar.'

The other men at the table found it hard to hide their disgust. 'Did you make a leap, is that how you met him?' Jack asked.

Tannis shook her head, 'God no, if my mother had caught me doing that, she would've punished me worse.' Tannis wrung her hands at the thought, 'I just curled up in a ball and cried, the next thing I knew, there was Louis holding a candle, he told me that he would watch over me when I needed him,' she looked across at her brother now. 'The next morning, I told my brothers and sisters, but they didn't believe me, and my mother told me it was all in my head, then when my father told me he had an imaginary friend when he was a kid, I thought that was what Louis was.'

'Maybe he's genuine after all,' Ben looked at his wife sympathetically thinking of the cruel childhood she'd had.

'When was the last time you saw him?' Hennessey asked.

'I think I was about five or six, Dad took an interest in my training then, and things weren't so bad.'

'So why leave it so long?' Jack thought aloud.

'Maybe because as we get older, we ask too many questions,' Ned mused, 'he couldn't stay a so-called figment of her imagination forever.'

'And maybe now his DNA won't let him leap to Atlantis,' Jack added.

'Did you have a way of calling for him Tannis?' Hennessey was getting back to business now.

'No, he just showed up when I needed him,' she admitted.

'So, we still have no way of making contact,' Hennessey frowned.

'Maybe there is a way,' Ned typed at his keyboard and produced his finding on screen for all to see. It was a copy of an old letter as Ned explained, 'England 1745, this is a letter from Horace Walpole to his father, Robert. It's personal stuff mostly but if you look here,' he pointed part way down the page, 'the letter mentions the Comte de Saint-Germain being arrested in London on suspicion of espionage,' he looked at them all, 'this was the time of one of the Jacobite rebellions, anyway he was released without charge,' he shrugged, 'shouldn't be too hard to trace back time and place.'

'Very well 1745 then,' Hennessey was bringing the meeting to a close as he began to rise, the others following suit, all but Tannis who piped up. 'What if we haven't met yet?' They all paused and looked at her as she went on, 'When we go back to 1745 what if he hasn't been to Atlantis at that point in time?'

'Good point,' Ned said as they all retook their seats, 'it could throw a spanner in the works, it could stop him from making the leap for one reason or another and you'll die back in that cave.'

'Then we'll err on the side of caution, Colonel Marsters and Major Rhodes will make first contact,' Hennessey planned aloud, 'Tannis you will remain hidden close by to ascertain if he is a threat or not.' The meeting was over.

'Well, the smell hasn't improved,' Jack wrinkled his nose as he looked down at the raw sewage in the gutter. He and Ben were both dressed as well to do gentlemen in their period costumes. Tannis was also dressed to complement their position, as they escorted her down the street towards their accommodation and as it was not a time change order, she and Ben could travel back as man and wife with

Jack once again acting as her brother. It was July 27th, 1745, another hot summer's day in the busy poorly aired streets; they had made their leap back to the day before the Comte's arrest just to recon the area and sound out the locals. It seemed pretty straight forward there was only one way out of the prison where the Comte would be held, and the nearby market would afford Tannis plenty of cover to observe with a clear line of sight.

Back in their lodgings, she turned her back quickly to Ben for him to loosen her dress and corset, this done she let herself fall back onto the bed, nothing was said, her teammates knew her feelings towards the costumes of the day. They ate in their room then stayed up late pondering the next day's possible events.

During the night, a gale blew rattling the windows, at one point the panes rattled so loudly it woke Jack, and in that state between sleep and wake he thought he saw someone looking in through the glass. He blinked as he sat up, and the image was gone, so he shook his head and settled back down reminding himself they were on the first floor. He looked across at Ben and Tannis sleeping soundly and closed his eyes.

Next morning Tannis waited across the way from the prison well hidden in the throng of market stalls as her teammates waited near the doors for them to open. As she casually picked up ribbons and pieces of cloth Tannis shuddered, *'someone walk over your grave?'* She heard Ned's usual explanation in her head as she turned quickly but saw nothing unusual, just people shopping and paying her no particular attention.

She snapped out of it as the sound of the huge iron bar that secured the prison gate slid across; it seemed that this must be a normal occurrence as no one even bothered to pay it any mind. From the corner of her eye, she watched as a dirty road weary beggar was shoved out into the street, closely followed by another; then she saw him. Louis made his exit sedately without so much as a second glance behind him.

He made to walk on then stopped; he hadn't given Jack and Ben the chance to start to tail him. Paying them, no never mind, he headed toward the market stalls. Tannis moved away not wanting to be seen, she turned to leave and walked straight into him, how had he changed his position so quickly. Having lost sight of him too, Jack and Ben hurried to where Tannis would be and found them both standing face to face. 'You shouldn't have come Cherie,' Louis took her hand and kissed it, 'but it is good to see you well,' he looked over her shoulder at her teammates, 'gentlemen a pleasure once more. But perhaps we should continue our reunion somewhere more appropriate?' He glanced around, 'I have a modest townhouse not far, shall we?' He took Tannis by the arm and led the way.

It was a short carriage ride during which no one spoke as the ride was open top and the driver was in earshot. So, it was a relief to all when the horses were brought to a stop, and they alighted with Louis leading the way into a beautiful Georgian townhouse, the door was opened by a footman who took care of the carriage driver, while the butler showed them all through to the drawing room. There Louis dismissed him, and finally, they were alone.

'And now we can talk,' Louis smiled, his hands open and apart. 'Child, you have grown into a beauty, and with a soul so pure,' he took Tannis' hands in his and shook his head then sighed and released his gentle hold and gestured for them all to be seated as he sat himself in an armchair. Jack did the same opposite his host while Ben and Tannis sat together on the chaise longue. 'I assume you have a few questions?' He spoke with his soft French accent.

'Who are you Louis and where are you from?' Tannis asked the first of what would be many, 'and shouldn't your accent be German?'

He sat back in his chair. 'I have gone by many names, but Louis has been my favourite since you named me with it and my accent. Well, I have spent more time in France than anywhere else, I suppose I just picked it up,' he mused, 'now you are old enough to understand I can tell you; I am from your very distant future.'

Jack sat up in his chair, 'Time travel is outlawed in the future,' he was on the alert.

'That is true Colonel,' Louis reassured, 'but as with your Phoenix, shall we say we too have some rotten apples.'

'So, you're us in the far-off future?' Ben summed up.

'More so than you think, Major,' Louis smiled thoughtfully. 'I am a direct descendant of the two of you,' he looked from Tannis to Ben.

Tannis' jaw dropped, this made Louis laugh, 'Yes Cherie the two of you will have the children you long for.'

'So, you're part of a team too?' Jack tried to bring the conversation back around to the mission.

'Alas there are not enough of us, we are forced to work alone,' he sighed, 'and before you ask, our targets are not like your Phoenix agents, they have no interest in changing time, they have darker motives.'

'You don't wear a timepiece?' Tannis pointed out.

'As you do not need yours Cherie,' he inclined his head.

'So why are we not aware of your enemies?' Tannis frowned, 'I don't understand.'

'As I said, Cherie, my race is from your very distant future - humanity has evolved on to a spiritual level, where we no longer need a physical form.'

Alpha team flinched back simultaneously.

Louis couldn't fail to notice, 'I see you have a problem with this?'

'We have, shall we say, a couple of spiritual beings from another dimension giving us problems any chance they get,' Jack explained. 'They take humans as hosts mostly against their will.'

Louis nodded, 'Perhaps if you saw me in my spiritual form, it would alleviate your concerns?' He offered then leaned back into his chair and slowed his breathing, his eyes closed, and his mouth opened and from it came a beautiful shimmering golden glow, almost like gold dust caught in a ray of sunlight then the body breathed in gently, and the spirit was drawn back inside. Louis opened his eyes and looked at his guests, 'Did that help?'

Tannis smiled, 'You're beautiful, is that what a pure soul looks like? I've never seen anything like that before.'

Louis just nodded.

'Exactly the same came from you when Billy shared your powers with us,' Jack told her.

Tannis lowered her head, Ben knew what she was thinking as he took her hands in his and told her, 'Hey, we're past all that remember?'

She looked up at him and nodded, Louis seemed to sense their emotions too, and was pleased that she was no longer alone in life as he looked directly at Ben and inclined his head, 'Merci,' then he addressed them all once more, 'now I should explain that when we take a body, it has to be close to death, we are unable to share a consciousness the spirit must be absent,' he looked down at his body, 'this poor soul was from your Roman times and died of malaria.'

'So, who are you fighting if they don't want to take over the world and can't take a live host?' Ben frowned.

A wave of sadness washed over Louis as he spoke, 'In my time there was a civil war, and the two factions were the Puritys of which I am one. We live on a higher spiritual plane where we do not eat or drink and do not indulge in any of the pleasures of the flesh; we exist to learn and evolve. However, some were not so disciplined; they are the Feeders who sampled the old ways, leaping back into the past and taking hosts so that they may live among you.'

'I can understand you don't agree with their choices, but if the hosts they take are practically dead already, I should be asking where's the harm?' Jack sat back in his seat, 'But I'm guessing there's more to this?'

'You are an intelligent man Colonel,' Louis acknowledged, 'yes there is a sinister side to their time wanderings,' he looked at his hands then to his guests, 'as long as my spirit remains pure, this body and I will live in harmony, but when a Feeder takes a body because their spirit is corrupted, they need more than just your food and drink to exist.' He looked down ashamed now, 'They must feed on the life force of humans.'

'Like Vampires?' Ben didn't mean to speak his thoughts aloud. 'Very much so Major, have you never wondered where the legends started of your vampires and werewolves, then evolving into serial killers?' He looked at Ben, 'In fact that is how I track them, rumours and legends dating them back through history.'

'So how come we've never come across them if they're moving through time killing people?' Tannis frowned.

'Once their souls are impure, they lose the ability to travel through time and must just live through it,' he winked at Tannis now, 'and maybe we're not too bad at our jobs like you, but mostly it's down to the book work.'

Tannis smiled, 'You'd get on well with my brother Ned, but then again on an evolutionary scale you'd probably see him as prime ordeal slime, he's fathered nine children, cooks and eats the most disgusting food and gets pissed on a regular basis.' She froze, 'Christ, is that what you were doing on Atlantis when we met, were you hunting Feeders?' Tannis shuddered.

'No Cherie, you were my first mission. I was to protect you at all costs if a Feeder ever picked up on your life force, they would see you as a great prize. So, I watched over you while you were unable to take care of yourself and when The Eldridge arrived no Feeder could make it to Atlantis, so my mission was changed.'

'But the nights you came when I was in the cellar....' Tannis didn't finish.

'I watched over you from the day you were born Cherie; I could not allow such an act.'

The room fell silent for a while with each, and every occupant lost in their own thoughts.

It was Ben who broke the silence, 'If, like us, you have an anonymous job to do, how come you're so prominent in this century?'

'An excellent question Major,' Louis admired. 'For reasons known only to themselves a group of Feeders have gathered in this century. Maybe for protection, I can't say; typically, they hunt alone but tracking them here. I have discovered a nest of six, and my task is made more difficult as others like me are needed elsewhere and cannot assist me, so I must try and lure the Feeder's out into the open using myself as bait.'

'That's why you got yourself arrested,' Jack raised an eyebrow, 'dangerous path Louis, six against one.'

'I have little choice Colonel; I cannot leave the people of this time to the mercy of these beasts.'

'Well, it so happens that we're at a bit of a loose end and we do owe you one,' Jack looked at his team who nodded their agreement.

Louis pursed his lips, 'Thank you, Colonel, but I cannot accept, I cannot put a human life in danger for my own gain. Also, I am guessing that your coalition may be looking to add to their alliance and this I must also decline, my race, were sent back to fight the Feeders, and cannot interfere in your timelines.'

'But you saved me in France?' Tannis looked at him questioningly.

'Ah, an altered timeline is such a grey area don't you think?' He winked at her again and made her smile.

'Fair enough, no harm, no foul,' Jack accepted Louis's refusal. 'But we'll still hang around and give you a hand, now that we know there's a threat we have to act.'

Louis inclined his head, 'In that case I thank you, and you are welcome. However, I fear it will not be my presence the Feeders are now drawn to,' he motioned toward Tannis. 'I sensed your presence yesterday, Cherie, and any Feeder worth its vile breath will have sensed you too, your life force will be like a drug to them, I think by now you are their prey.'

Jack was jolted back to his awakening the night before, 'Last night, the wind rattling the window half woke me, I could've sworn I saw someone looking in, I thought I was dreaming when I looked back there was no one there.'

'So, it has begun,' Louis stood. 'We must prepare.'

'I suppose holy water and crucifixes are just part of the folk tales?' Ben had to ask.

'I'm afraid so and judging by the breath of some of them they are quite fond of garlic,' Louis added. 'But know this, although they are faster and stronger than most humans, they can be killed in the same way, like yourselves though I am forced to use the weapons of the time that I am in.' He gave Tannis a serious look now, 'And no matter what, you must not dispatch them to another dimension, the problem must be contained here.'

Tannis pulled a face 'But I know a really nasty one.'

Louis merely raised a finger and shook it gently at her; she smiled remembering this gesture he would make from her childhood.

And so, knowing that the Feeders were already aware of Tannis it was decided that they should go about their normal day of shopping and take tea in the park while Louis kept a close watch. As the uneventful day drew to a close and they made their way back to their lodgings, their night plan came into action. Louis would keep watch outside in the backyard where the Feeders were more likely to enter from as they had done the night before, meanwhile Jack and Ben would be positioned inside but downstairs. With a good view of anyone coming in. Tannis would then get herself ready for bed and literally lie in wait, but it was too early for that now, and she was getting bored as she waited for the Innkeeper's wife to bring her evening meal up to the room.

She walked over to the window and tried to look down into the stable yard below. But she could see nothing in the darkness; moving over to the table now she smiled to herself, all those years Louis had been watching over her, and she never knew. Now here he was doing it again, she felt a little sad for him being almost exiled from his true time in the future. Good job he's immortal, she thought to herself, these things had a way of dragging on. Tannis roused herself from her thoughts when there was a knock at the door; it was the Innkeeper's wife with her tray of food. Tannis thanked the woman and closed the door behind her as she left and sat down to eat.

Downstairs Jack and Ben too ate their meal, their eyes constantly on the alert moving from face to face, checking everyone who came through the door, but nothing so far and after an hour or so the room began to empty as the guests made their way upstairs. From behind the bar half hidden around the corner the Innkeeper's wife was signalling nervously for them to come to her. Both men stood cautiously and made their way over as she led them into a back room where the poor woman broke down in front of them 'Oh sir's you must forgive me,' she sobbed. 'They've taken my husband you see; they made me do it.'

'Do what, what have you done?' Jack didn't know why he was asking; his gut told him it was the Feeders.

She looked at Ben as she wrung her hands, 'Your lady wife, they made me slip something into her dinner to make her sleep, then I had to let them in up the backstairs,' she stammered. 'They rolled her up in a blanket and carried her away sir.'

'How long?' Ben snapped.

'No more than an hour sir.'

The two men raced out of the room leaving the trembling woman calling after them her voice wracked with sobs, 'They have my husband, I had no choice.'

Upstairs Ben kicked the door to their room open. Tannis was gone, Jack hurried over to the window and called out, 'Louis get up here,' he had only closed the window and taken a few paces across the floor when Louis entered the room.

Jack told him what had happened as Ben searched the room for any clue as to where they may have taken her. 'Nothing,' he said bitterly, throwing the pillows back on the bed.

'Do not lose hope, I can still sense her faintly now, we can track them,' Louis made to leave the room. 'We will need horses, hurry my friends and do not worry; it was not Feeders that took her, or I would've sensed them, paid kidnappers are at work here, once they hand her over, the Feeders will feast on them. They will not feed on one like Tannis straight away when her system is full of drugs, they will encourage her life force to be at its fullest.'

They helped themselves to the three best horses from the stables and rode out, giving Louis the lead. He took the road south out of London, and they raced full speed into the night.

The men had been riding hard for an hour when Louis finally slowed their pace, the horses covered in sweat. They were in a wooded area, through the trees Louis pointed to an enormous stately home, 'Tannis is inside,' he whispered.

The men dismounted and moved cautiously towards the property. There were no guards on the outside and from what they could see through the windows, no servants inside either. 'They will keep their presence low-key, no witnesses,' Louis said coldly.

The three of them reconnoitered the area and once satisfied their presence remained undetected, they moved silently around the back of the property. Steps leading down to the cellar seemed the obvious way inside.

Jack picked the padlock easily and opened the door, as soon as he did so the stench hit them, it was unbearable and made them gag. All three men had smelt it before, but no one spoke as they continued into the darkness. As the smell of decomposition even permeated their clothes, from nowhere, Louis produced a lit candle.

'Handy party piece,' Jack whispered.

'Merci,' Louis acknowledged, but that was the limit of the jest, for as the candlelight emanated across the cellar, the reason or reasons for the stench became apparent.

There must have been at least thirty bodies dumped down there, all at various stages of decay, as they made their way past the gruesome sight, they noticed the most recent deposit. It was the body of the Innkeeper, and two others, no doubt the kidnappers. They continued on their way in silence up some stone steps that would gain them access to the main house. Once at the top of the stairs Jack opened the door a crack and looked through, he signalled that the way ahead was clear, and they stepped inside. They were standing in the kitchen now; it was dust covered yet with nothing out of place after all Ben thought to himself, they had no need to cook their food.

'Colonel, with respect I will move faster alone, bon chance,' and with that Louis was gone.

'Just us mortals then,' Jack whispered as the two men made their way along the corridor that led from the kitchen to the main rooms of the house. As they moved through the hallway, they came across the body of a woman, her neck had been broken, and there were visible signs of a struggle.

'A Feeder?' Ben looked at his CO.

'Looks like the one I saw at the window,' Jack confirmed. 'I guess they didn't realise drugs don't last long on Tannis,' he grinned at his teammate. Ben crouched down, there was a small broken phial on the floor where a few drops of the liquid remained. He dipped his finger in and smelt it, 'I guess she was outnumbered, looks like they drugged her again.'

'Yeah, little buggers are quick,' Jack pointed to the stairs now, it looked like something, or most likely someone had been dragged towards them.

The house was decorated in gothic tastes that bordered on the creepy; Jack thought to himself as he looked at their surroundings, then he froze as he saw something out of the corner of his eye. Ben also noticed it too, but by the time they realised four Feeder's were rushing head on at them, it was too late to raise a weapon. Both men were knocked clean off their feet and out for the count.

It was Ben that came around first, he slowly opened his eyes and took in his surroundings. His hands were tied above his head, suspending him from a hook mounted on a wooden panelled wall. Opposite, the whole wall was a huge mirror. Jack was in the same position next to him, he began to stir now too and looked around as he got his bearings.

'Situation normal then,' he groaned, his head was sore.

Before either of them could say or do anything more, the lights in their room went out, and the mirrored wall in front of them turned transparent allowing them to view the bedroom on the other side of it.

Inside lying on a four-poster bed seemingly sleeping was Tannis, she had been stripped of her clothing and now lay wearing a bra top made of strands of pearls and precious jewels. Her small panties were of the same design, the only part of her clothing that remained were her stockings. Her eyes had been lined heavily with black kohl eyeliner and her hair intricately adorned with jewels.

The door to her room opened, and in a flash, a Feeder was on its hands and knees crawling up the bed towards her.

From the other room, the two men struggled with their bindings, but it was useless. They tried to call out, but Tannis never moved, all they could do was watch.

The Feeder, a female, raised herself above Tannis and ran her tongue down the sleeping woman's throat and between her breasts, down towards her stomach, allowing her hand to rest between Tannis' breasts as she did so.

In the next room, the two men stopped their struggle for freedom for a moment. Jack exhaled slowly, 'Bloody hell,' was all he could say about the erotic sight unfolding in front of them. Ben too stared for a moment before resuming his struggle.

Tannis moaned softly now, as the Feeder's tongue reached the top of her panties. She slowly began to sit up, her mind full of fog, where were they, why had Ben brought them here? She looked down at the hand resting between her breasts, that's not Ben, she struggled to sort her thoughts. Her head was still full of cotton wool, and with an awful drunken sensation, she was now face to face with the Feeder who opened her mouth for a kiss, no doubt literally a kiss of death. But the Feeder got more than she bargained for, Tannis reared her head back and brought it down fully on the Feeder's nose. As she gasped in pain Tannis grabbed her head and twisted it, breaking her neck. Pushing the dead body away from her, Tannis looked towards the door, in the other room Ben and Jack followed her gaze. Louis stood in the shadows.

'And you were gonna wake me up when?' Tannis frowned, her speech slurred.

'You had the situation under control Cherie,' he inclined his head to the dead Feeder, 'your second kill whilst drugged, very impressive.'

Tannis looked down at her state of undress now, 'What the hell?' She touched the pearls then looked at her bottom half, 'What the hell?' She half slurred; half shouted now. 'Gimme your jacket,' she shoved her way toward the edge of the bed.

Louis hurried over, 'Cherie do not try and stand yet,' his advice came too late. Tannis had swung her legs over the edge and tried to stand, resulting in a dull thud as she hit the floor. Louis was there in an instant helping her up. 'Your system is still full of the drug; you need to rest.' He made sure that she had her balance, then let her go as he removed his jacket and put it on her, buttoning it up as it took most of her concentration just to remain upright.

Louis smiled 'Come, Cherie, we have work to do.'

'Where's my team?' she rubbed her temples now trying to clear the fog.

'I fear the Feeders have them.'

'Then we must find them first!' Tannis insisted, trying to sound firm while slurring didn't seem to have the desired effect.

'We came to hunt the Feeders, Cherie.'

'I will find my team first!' She was adamant as she stamped her foot like a petulant child. Then, losing her balance, she fell backwards into the mirror behind her. It smashed and gave way. Tannis fell flat on her back into the room where her team were imprisoned. Looking up she saw them both, 'Found em,' she groaned as Louis stepped over her and freed her teammates.

Ben helped her to her feet, and she hugged him tightly, then wrapped her arms around his neck and kissed him. Ben gave his CO an apologetic look, but Jack just shook his head as a sign for Ben to let it go. Tannis wasn't herself for the moment.

'Come on,' she took Ben by the hand, 'we're going vampire hunting,' she slurred again. Jack stood in front of her now and took her face in his hands, using his thumbs to gently raise her eyelids. 'She's high as a kite,' he sighed.

'We can't leave her,' Ben hugged his wife again now as she had wrapped her arms around him once more.

'Keep her close and quiet,' Jack ordered as they made their way out of the room.

'So, there are four left,' Louis looked across to Jack.

'Three females and one male,' Tannis was lucid for a moment. They continued along the hallway, empty suits of armour staring down at them in the dim candlelight. Tannis felt her husband's hand slip quickly from hers as he was hit head on again by a Feeder and pushed up against the wall. Jack too was being attacked.

Louis was more evenly matched to the pace of the Feeder that set about him and was therefore able to fight hand to hand with her.

Tannis, her senses still dulled by the drug inside her, stood for a moment taking in the scene. Ben's attacker repeatedly bashed his head back against the wall to stun him into submission, all he could think about as the Feeder's mouth moved towards his was, who would look after Tannis. He came to his senses as the Feeder released her grip and he fell to the floor, then he saw the reason why Tannis stood over the body, sword in hand, borrowed from a nearby suit of armour. Seeing his CO was in trouble Ben took the weapon from his still groggy wife and threw it, the Feeder whose lips were almost on Jack's, fell dead in an instant.

Louis too finished his assailant with a dagger to the heart. Tannis had slid to her knees by the time her teammates re-joined her, they pulled her to her feet and helped her on their way. Maybe realising that his prize was getting away, or perhaps just needing to feed, the last remaining Feeder rushed towards them and took Tannis from their grasp. She didn't make a sound, there was just a rush of air, and she was gone. Louis took off after them at speed, leaving Ben and Jack to follow as best they could. It wasn't a difficult trail to follow as Tannis had had the presence of mind to dig her heels into the rugs that lined the wooden floor. There was the sound of a vicious fight as the two men caught up. Armed only with swords and a grim determination they rushed in. Tannis was bound and gagged and lay helpless on the floor while Louis and the male Feeder were going at it hammer and tongs, they were both moving too fast for either Jack or Ben to take a swipe in case they hit Louis. Still, he seemed to be holding his own, so they went over and freed their teammate. The drug had worn off completely now as she stood independently and glared in the direction of the Feeder, who at that moment got in a lucky punch and knocked Louis to the floor. It knelt over him and made to feed.

'Hey dog breath,' Tannis yelled as she ran along the corridor 'Hungry?'

The Feeder seemed unsure for a second or two, he wanted Louis dead and could feed off Jack and Ben, but the prize, the greatest feed, was getting away. Recognising his distraction, the two men rushed at him brandishing their swords, but the Feeder was already on his way.

Tannis hid in an alcove along the huge hallway. She knew her cover wouldn't last long, but also knew that her team would back her up. From her vantage point, she could see the Feeder making his way hungrily in her direction, sniffing the air. Ben was closing in behind it, it sensed his presence but needed to feed now and couldn't risk a fight in its weakened state, so it continued after its prey. Tannis left it as long as she could, then when he was close enough, she ran out into full view and raced around the corner with the Feeder close behind. Ben was joined by Louis now; the two men hurried after them, to see Tannis standing next to Jack, he had impaled the Feeder on his sword as it had run around the blind turn after Tannis. Satisfied it was dead Jack let him drop to the floor, he looked at Louis now, 'We may not be as quick as you lot, but we're a bloody good team.'

They checked the rest of the house for possible prisoners but found no one alive. So, they doused the place with lamp oil and let it burn, watching from a safe distance in the woods.

'Where will you go now?' Jack asked Louis.

'Same as you Colonel,' he sighed, 'on to the next mission.'

'You must have a base then, something like The Eldridge?' Ben looked at their ally.

Louis nodded, 'We do, but it's on a spiritual level, like your Atlantis, only the invited can enter.'

'Will we see you again?' Tannis gave him a concerned look.

'Ah Cherie, I should think so,' he smiled like a doting father. 'Now that Alpha team are the friends of the Purity's, I'm sure that we will announce our presence when our paths cross in future.' With that, he shook hands with the two men. Then took Tannis by the hand and kissed it in farewell, 'Au revoir Cherie,' he smiled, and with that, a golden glow emanated from his body, and for a moment a fact that they all confirmed later, they all felt a warmth inside them and a feeling that no matter what everything was going to be ok. Then Louis was gone.

'Let's get out of here,' Jack looked at Tannis standing in Louis' jacket and her stockinged feet. She frowned, 'What?' Then a look of horror washed over her, 'Oh my God, did you see what that pervert Feeder was trying to do to me?' She looked from one man to the other, they didn't have to say anything, the looks on their faces were enough.

'You're not going to put it in your report, are you?' She was mortified.

'Well if I did, it would be the most read report ever,' Jack mused.

'What!' She glared at her CO.

'Big tick in most bloke's life boxes that one,' his tone didn't change.

'But nothing happened,' she protested, then looking at Ben's grin, she realised they were having her on, 'Bastard,' she gave Jack a shove. He laughed as he walked over to set the horses loose.

Tannis took her husband's hands in hers and looked up at him, 'I didn't know what was happening, I thought it was you,' she tried to explain.

Ben smiled, 'Babe you were drugged, and nothing actually happened, it was great really.'

Tannis gave him a surprised look then raised her eyebrow, 'Ben Rhodes?'

'I mean,' he gave her an apologetic look. 'Well, it is most guys fantasies, not that I want it to happen again, but …' he made sure Jack was still busy with the horses, 'I really need to get you home as soon as possible,' his voice was husky with desire.

Tannis smiled, Jack was out of view behind a tree, she leaned forward and kissed her husband, letting her tongue probe his mouth. He pulled away slowly and swallowed hard, 'Colonel; we're good to go when you are,' he called out.

Chapter Seven

On a rare day off, Ben took Tannis out into the harbour on his pride and joy jet ski, work had been oddly quiet, but no one was complaining. He brought the machine to a stop right next to the force field that protected Atlantis. It was almost invisible to the naked eye, only occasionally making its presence known with the odd small blue flash. Ben reached out his hand and touched it; it wouldn't give an inch, just remained constant like a solid brick wall.

'Penny for them?' Tannis rested her head against his back, her arms around his waist.

'Oh, I'm way more expensive than that,' he pulled his hand back and rested it on hers. 'I was thinking how safe you were here until we came along and screwed it all up,' he sighed.

'I think bored is more the word.'

'Maybe, but if we hadn't messed with that timepiece, Kira and Nyra would still be locked up safe, and so would Phoenix.'

Tannis rested her chin on his shoulder 'Ben; there are timepiece's still out there waiting to be found, it was bound to happen at some point, besides how else would we have met,' she kissed his neck, 'although you really were hard work, so standoffish in the beginning,' she laughed as she teased him.

'I think time travel has clouded your mind Mrs Rhodes,' Ben reached his hand behind him and grabbed her ribs, Tannis yelped, she hated being tickled, as she struggled to free herself, they both fell into the water. He pulled her close and kissed her; they were still like that when a speed boat approached them, they pulled away to see a young Ensign salute, 'Sorry sir, ma'am, Admiral's orders Alpha team is to report to the briefing room immediately.'

'Very well Ensign, take the jet ski back,' Ben sighed, 'and be careful with it,' he ordered.

'Yes sir,' the young recruit saluted, then watched in awe as the two of them made a leap.

First Tannis leapt them to their apartment to change, then straight to the briefing room. Ned and the Admiral were already there, and Jack had been collected by one of the crew wearing a timepiece.

They all took their seats, not one of them looking pleased to be called in on their day off.

'Well, I'll get straight to the point,' Ned said in an apologetic tone as he looked at them all, 'as you are aware three weeks ago Echo team were listed MIA when they were sent back to 1908 to check out some electromagnetic activity in Paris, France.'

This struck a chord, and visibly the team stopped feeling sorry for themselves and thought about Echo team; the first team lost without trace.

'Well, as you know we also monitor all archaeological activity too these days, and it seems that the ruins of a small rowing boat have been uncovered in the Azores. Along with what's left of the vessel, three skeletal remains were found,' he looked at Alpha team. 'That's when we got involved, tests showed that the boat was from the mid to late 19th century, but the human remains were much younger than that. DNA tests have confirmed its Echo team.'

'No wonder we couldn't find them in Paris,' Ben frowned.

'How the hell did they wind up in the Azores thirty-six years earlier?' Jack was puzzled.

'That's where the plot thickens,' Hennessey spoke now, 'for some reason, Echo team weren't in Paris in 1908, they were on a ship in 1872.'

'Oh, God it sank didn't it,' Tannis groaned.

'Actually, no Tannis, you'll be pleased to know that this ship remained afloat,' Hennessey added.

Tannis looked at her brother, 'There's still something hinky about it,' she could sense it.

'It was the Mary Celeste,' Ned put her out of her misery.

'Knew it, bloody boats,' she cursed.

'Ships,' her brother corrected.

'Close enough,' the Admiral never corrected her since *The Gustloff* mission.

'Ha!' she looked smugly in her brother's direction, 'hang on, how do we know they were on board?'

'One of the sets of remains was holding a page of the ship's log.'

'As there were no survivors, you will travel back combat ready and bring Echo team home.' Hennessey was keen to get this mission started, 'but be on your guard Alpha team, none of this makes any sense, no time change has taken place, no threats detected, you will be going in blind.'

'On the plus side, not only does the ship not sink, but you don't have to wear a corset,' Ned teased his sister. Tannis said nothing, just mouthed the words, Fuck off.

The mission plan was discussed, Alpha team would leap into the hold and stow away as best they could if they couldn't go on board as passengers, and take it from there, their only objective; to secure the safe return of Echo team.

'If we can't go on board as passengers, how did Echo team end up there?' Ben looked around the table for any ideas.

'If Phoenix are on board, who knows what happened,' Jack shrugged.

'It's going to be a tight space for a fight,' Tannis looked at the image of the ship on the main screen.

An hour later in the hold, Alpha team were armed and ready to go. Ned had already said his goodbyes to his sister; they now waited for the Admiral to join them and give his permission for the leap. They didn't have to wait long, he strode into the hold and stood in front of them, 'Alpha team I have just spoken with the Joint Chiefs, your priority is to bring our people home. Should you run into any threat on the way, the order is to terminate, no prisoners for questioning.'

'Finally,' Tannis put her hand to her mouth realising her outburst, about time though, she thought.

'Yes sir,' Jack acknowledged, also thinking the same as his teammate.

It was cramped, hot and humid in the cargo hold, the three of them had to split up as it was impossible for them to hide together. Jack looked down at his boot and grimaced as a rat scurried across it. They kept in contact through their earpieces; nothing had happened so far, all was quiet, it was the 24th of November 1872, and whatever was going to happen it was going to be soon. At least that's what he hoped, there wasn't much air down there, and what there was, wasn't fresh.

The night was as uneventful as the day, it was only as the sun began to rise did, they hear the noises on the deck above, then a woman screamed, and a child started to cry, that was their cue.

'Move out and watch yourselves,' Jack whispered.

The sight on deck took them by surprise as they made their way up there, there must've been at least two hundred people milling about, a lot more than the eight crew and two passengers that should've been on board.

The people were confused and frightened, dressed in clothing from almost every century throughout history. The confusion, however, made it easy for Alpha team to find their colleagues, 'Come on Major Ross, it's time to leave,' Jack whispered in Echo team leader's ear. Without turning, the Major pulled down his collar enough for Jack to see he was wearing a manacle of some sort around his neck, 'We all have one sir, set to detonate, if we try anything.'

Before he could say more, Tannis looked through the crowd and saw them, 'Should've known,' she nudged her teammates to look in the same direction.

'No wonder there were no time changes,' Ben rolled his eyes as they watched Richardson and Hicks shove their way to the front of the crowd; noticing that Richardson was carrying something familiar made up from Echo teams timepieces.

'They keep cobbling them together,' Jack whispered.

At the bough of the ship Richardson activated the device, at first it did nothing; then slowly a portal began to open in front of the bow, on the other side there was a cave of some sort. Hicks wasted no time in forcing the frightened people through. Tannis sent a small power surge from her fingertips to each of Echo team's manacles and disarmed them; then Alpha team gave them their timepieces. 'Sir, we won't leave you,' Ross began.

'It's an order Major, and believe me it's for your own good, staying here won't serve any purpose,' Jack dismissed them, and they were gone. 'Fancy a stroll?' Jack gestured toward the portal as he mingled in with the crowd and his teammates followed suit.

Once on the other side they were stunned at what they saw, hundreds of people all in some sort of stasis; freely suspended in the air, but alive. 'They're harvesting hosts,' Tannis whispered.

The terrified crowd began to jostle one another trying to find a way out of the nightmare. But Hick's and Richardson, both so cold and calculating, moved through them with a small pen-like device each and jabbed them in the neck, rendering them helpless in an almost catatonic state; just standing in silence, staring into nothing as they awaited their fate.

'Sir, look,' Ben pointed to one of the bodies already in stasis.

'Isn't that one of the Joint Chiefs?' Tannis thought she recognised the man.

'Oh, yeah,' Jack looked at his team, 'we've got to get back to The Eldridge and report this.'

'Sir we should get out of here soon,' Ben could see Hicks and Richardson getting closer, 'unless you want to take them down now?'

'I'd love to, but those two wouldn't think twice about using these people as cover, or hostages, we need to come back when they're off collecting more,' Jack said hurriedly. 'Then we can plan a nice little welcome for them.' With that Tannis took their hands and they were back on The Eldridge.

Once more in the briefing room, Ned and Hennessey sat with Alpha team as they were debriefed; the two men listened as the team retold their short mission.

Hennessey nodded, 'It seems the Joint Chief that you saw is yet to be reported missing as he is sailing the Med, in supposed secrecy. We must assume Kira and Nyra have used him to gain information for any missions that they could intercept and steal timepieces; as in the case of Echo team,' he looked at Alpha team, 'and well done for their safe return. They were a little shocked when they were told of their alternative fate; I believe they would like to buy you all a beer later,' Hennessey smiled to himself; his teams faced so much danger on every mission; saved each other countless times that now their thanks came down to a beer after work, as personal gratitude's were no longer necessary. 'As for the Joint Chief in question, you will as you have already said, return and secure his release, then if Hicks and Richardson cannot be brought back for trial, they are to be terminated; is that clear?'

'Clear,' all three chorused.

'Sir, what about the other's, there could be over a thousand of them?' Jack was worried about the reply he was going to get.

'These people have no place in time Colonel, they were lost at sea, you know this,' it was evident the Admiral was uncomfortable with the thought too.

'No,' Tannis spoke up, 'these people were lost, never found, Hicks and Richardson took advantage of this, for all we know they took these people from their timeline making history this way.'

'Tannis, you know we can't let these people back into the world, we would be changing history ourselves then,' Ned said awkwardly, 'that was the reason you did what you did on *Titanic*.'

'No,' she swallowed hard and refused to let the tears come, 'the people who died on *Titanic* were mostly found, history killed them.' She still had trouble convincing herself of that sometimes. 'Those people in the cave are innocents, and I will not kill innocents, nor will I allow them to be killed.'

'Couldn't they live on Avalon?' Ben suggested, 'it's more than big enough.'

Tannis smiled at him; he knew what she wanted to say to him, he just winked his reply.

'An excellent solution Major,' Hennessey was visibly relieved. 'I will inform the Joint Chiefs of our decision,' he smiled as he stood and left the room.

'Do you think they would've had those people killed?' Ned asked as he stood and picked up his paperwork.

'Not on my watch,' Jack replied bluntly as he and his team left the room.

The remainder of the Joint Chiefs not only endorsed the plan to relocate the hostages to Avalon but also insisted that teams would be sent through with them to help them settle in and adjust to their new lives.

Alpha team sat together in the Mess, no one really said much, they were busy eating their meals and thinking about the mission ahead. This often happened, it wasn't an uncomfortable silence; they were at ease in each other's company. Something, however, caught

Ben's attention, as he stopped eating and looked at his wife. Jack stared at her too, 'What?' She mumbled her mouth full of food.

'Hungry Babe?' Was all Ben could say as she continued to eat as fast as she could.

'Uh huh.'

'Since when did you like meatloaf?' Jack watched the last of it disappear.

'Dunno, just really hungry,' she said, reaching over and pulling her dessert toward her.

The tannoy calling them to the hold brought the conversation to an abrupt end, but both men still noticed Tannis grab some fruit as they left the room.

Richardson and Hicks were noticeably absent from the cave when Alpha team along with two other teams made their return leap into the shadows, and this time they were joined by medics. Who upon Jack's orders began to wake the sleeping prisoners; the Joint Chief to be the first, he was brought safely round and quickly placed in the most capable hands of Major Charles, who had been brought in especially for the task of taking the man safely back to The Eldridge.

The prisoners were only brought to a state of semi-consciousness to avoid panic when Tannis sent them on their way; she had already sent a team of thirty coalition members out to help with rebuilding and medical care etc. Now, she began sending the first groups of freed prisoners through.

Jack had the whole cave covered with various personnel, if Richardson and Hicks turned up, they wouldn't be going anywhere.

Tannis was getting tired but wouldn't stop for a break; she wanted these people out of the cave and into safety. But it was Ben who put a stop to it as he saw her sway a little after she had sent more on their way. 'Time for a break, Babe,' he led her to the side of the cave and sat her down.

Jack joined them and gave her a protein bar, which she ate hungrily.

'That why you were stuffing your face back on The Eldridge, building your strength up?' he asked as he sat on the other side of her as usual.

'Maybe,' she shrugged as she reached inside Ben's jacket and took out his food bar too, she had already eaten hers.

It wasn't long before she was up and back at her task. Finally, she sent the last through, and the rest of the personnel began to leave too; until Alpha team were the only ones left.

Tannis was weak, sitting and leaning against the cold wall. 'When you're ready, get yourself back to The Eldridge,' Jack told her, 'We'll handle those two.'

Tannis shook her head, like she was ever going to leave her team. 'I'll be okay in a minute, I just feel a bit sick,' she said quietly as she tried to stand up, she cried out in pain as she clutched her stomach and fell to her knees. Ben hurried to her side, 'What is it?' He couldn't hide the concern in his voice. Jack too knelt by her side and helped Ben lower her gently to the ground as she slipped into unconsciousness.

They had no time to check her out, Hicks and Richardson were back. Ben set Tannis' timepiece and lifted her hand, so that when he let it fall it would hit the button and get her back safe to The Eldridge. He did this just in time as he felt something hit him square in the back, it was Kira, Jack too was hit by Nira.

Tannis' eyes flickered slowly open, she was in the infirmary, with Ned standing over her, 'Where's Ben?' she asked groggily, she still felt nauseous.

'You came back alone,' he said awkwardly, 'the Admiral sent a team back, but the cave was deserted.'

Tannis sat bolt upright now, 'I have to find them,' she grabbed the cardboard receiver next to her and vomited into it.

'You're not going anywhere,' her brother said firmly, 'look at the state of you.'

'I'll be fine, my team are in trouble, and they need me,' she argued.

'And where will you look?' Hennessey's voice preceded his entrance.

'There has to be a trace, something they left behind in the cave,' her mind raced.

'Nothing,' Hennessey sighed.

'Well, I'm not just going to sit on my arse and wait for archaeologists to find them,' she pulled the covers from her and swung her legs over the bedside.

'Ahh, the patient is awake,' O'Brian poked his head around the curtain. 'Gentlemen, would you let us have some privacy please?'

When Hennessey and Ned had left, O'Brian sat down next to her on the bed; he knew that she would go after her team regardless of what anyone said, 'I can give you something for the sickness, but how will you know where to look?'

'There's someone who owes us a favour, he should be able to help me,' she took the tablet the doctor gave her, then as an after-thought, 'Doctor, I don't get sick.'

'Oh, you're not sick Tannis,' the doctor smiled. 'You're pregnant.'

Tannis almost fell off the bed, 'I can't be, you know that' she stammered.

'And nothing is 100%, you know that' he laughed.

'Who else knows?' She pulled her thoughts together now.

'Just us,' he frowned, 'Tannis, you have the right to patient confidentiality as much as anyone.'

She beamed at him and then hugged him, 'Thanks, Doc.'

He returned her smile and whispered, 'Now get out of here and find your team, that husband of yours needs to know he's going to be a father.'

'Err, I'd rather not do it with my arse hanging out the back of a hospital gown,' she looked around for her clothes.

'In the bedside locker,' he whispered as he left her alone, closing the curtains behind him.

Tannis was relieved that the tablet had stopped her from feeling sick, it had already started working when she made the leap. She stood in the open air now, the sun beating down on her 'BILLY!' she yelled as loud as she could, no reply 'BILLY!' she carried on regardless.

'Alright Missy, no need to shout, Billy's not deaf you know,' the aboriginal smiled. 'Your fella's in trouble?' He already knew, 'better get you inside, a woman in your condition,' he grinned again.

'Do you know everything, Billy?' Tannis asked as they walked on together and vanished, reappearing inside his cave.

'No idea about the offside rule in football,' he said as they sat by the fire.

'You help me find my team, and I'll get Jack to explain it to you.'

He thought for a moment, 'Billy can help you find them, but it will be your spirit I send looking, not your body.'

'You mean like in Dreamtime?'

'Pretty much, but you can't stay out of your body for too long, or you won't find your way back.'

'Will I be able to help them if they need me to, you know, fight?'

'You will have to use your cunning, not your strength, take it or leave it, Missy, I can't help you harm others, no matter what they done.'

'You weren't the pacifist when Phoenix were kicking the shit out of us in Dreamtime,' Tannis said bluntly.

'No one was hurt then, and as I remember, it was Alpha team doing the shit kicking.'

'Why not send my spirit to find them, then I'll leap there in my body?' Tannis reasoned.

'You can't risk that little one in there,' Billy pointed to her womb. 'Billy, I won't stop the fight, you know that.'

'You'll have no choice when your belly gets big.'

Tannis sighed, this issue would have to wait, she needed to help her team first, 'Fine then, we'll do it your way, but can we hurry it up please.'

This time Billy laid her on a bed of dry grass; he painted her face again, and before she knew it, she was looking down at her own sleeping body. Billy looked up at her, 'Now Missy, clear your mind and think only of Ben.'

She did as she was told, but she was worried, all she could think about was him being hurt and in pain. Billy picked up on this, 'You can't think like that, get your thoughts all messed up, and you're no good to him.'

Tannis nodded and concentrated hard, she closed her eyes, but they didn't stay that way for long, she soon flashed them open.

'You see him?' Billy asked.

'I feel him; I can't see him.'

'Good enough, off you go, I'll bring you back when it's time, so be quick.'

It was the strangest sensation she thought; it was almost as if she were being sucked down a plughole, her breath was dragged from her, she didn't know how long she could last when suddenly she was hurled out the other side.

It was like in her Dreamtime experience, she was standing on some grass, but she couldn't feel it, there was a breeze, she could see the trees swaying gently, but she couldn't feel that either. Kneeling Tannis tried to pick a small flower, her hand passed right through it 'Lot of good I'm going to be here,' she said in a whisper, then tried her powers, she couldn't risk being heard if she managed to blast something, so she tried to bring the sensation on; she felt the tingling start in her fingers, 'promising,' she smiled as she walked on her way. There was a log cabin ahead; it was getting dark when she drew closer and peeped in the window.

She was relieved to see her teammates were inside, and appeared to be unharmed, but were both bound tightly back-to-back on two chairs.

Richardson and Hicks were inside too, Richardson walked over and stood in front of Ben, 'Why wasn't Tannis with you in the cave, have we had a little lovers tiff?' She sneered, 'never mind, we'll let her find you soon enough when you're a host, you will travel back, and after a tearful reunion, you will drive a knife straight through her heart.'

'Go to hell,' Ben glared.

'Such harsh words,' she tutted, 'when you and I are going to be such close friends,' she stroked the side of his face, he pulled away roughly.

Hicks stood in front of Jack, 'Got big plans for you too, a man with your clearance, it will be easy to arrange a meeting with the Joint Chiefs, another promising group of hosts.'

Jack said nothing; his mind was focused on finding a way to escape. Also, the device that had been constructed from Echo team's timepieces sat on the table to their left; that too had to be neutralised.

Finally, Richardson left Hicks to watch the prisoners as she went upstairs to bed.

Their jailer soon dozed off in the chair, and Tannis made her move, still not sure what she was going to do, she tried to put her hand on the doorknob, but it just passed straight through. 'So, I should be able to pass right through the door,' she reasoned, and took a small run, heading straight for it. Her reasoning was right.

Both Jack and Ben who were still awake had been looking in the direction of the door when Tannis came through it, they almost jumped out of their skin but managed not to make a sound, so Hicks slept on.

Jack motioned his head toward the mantle above the fireplace; a knife rested on it. Tannis knew what he wanted her to do, but she shook her head helplessly as she knelt by their side. She made to touch them, and her hand passed right through, they could see the painted marks on her face, 'Billy?' Ben whispered.

Tannis nodded, 'He was my only hope of finding you,' she whispered back.

'Well now you've found us, can't you get your body and come back?' Jack frowned.

'No, this was part of the deal, he won't help me do harm to others,' she looked over to where Hicks sat snoring, 'there's something else,' she looked at Ben now, 'I'm pregnant, he doesn't want me risking the baby.'

Even though the odds were against them in an impossible situation, Ben gave her the biggest grin, 'Pregnant?'

She smiled and nodded.

'That explains the appetite,' Jack smiled, 'congratulations mate,' he leaned his head back towards Ben.

Back to business, Jack asked Tannis 'If you're like we were in Dreamtime, do you still have your powers?'

'I can't make a leap, but I think I could blast something, but not far.'

'Can you do anything with these ropes?' Ben struggled with his bindings.

'Probably not without waking those two up.'

'We'll take our chances,' Jack confirmed.

Tannis put her hands as close to the ropes as she could without them passing through and felt the power build in her body. A loud crack woke Hicks from his slumber, just in time to see Ben and Jack shaking the ropes loose from their bodies and standing up. He pulled his sidearm from its holster and opened fire on the two men, wondering how the hell Tannis had found them. Before the threat became credible, Tannis placed herself in front of her team, palms out and stopped the hail of bullets. At this moment, Richardson, no doubt startled from her sleep, ran down the stairs. Her first instinct, as usual, was to kill Tannis, it didn't even occur to her to wonder how she had found them, she just opened fire, her jaw dropped as she pumped a clip full of bullets at her enemy, and they just passed right through her.

Tannis knew she couldn't do much else, so she marched straight towards them both, typically in their cowardly way, the two of them made a leap and were out of there. 'Shit,' Tannis cursed, had she had form; she would've managed to grab Richardson.

Ben went over to the sideboard and picked up his and Jack's timepieces, at least they hadn't managed to take them when they had made the hasty leap.

'I guess this is bad?' Jack looked at the device constructed from the stolen timepieces; it had begun to hum.

'You should get out of here; I'll take care of this,' Tannis stared at the apparatus.

'How, if you can't even touch it?' Jack took his timepiece as Ben passed it to him.

'If I can't blast it into another dimension, I can bloody well blow it up,' she argued, 'now go, Billy said I couldn't stay here for long, or I won't be able to find my way back.'

Ben shook his head, 'I won't leave you.'

'Ben, when I blow this thing, the two of you will be killed, what can it do to me?' She tried to touch his hand.

'Ok,' Jack agreed. 'Blow it, and get back to your body, clear?' 'Clear,' Tannis said hurriedly as she began to bring her power to bear. Reluctantly, her teammates made the leap, and she was alone, she let the full force of her powers unleash onto the device. There was a huge explosion, and when the dust settled, nothing remained, not even Tannis, just a massive crater in the ground.

Jack and Ben didn't return to The Eldridge but went to Uluru. 'Billy!' Ben yelled and Jack too joined in.

'You're as bad as Missy for shouting,' Billy appeared and led them into his cave. Ben rushed over and knelt at his wife's side. 'She's right mate, back in a few minutes,' then Billy turned to Jack, 'now Missy made a deal with Billy,' he led Jack to sit with him around the fire, while Ben sat with his wife and waited.

'So, what's the goalkeeper's position then?' Billy frowned.

Jack exhaled slowly, he had been trying to explain the offside rule to Billy and seemingly not doing well, 'Billy, you're an all knowing, all seeing being, and you can't get the offside rule.'

Billy shrugged 'I'm a Rugby Union man myself.'

Their discussion was interrupted as Tannis sat up, 'Christ, that was weird,' she gasped, then turned to see her husband and was in his arms. They both stood as Jack and Billy came over to join them.

'Well, if it isn't the ghost of Christmas present,' Jack grinned as he hugged Tannis.

Billy stepped a little away from them all. 'There is a decision to be made before you leave,' he looked at Tannis and pointed to her belly. Instinctively Ben and Jack placed themselves in front of Tannis and totally out of character, she let them.

Billy looked put out, 'You know, Billy can never harm a life, but look at you, Missy. Your men are protecting you, and you're letting them, Alpha team will be no use to anyone like this.'

Tannis stepped out and stood side by side with her team as Billy spoke to her now, 'I told you; you can't fight when your belly gets big.'

'So, what are you suggesting?' Tannis eyed him warily, she had to agree, she was never going to stop the fight, but also had to protect the baby.

'When bushfires come through, everything looks dead and burned, but Billy knows better, I put the seeds to sleep, they can stay like that for years until the time is right, then Billy wakes them up.'

Tannis raged at the helpless situation as she stormed to the other side of the cave, Ben followed her. Jack and Billy remained where they were giving them time alone.

'They ever going to get a break?' Jack sighed at the situation.

Billy thought for a moment, 'The future is bright Jack, I can't say more.'

Ben held his wife as she sobbed in his arms, they both knew what had to be done, didn't mean they had to like it though, after a while, they went back and joined the others.

'So how does it work?' Ben tried to keep his voice calm, Tannis still couldn't trust herself to speak.

'I just slow things down so much that baby just sleeps, doesn't grow, just sleeps until I wake him up.'

'Him?' Ben smiled.

'Whoops; spoilers,' Billy gave them a sheepish look.

Tannis drew a breath, 'Do it.'

Billy nodded and stepped closer, he placed his hand gently on her stomach and closed his eyes, then stepped away, 'Little fella sleeping now, no harm can come to him, not even from that Gunther bloke.'

Tannis nodded her thanks, and Ben shook Billy's hand, 'It won't be for long you know, the little fella in there is just the first for you two.'

They said their goodbyes and Billy took them outside, waved farewell and vanished.

Before they made the leap back to The Eldridge, Jack turned to Tannis, 'Who else knows about the baby?'

'Just Dr O'Brian,' she was still a little upset.

'Right, well he's a good bloke and can be trusted to keep quiet,' he looked at them both. 'What I'm saying is, it's up to you who else knows about this, it won't be in my report if that's the way you want it, this is nobody's business but yours.'

'I think it would be for the best if we kept it to ourselves,' Ben thought aloud, 'I don't want Tannis put in any more danger.'

Jack nodded his understanding, 'Mum's the word then,' he grinned as he nudged Tannis, 'see what I did there?'

As usual, he did the trick and made her smile, then blink, they were gone.

Chapter Eight

'Oh God,' Tannis cried out in pleasure as Ben pushed harder inside her. He too moaned as the sensation between them became more intense, his lips were on hers, hard and demanding, his tongue in her mouth; when he stopped suddenly, their cell phones were ringing. Tannis pulled him back down on her mouth. 'Could be important,' he whispered, still not wanting to stop as the phones sounded again. Tannis shoved her hand out and fried them. 'But not as important as this,' he grinned as he took her nipple in his mouth and moved inside her again.

Tannis timed their leap outside the briefing room to perfection, to the others it would seem like they had just been messaged. Jack gave them a start as he stuck his head around the door, 'Hey, c'mon the eggheads have got a bee in their bonnet about something,' he had already been onboard; his afternoon off had been cancelled as Admiral Hennessey had made a trip to the real world, so as the most senior officer next in line, Jack had to assume command. Although that had now cancelled itself out as the Admiral had returned early to see what the fuss was about.

They followed their CO into the briefing room and saw that not only Ned and the Admiral were there, but Dr Kelsey had joined them too.

'Amanda hi,' Tannis greeted her, they had become good friends after their first mission together; Ben too nodded a greeting as they all took their seats.

'So, what's up?' Tannis looked across the table at her brother. 'Ok, well a bit out of my league this one as A) Phoenix haven't actually done anything and B) there's no actual time travel involved,' he explained.

'So, I'm guessing by the good Doctor's presence; it's a science mission then?' Jack pursed his lips. The last two missions involving scientists had both gone badly, and judging by the look on his team's faces they were thinking the same thing too. On the other hand, he had nothing against Dr Kelsey, after all, he had recommended her for duty on The Eldridge. She and Doc O'Brian were the only two scientists he had any time for.

'Doctor Kelsey, perhaps you could explain,' Hennessey looked at the nervous young woman who sat next to Ben. She was a little reluctant at first, but the attentive expressions on the faces of her captive audience soon made her feel at ease. So, pressing the button on the remote in her hand, the screen lit up, and Amanda began. '*Castle Ludendorph*, Germany,' she explained as the image of an imposing mediaeval structure flashed onto the screen, 'famed to be one of the most haunted places in the country,' that was when she noticed her audience's expressions change from interest to scepticism. 'Just hear me out,' she raised her hand.

Tannis rested her elbows on the table in front of her and put her chin in her hands, 'Hey, you go girl, no one listened to me when I said there were monsters out there, and we all know how that one went.'

Amanda wasn't sure that was the kind of support she needed, but right now she would take what she could get. So, she pressed on, 'As you know, we regularly monitor for a particular type of electromagnetic activity for weaknesses in time and dimensions, etc.' She looked back to the screen now, 'and well, this place is going off the scale lately. Nothing prolonged, but definitely getting stronger and as the day's pass, lasting a little longer each time.'

'You think someone, or something is trying to come through?' Hennessey sat forward.

'I couldn't say sir, but from my calculations, we can expect the events to peak at 01.00 on November 1st, and whatever it is, it will be big,' she concluded.

'That's this Sunday. Hence no time travel,' Jack nodded to himself.

'And we have no idea what the threat could be, or where it's coming from?' Ben asked as he fiddled with his pen.

'Go on then,' Tannis frowned at her brother, you're obviously busting a gut to tell us something,' she was referring to the fact that he had constantly been fiddling with his paperwork, waiting for the chance to speak.

Ned choked back a laugh, 'The castle has been empty for some time now, something to do with so many ghost sightings. But unfortunately, the weekend in question, the castle has been hired out for a Halloween weekend of ghost hunting by a parapsychologist and three others.'

'You have got to be kidding me?' Jack rubbed his hand over his face in disbelief.

'Sorry Jack, but the best we could do was buy the four of you a weekend there too,' Ned stifled another laugh as he went on to explain that they would go in as married couples. It was to be Ben and Tannis' honeymoon, and they had wanted something different.

Tannis looked across at her husband as she flopped back in her chair, 'Oh darling, how romantic,' she teased.

'Well, you know, I try,' he sighed as he shook his head.

'So,' Tannis rolled her eyes and looked at Ned, 'can we leap there, or do we take the Mystery Machine?'

'Tannis, this is not an episode of Scooby Doo,' her brother chastised gently.

'Tell me about it,' she fired back, 'all hell's gonna let loose in there this weekend. With God knows what coming from God knows where and to top it all off we'll have four civilians to watch out for too.'

'Very well Alpha team, Doctor Kelsey, we will leave you to read your files and discuss the mission,' Hennessey told them as he stood and left the room. 'Oh here,' Tannis threw the fried cell phones to her brother. 'Another two, what the hell do you do with them?' He frowned as he followed behind the Admiral. Ben said nothing, just remained poker-faced as Tannis shrugged and smiled sweetly at her brother.

The four of them sat reading through their files in silence. Tannis dropped hers down on the table, 'A parapsychologist, his assistant slash wife and some T.V. fake medium with his agent. Ned was wrong, this is an episode of Scooby Doo.'

'Jinkys,' Jack wisecracked as he too laid his file down.

'And there's no clue as to what we're up against?' Ben looked at Amanda. 'No, sorry Major, it was just through routine monitoring that I found the power surges,' she replied.

'You know what that means?' Jack sniggered. Tannis chuckled too as she followed his train of thought, 'They would've got away with it too if it wasn't for those meddling scientists,' they chorused. Ben rolled his eyes and gave Amanda an apologetic look; his teammates were always joking around. But he knew when it came down to business, he wouldn't want to be with anyone else.

They were given permission to leap into a nearby forest a few hundred yards from the castle, dense enough to cover their arrival. It was Saturday 30th October, and it was already getting dark. The castle loomed in front of them when they arrived, its high towers, round turrets and narrow windows added to the imposing effect.

Tannis just stood and stared as a feeling of dread washed over her 'This place gives me the creeps,' she whispered.

'Come on there's a path over there,' Ben pointed out in the half-light as he led the way, Dr Kelsey behind him. Jack picked up his gear and began to follow too, quickly noticing Tannis was still staring at the castle. He walked over and stood by her side to get the same view she had, 'Tannis c'mon, we're moving out.'

'I am,' she whispered.

'Your feet aren't moving,' he whispered back.

'They're scared.'

'Well tell them not to be, it's your arse you should be worried about,' he side-eyed her now. Tannis snapped out of her stare and looked at her CO 'Why?'

'Because if you don't move it and catch up with the others, I'm going to kick it,' he told her and backed it up with one of his looks.

Once inside the castle, they were shown to their rooms by a very polite housekeeper. She was in her fifties and overweight, but friendly, and was very impressed that the four of them spoke fluent German. She explained to them that she had only agreed to take the position of housekeeper on the understanding that she could leave every day before dark, not returning until morning. 'I grew up in the village you see, I know the tales of the castle. No one ever stays long, not even the staff.'

Once inside their rooms, she went on to tell them that a cold supper had been prepared in the dining room. Then she hurriedly excused herself, 'There will be no staff over the weekend,' she told them as she left, 'the other guests have requested no interruptions. So, I will not return until Monday,' then she turned back and gave them a concerned look, 'have a safe and peaceful stay.' With that she closed the door softly behind her. 'Well, we sure got the full tourist show there,' Ben took Tannis' case and put it on the bed next to his. Jack and Amanda would be in the adjoining room. Tannis looked around the chamber; it was the same throughout the castle, or what they had seen of it so far, bare stone walls and floorboards and bare stone floors downstairs. Stern looking family portraits glared down at them at every turn only occasionally blotted out by a dusty suit of armour, or a very pissed off looking stuffed animal. 'And I thought this place looked creepy on the outside.'

Jack followed Amanda into their room, above the fireplace was the mounted head of a deer, the doctor turned her nose up at it. Jack gave it a quick glance as he passed, 'Christ, he must've been running bloody hard when he hit that.'

Amanda laughed and began to relax as she dumped her case on the bed. Why had she been so nervous about posing as the Colonel's wife, she had worked with him before, and he had been nothing but professional. It would be weird though, sharing the same bed but she guessed he must feel the same way too. Besides, she had met his wife a few times now in town and at Ned's parties, and she was one of the few who knew what Tannis had done, travelling back and saving the whole family; although that was strictly a taboo subject on base, no one could even mention the matter.

They unpacked and as well as their clothes, inside hidden panels in their cases, they checked their weapons and armed themselves discreetly then went down to dinner.

'This should be fun,' Tannis walked with Ben hand in hand, 'I've never met anyone who converses with spirits.'

'I doubt you will tonight, I've seen Gerrard's TV show,' Amanda sighed.

'What's he like?' Jack offered her his arm, she took it and smiled 'He's a dick,' she replied bluntly.

'That a scientific term?' Jack raised an eyebrow.

'Absolutely, we use it all the time at work to describe particular types of people,' she was cautious not to say too much as they were close to the dining room now.

Behind them, Ben whispered in his wife's ear, 'Bet Harmon's at the top of that list.'

Inside the dining room, the other guests were already there. 'Hello, and welcome,' a small rotund middle-aged woman semi waddled towards them. 'I'm Amy Colson,' she introduced herself, 'oh it's so nice to have ordinary people to share the weekend with.' The four of them introduced themselves, then Amy made the introductions for the other guests. There was her husband, the parapsychologist, middle aged, the same as his wife, but stick thin with a hook nose and eyes that seemed to be everywhere.

The TV medium didn't need any introductions; he was dressed in a black velour suit with a white ruffle shirt; his wavy hair was swept back perfectly as he tried to strike a pose by the enormous fireplace. Then there was Lou, his agent, a fat sweaty man who showed no interest in anyone or anything that couldn't further his star's career. He spoke quickly and if you showed no potential, dismissed you just as fast.

They sat down at the oversized dining table and helped themselves. Amy made sure she was sitting near the happy couple 'So tell me, was it love at first sight?' It seemed she was glad to get away from the conversation at the other end of the table, which appeared to consist of the medium and the scientist poo-pooing one another's theories.

Tannis smiled at the older woman, 'Absolutely; I fell into his arms the second time we met.'

'Yeah, what can I say Emma swept me off my feet that day,' Ben used his wife's cover name.

Jack smiled to himself as he cut into his cold meat, they were telling the truth after all.

'Was that in America or England dear?' Amy asked, clearly picking up on their accents.

'America,' Tannis replied, 'I had taken a short trip there, and Michael had just got back from Iraq,' she stuck to the truth as much as possible; the best way to remember your cover.

'Oh, fate is a mysterious thing,' Amy clapped her hands together, 'the two of you travelling so far and then meeting by pure chance.'

Tannis smiled as she looked at her husband, he winked at her, and they continued their meal as Amy then directed her questions toward Jack and Amanda.

After dinner, Alpha Team and their temporary addition took their drinks and sat close by the fire. Tannis cuddled up to her husband, it was a nice change to be able to relax as a couple; after all, they were on their honeymoon.

Jack and Amanda too were convincing, and they played their parts well. They were engaging in polite conversation once more with Amy, when from across the other side of the room the psychic gasped and swooned a little. His agent hurried to his side, helping him to sit down on a clearly stage-managed nearby chair. 'The spirits are coming to him,' Lou explained.
'Oh Lou, the tormented souls are calling to me,' Gerrard hammed it up.

Amy looked at her new allies, 'Only spirit that one comes close to is out of a bottle,' she whispered as her husband came over to join them. 'I bet he can feel a séance coming on,' he sighed, then excused himself, 'I'd better get my equipment, make it look as though I'm interested.'

Lou summoned them over, 'The spirits wish to communicate with us through Gerrard,' he said, as he pulled more chairs into a circle around his client.

'Why not, that's what we're here for after all,' Jack said half-heartedly as the others followed him over and took their seats. Lou turned out the lights, so now the room was lit only by the dancing shadows thrown up by the firelight.

'Hurry Professor,' Lou chided as the scientist walked back into the room carrying his equipment. 'Doubt I've missed anything,' he grumbled, as he laid his laptop down on the table and plugged what looked like a small satellite dish into it; then he began typing. It seemed that was Gerrard's cue to go into his trance; he rolled his head from side to side, groaning, this went on for some time, then he began telling them that the mists were clearing, followed by more groaning, then, he could see a little boy. 'Oh, his spirit is tormented, I can feel him falling, ahh no, the water is so cold, I can't breathe,' and with that he slumped in the chair, indicating the show was over.

Professor Colson tutted and switched off his equipment as the others moved back to their original seats by the fire, 'I guess that would be little Ludwig von Ludendorph, who tragically drowned in the river two hundred years ago,' Ben looked at his team.

'I see you, along with Gerrard, have read up on the castle's history?' Professor Colson sat with his wife now.

'Not really, it was just on one of the little flyers in our room, tells about all the supposed restless spirits,' he replied.

'And wait until Gerrard's next instalment, that too will come from print, not spirit,' the professor shook his head.

'You don't believe in mediums?' Amanda asked.

'I am willing to believe that little green men live on Mars if someone can prove it to me. But for all the years I have spent on research, all I have proved is that the world is full of frauds; taking advantage of the bereaved and lonely for profit,' he looked Gerrard's way once more.

Although the professor had shut his laptop down, the rest of the equipment had remained on standby; and as they all sat staring into the flames during a brief interlude in the conversation the electronic devices began to beep, their attention-grabbing noises getting louder and faster.

The professor jumped out of his seat and hurried over to the table 'Good lord!' he exclaimed, almost surprised something had happened for a change; he checked the instruments, 'This is huge, I've never seen such a high electromagnetic surge before.' Alpha team exchanged glances, 'What does that mean Professor?' Amanda innocently asked.

'I'm not sure,' the professor hurriedly detached his portable gadgets from their charging points and hurried out of the room calling back, 'Amy bring the torches.'

Amy quickly did as she was asked, as Jack stood now too, 'Shall we?' He led his team out of the room, 'Ok we'll take the attic and work down,' he looked at Ben now, 'you and Tannis take the cellar and work up.' Ben nodded and they split up.

The entrance to the cellar was along the hallway that led to the kitchen; the smell of damp hit them as soon as Ben opened the door. He reached around the wall for the light switch, located it and flicked it on, nothing happened, 'Of course not, why would it?' he muttered about the broken or missing light bulb. Tannis reached into her rucksack style handbag and took out a torch, passing it to her husband and closing the door behind them as he turned it on.

'Careful,' he shone the light onto the stone steps, they were wet and slippery. 'Oh, you take me to the nicest places darling,' Tannis teased as she followed him. 'Well, you know with it being our honeymoon and all, I wanted to make it special,' his tone followed hers.

The attic landing was sparse, to say the least; the floorboards creaked as they made their way toward the next room to check it out, and as Amanda passed by a small window, it moved a little as the wind outside picked up, she jumped, momentarily startled, but soon pulled herself together as Jack grinned 'Jumpy?'

'Well, our last outing together wasn't exactly run of the mill, was it?' She tried to calm her tone.

'They never are,' he sighed.

'Besides, haven't you seen enough horror movies where the group split up, search opposite ends of the place, so neither can hear the other scream?' She tried to sound lighthearted.

Jack put a calming hand on her arm, 'Alpha team doesn't scream, we may get a bit rowdy and curse, but we don't scream; and believe me, those two can take care of themselves.'

Ben and Tannis hadn't reached the bottom of the cellar steps when something brushed past their legs. They froze, then gave one another a dumb look as they watched a black and white cat hurrying down the last few steps in front of them. Ben turned to speak but quickly faced forward again as a voice came out of the darkness ahead of them 'There you are cat, I've been looking for you everywhere,' a little girl stepped out into the torch light, picking up the feline wanderer.

Her dress looked probably seventeenth century; she could have only been about eight or nine years old. She continued to chastise the now submissive cat as she carried it, 'Papa will be furious if he catches us down here,' and with that, she walked toward the wall across the way and disappeared straight through it.

They both hurried after the child, only to find the wall made of solid stone, Ben shone the light onto the floor. The stones had furrows dug into them that continued right up to the wall, 'This wasn't always here,' he looked at his wife, 'and we both felt the cat touch us.'

Tannis nodded, 'Time is mixing, it wasn't strong enough for the little girl to see us, but if Amanda is right and the power is getting stronger,' she gave Ben a concerned look, 'this will be a really bad place to be.'

Ben took her hand, 'C'mon; we should tell Jack about this,' he said as he led her back up the stairs.

They stood in the passage leading to the kitchen, grateful for the better quality of air. Ben closed the cellar door as Tannis put the torch away. They both turned quickly as they heard a sound coming from the kitchen and almost jumped out of their skins as Amy hurried around the corner, straight into them. She was breathless from her exertion as the two of them took an arm each, leading her out into the large entrance hall, easing her down onto her chair. 'Oh, my goodness,' she puffed, her hand on her ample bosom. 'I was in the kitchen, making some warm milk when I turned around, there was a man standing behind me, dressed like one of these lot,' she pointed to one of the huge portraits hanging on the wall depicting the castle's ancestors from centuries past. She had calmed her breathing now, 'I don't know how he got in, all of the doors are locked.'

'You go to bed Amy, we'll take a look,' Tannis touched the trembling woman gently on the arm.

'Well, be careful,' she fussed as she got up from her seat.

'Probably one of your husband's ghosts,' Ben smiled.

'Oh, no such thing,' Amy shook her head.

'You don't believe in ghosts?' Tannis was surprised.

'Oh, I believe in the afterlife and the spirits there,' she looked directly at Tannis, 'your brother is trying to contact you, has been for some time.'

Tannis was not convinced, 'Well you had a pretty even chance guessing I had a brother.'

'It's not a guess my dear.'

'C'mon, you'll be telling me you have a message from my mother next,' Ben said sceptically.

'No dear, sorry, but your grandmother is watching over you and is very proud,' Amy placed a hand on each of theirs now, 'You're good people, and I respect your wishes,' then she left them and headed towards the stairs, 'but when you're ready to talk, Will has something important that he needs to tell you.'

Tannis and Ben just stared at each other, 'How could she know?' Tannis whispered nervously.

Ben was just as uncomfortable with what Amy had said about his grandmother; he took his wife's hand in his. 'I don't know, but right now we need to focus on the mission.' She leaned into him, he held her tightly and whispered, 'we can go see her later, if you want to.'

Tannis just nodded, and they went to do a quick check in the kitchen, and once ascertaining whoever had been there was gone now, and the place was secure, they continued on their way to the attic.

Jack opened another door and went inside, the rooms that they were checking must've been used as servant's quarters; this one was a long dormitory used for storing furniture and old paintings now by the look of it. Most of the contents were covered in dust sheets, so they went in a little further to make a proper search. Jack's trained ear heard Tannis and Ben on the landing almost outside the door; after all, they weren't trying to be stealthy, he moved silently over and opened it quickly.

'Boo,' he said dryly.

Both his teammates jumped as Tannis laughed, 'Jesus Jack.'

'See, told you they don't scream,' Jack gave Amanda a satisfied look, as Ben and Tannis exchanged a confused glance and stepped inside. Ben filled them in on what had happened both downstairs and, in the cellar, leaving out the part about Will and his grandmother.

'Well, nothing's going on here,' Amanda looked around the room once more, instantly regretting opening her mouth as from the far end, a heat haze seemed to appear, it covered the width of the room and was moving toward them.

'Doctor?' Jack looked at Amanda for an explanation.

'I've never seen anything like it before,' she stammered.

'I have,' Tannis grabbed Ben's arm and stepped back towards the door, 'we need to leave now!'

The haze gained momentum as they ran for the door. Jack was last out, making sure his people were clear as usual, he grabbed the door handle and slammed it shut.

The four of them stood on the landing, Tannis held on to her teammates and called to Amanda, 'Grab onto Jack,' she did as she was asked, but the threat came no further; they relaxed their grip on each other, and Jack stepped forward and slowly opened the door. 'Shit!' was all he could say as the sight in front of them unfolded when the door swung open; the room was now full of beds all neatly lined up in rows, and those beds belonged to a group of Nazi soldiers all getting changed.

'The little girl couldn't see us, maybe they can't,' Ben whispered. His thoughts were put down as the soldiers inside noticed them and, picking up their weapons, took aim. Jack grabbed the door handle and slammed it shut, as Tannis stepped in front of them all and thrust her hands out ready to stop the hail of bullets coming their way. But the door swung open of its own accord, and the room was empty once more. Tannis heaved a sigh of relief as Ben and Jack put their weapons away.

'Definitely getting stronger,' Amanda looked at Tannis who just nodded.

'So, what was that haze?' Jack too looked at Tannis, 'you said you'd seen it before?'

'It washed through Atlantis when the folks sent The Eldridge back,' she bit her lip, 'and we all know what happened to the island.' They headed down to their rooms now as Amanda pondered, 'I doubt it's something with such a power source as The Eldridge, but if someone or something has the ability to manipulate time, we need to find it fast if we want to either stop or contain it.'

They decided to call it a night, their search of the house had turned up plenty, but not the power source they were looking for.

They would sleep fully dressed, just to be ready, Ben jumped on their bed and flicked the TV on, 'Whoa, they got the fight on satellite.' Tannis poked her head around the bathroom door, still brushing her teeth as Jack hurried in and pulled up a chair next to his teammate, 'How come you got a TV?' He frowned.

'Honeymoon outranks all this time,' Tannis laughed as she walked over to the window and closed the curtains. There was a storm brewing outside, the wind was getting up. She drew them tight and walked into Amanda and Jack's room, 'Blown out on my own honeymoon for a boxing match,' she bemoaned to her friend, who threw her a magazine to read. The two women sat on the bed and talked.

Jack and Ben could hear them laughing in the next room 'Those two seem to get on well,' Jack observed.

'Yeah, been meeting up since Amanda got transferred,' Ben replied casually.

'What, girly shopping trips, that sort of stuff?' Jack was pleased Tannis had a female friend, she only had Elea since her sisters were killed, and she was always busy with the brood.

'Yeah, pretty much,' Ben settled back putting his arms behind his head, 'and a few ass-kicking lessons.'

'Basic training not enough?' Jack gave his friend a sideways look. 'A girl needs to be able to take care of herself, that's what Tannis told me when I said the same.'

In the other room, Amanda confided in Tannis that Major Harmon had been flirting with her, flowers, chocolates, the works.

Tannis wrinkled her nose, 'Amanda, you're not gonna fall for that, I mean if you like him, well…'

Amanda laughed, 'God, no that scientific term I used earlier to describe Gerrard, well you know who it was invented for.'

Tannis laughed out loud 'Major Harmon.'

This made her teammates prick up their ears, 'Ladies; I hope you're not being indiscreet in there,' Jack gently warned.

'No, Amanda was just explaining a scientific term,' Tannis called through, in her best innocent voice.

The two men looked at each other and held back a laugh; they knew exactly what the girls were laughing about now.

The fight wasn't all that great, so they decided to get some sleep, they would need whatever they could get for whatever the next day brought.

Tannis walked back into the room she was to share with Ben, and whacked her toe on the door frame, 'Swine!' She yelled as a huge clap of thunder rumbled, and lightning flashed, then the lights went out.

'Oi,' Jack growled as he turned his torch on to see Tannis still hopping about on one foot.

'Don't look at me,' she snapped.

Ben walked over to the window and looked out, 'Village has still got power, must be the trip switch,' he grabbed his torch and walked over to his wife, 'you ok now?'

She nodded and tried her weight on her foot, 'Stupid place to put a door frame,' she grumbled.

'Yeah, right around the door,' Jack rolled his eyes.

Tannis narrowed hers at him but said nothing. Amanda joined them now, bringing her torch too, 'C'mon, we'll all go, haven't seen the cellar yet,' Jack sighed, so much for sleep.

They were not alone as they stepped out onto the landing, the other guests were milling about by torch light too, 'Err, we'll go down and fix the fuse,' Jack offered as he led his team down the stairs. Gerrard seemed relieved as he immediately retreated to his rooms, with Lou in tow, Mrs Colson too thanked them and went back to bed, dragging her ever curious husband with her.

As the four of them headed along the corridor to the rear of the castle, that would lead them to the cellar, Amanda bent down and picked up a black and white cat that had been rubbing around her ankles, 'Hey gorgeous.'

'You know that cat is over four hundred years old,' Ben whispered.

She put the animal quickly, but gently back down on the floor, 'We should avoid contact with anything that comes through, if it goes back, it may take us with it.'

'Just so we're clear, anything like that happens, you leap back to The Eldridge immediately,' Jack ordered.

'Clear,' they all agreed.

Down in the cellar, nothing appeared out of the ordinary, Tannis held the torch for Ben as he fixed the fuse; meanwhile, Jack and Amanda checked out the grooves worn into the floor that they had been told about earlier.

'Got it,' Ben closed the fuse box. Jack shone his torch up to the ceiling, from where the light pendant hung with no bulb in it. But a crack of light that shone under the door at the top of the stairs confirmed Ben had resolved the problem. They made their way back to the stairs, just in time as the haze began to appear again, but this time it didn't move, it seemed to manifest itself on the wall that they had ascertained was recently bricked up. The haze settled and the wall was gone, revealing what was a well-lit and clinical-looking lab, complete with large cages and operating tables. A man was secured tightly to a table, he was unconscious, but that wasn't all, he was wearing a timepiece. The haze wavered, and the wall returned.

'Anyone recognise that guy?' Jack looked at them all in turn.

'Could be one of ours from the future, for all we know,' Amanda supposed.

'He's Phoenix,' Tannis blurted out, 'disappeared about ten years ago. We had a few run is with him, but none of us managed to kill him.'

'Still, doesn't help, what we just saw could be from decades ago,' Jack frowned, 'and if whoever's got him strapped to that table finds out what that timepiece is for, we could have a big problem on our hands.'

Amanda began to pace a little; it helped her to think, 'Maybe they already did,' she said to herself, then stopped walking as she noticed them all looking at her.

'Care to explain your theory there, Doc?' Jack leant against the wall.

'Maybe they did find out that the timepiece was more than just a watch, but in trying to find out how it worked, they tapped into the power source,' she offered.

'And now it's leaking like Cole's' Tannis' eyes showed her sadness at the memory of her brother.

They went back to their rooms and slept for what remained of the night, as morning came, the storm abated.

Jack woke first and washed and changed while the others didn't bother to move. As he came out of the bathroom, Amanda was waiting to take her turn, hearing no sound of movement from the other room, he decided to wake them up. As he stood in the doorway he felt as though he were intruding, they were both still dressed under the blanket, he knew that, but it was the way Ben had his arms protectively around Tannis, and as she lay within them, she seemed so small and fragile.

Jack shook himself from his thoughts as he knocked on the door frame, 'C'mon you two, we're on the clock remember,' he called as he went back into his own room. Ben opened his eyes, and seeing Jack had left, he pulled his wife closer and kissed her, she opened her eyes and smiled.

When they were all ready, they made their way downstairs to the kitchen to make their own breakfast; passing Gerrard and Lou on the landing, 'Tis all hallows eve,' Gerrard called to them dramatically, 'the spirits will be abroad tonight.'

Amy and her husband were already in the kitchen when everyone else arrived, Amy had kindly been preparing a massive fried breakfast for anyone that wanted it. The team gratefully accepted and sat at the large wooden table. 'I'll have a decaf skinny latte,' Gerrard commanded as he took his seat. Amy didn't bite; she just plonked a mug of tea in front of him. When everyone was served, Amy too took her place, ready to tuck in, she was pleased that the others had used their manners and waited for her to sit. She was surprised however when they all gasped with what didn't sound like delight. The reason behind their reactions soon became apparent when Amy looked down at her plate, all her food and everyone else's too had moulded and rotted; before anyone could speak their attention was then drawn to the foot of the table. There stood a man dressed in a doublet and hose, his face clouded with rage as he drew his sword, then vanished.

The smell of freshly cooked food drew their eyes back to their plates as there waiting to be eaten was breakfast.

Gerrard screamed and ran, Lou close behind him, 'They're real, oh my God, they're real,' the two terrified men raced straight out of the castle towards the village without looking back.

Professor Colson hurried out of the kitchen with his wife in tow, presumably to get his equipment. Jack looked at his team, 'Well, at least that's two out of the way. But we need to find that power source before this gets out of hand.'

They split into two's again and searched the grounds now. The outbuildings turned up nothing when Ben and Tannis checked them out, so they made their way into the courtyard where Ben led her over to the far wall, 'Automatic weapon fire,' he pointed at the markings on the masonry, 'what the hell happened here?'

'That would be from the war,' it was Professor Colson, 'there was a garrison of Nazi's stationed here,' he nodded, 'very curious though.'

'How so?' Tannis frowned.

'Well, the Germans were notorious for their paperwork and record keeping, and from records found pertaining to this place, the whole garrison just disappeared, probably sent to join other companies, but no records, very odd,' he shook his head as he turned to walk on, instruments in hand.

'When did they disappear?' Tannis asked.

'Well, the records end on 15th, May 1944,' he muttered, his attention drawn to a wailing sound coming from his equipment.

Ben gave Tannis a nod, and they set off in search of their CO, whom they knew would be searching the walled gardens and the outbuildings around there. They caught up with them on the lawn and filled them in on the news.

The sky suddenly darkened, and thunder rumbled, as they looked above them, the tell-tale blue flashes of time travel flitted around in the darkness.

'I don't think we will have to go back to 1944,' Tannis closed her eyes as if concentrating, then she opened them again quickly, 'it's coming to us.'

'Back inside,' Jack ordered.

'Jack, there's more,' Tannis grabbed his arm as they ran from the coming storm, 'dimensions have broken through too.'

Inside once more, they locked all the doors and hurried to their rooms, where they armed themselves appropriately. The storm outside showed no signs of abating, if anything it was getting worse. They went back out onto the landing, 'Get the professor and his wife out now; they have to leave,' Jack said as they all raced to the stairs, a noise behind them on the landing caused them to turn and look up. It was Professor Colson 'Professor, where's Amy?' Ben asked as he took a few steps back up the stairs, 'Oh, the dining room I believe,' he replied without looking up, he was busy with a hand-held device, seemed to be scanning for something, then it appeared in front of him, the haze.

'Professor, get down here now,' Jack shouted, but the scientist was too engrossed in the sight that had presented itself to him, 'My word, this is amazing,' he stepped closer.

'No Professor, don't!' Amanda yelled, but it was too late as the professor stepped closer again to the haze, it too moved closer to him, and he passed right through it; and although they could still hear him talking, he seemed oblivious to their calls.

Their blood ran cold as they then heard the unmistakable shriek 'Nightwalkers,' Amanda gasped as her hand went to her mouth. Jack was closest and tried to force his way through the haze, but it was like a solid wall now.

'How can that be?' Amanda pulled herself together, 'maybe once a weakness occurs, it strengthens itself.' This didn't help the professor though, and they were helpless to do anything other than watch as a *Nightwalker* stalked closer to the unarmed man, but this one was a little different from the others that they had come across before, this one was dressed in Nazi uniform.

'That's what the cages were for in the lab,' Tannis bit her lip nervously.

They looked on as the condemned man tried to talk with the beast, but it was no use, it was on him in an instant, ripping at his throat with its razor-sharp teeth, and claw-like nails. Then the haze faded, and the landing was empty as if nothing had happened.

'Amy!' Tannis shouted as she ran down the stairs, she looked over her shoulder to see where her team was, but she turned back too late. She had run right through a haze, she tried to shove her way back through, but it was no use. She couldn't see her team on the other side, but she knew they were there, so she decided to stay put where they could see her.

From the darkness across the entrance hall came the sound of movement, 'Amy?' Tannis drew her sidearm and froze as the reply came, it was the shriek of not one but two *Nightwalkers*, then another.

Ben began shoving at the haze, but it wouldn't let him through. They watched as Tannis backed up, her teammates knew these things were her worst nightmare, and now she was alone with them again.

'Make the leap, get out of there,' Jack shouted.

'Tannis, get back to The Eldridge,' Ben yelled.

Her closeness to her team made her almost aware of what they would be saying. 'I don't know if you can hear me, but I can't leap, something's stopping me, time's all wrong here, I …' she couldn't finish her sentence as the first *Nightwalker* rushed at her. She opened fire, and it fell dead, but then three more were on her, she killed two more, but the third knocked her weapon from her hand. It was close combat now; they fought hand to hand. Tannis held her own well for saying the superior strength of the *Nightwalker*, but then another joined the fight, running from the darkness right behind her, it clawed her back, and Tannis yelled out in pain as the beast's nails tore through her flesh. The other then saw its chance and went for her throat as she lashed out and kicked the one behind her.

From the other side of the haze, Ben and Jack both called out, but it was useless; the beast had its target in sight, it was so close now Tannis could feel its breath on her neck. Then a shot rang out. And the *Nightwalker* fell dead, Tannis pushed it from her and grabbed the knife from her boot and threw it at the one remaining, where it stuck in its neck, game over.

Then came the task of finding out who fired the shot. Tannis was on her knees in agony when the Marine leant down and offered her a hand, 'You're hurt,' he said as he pulled her up, he shoved the weapon he had picked up in his waistband. Tannis allowed him to help her stand, then she made her move, quickly reaching for the gun and aiming it at his head, 'Step away,' she ordered.

'Hey lady, I just saved your ass,' he complained as he stepped back.

'And you're still breathing,' she winced as the pain came again.

'I really should look at that,' he motioned to her back. 'I'm a doctor,' he told her and made to step closer.

'Not an option,' she raised her weapon again and motioned for him to stand aside, 'don't take it personally Doctor, there are very few people I trust with my back,' she moved now too and leaned against the wall.

'Ok, so you won't let me help you, maybe you can help me,' he folded his arms, he was around five feet ten, not in bad shape with light brown hair. Tannis had the feeling she had seen him somewhere before, but couldn't place him, 'If I can,' she agreed.

'Well, you know the thing is, I'm having the weirdest day, one minute I'm in Iraq working on a mass grave, then the next thing I know. I'm in this damn castle, but not just here with you, oh no, every time that damn haze moves, and I pass through it I wind up in the same place, but a different time. I've had mediaeval guys trying to torch my ass, and let me tell you, the Nazi's, well they just shot first, and I guess we're gonna ask questions later.'

Tannis placed him now; he was the scientist that went missing in Iraq when they found Cole's body, she had seen his photo on file; looking to where her team would roughly be standing, she raised an eyebrow.

'I can't help you there Doctor, I'm just visiting the castle too,' she shrugged. They both fell silent as Tannis leaned heavier against the wall, she was in a lot of pain now, and she could feel the blood running down her back.

'I'm forgetting my manners,' the doctor apologised. 'I'm Captain Logan Fraser, U.S. Marine Corp,' he raised a hand in a mock greeting.

'Tannis,' she said as she nodded a response.

'Got a last name that goes with that?'

'Rhodes.'

'Huh, one of the guys I'm working with in Iraq is called Rhodes, him and a British Colonel run the show, good guys too,' he mused.

Tannis just acknowledged him with a nod, she would say nothing, he may be who he said he was, but where else had he been along the way. Realising he wasn't going to get much of a conversation out of her, he turned his attention to the dead *Nightwalkers* and knelt to take a closer look at one of them, 'Have you ever seen anything like this before?' He looked back at Tannis as he gently opened the mouth of one.

'Don't get too close to the teeth,' she warned.

'It doesn't seem up to biting me now,' he grinned.

'It doesn't have to bite, catch yourself on one of those and you're looking at your future.'

'You're kidding?' he quickly stood.

'You think they all looked like that in the German army?' She frowned at him.

'But how, nothing like this has ever been recorded before,' he gave her a puzzled look, which soon turned to realisation, 'you're not the average tourist here, I saw you fight these guys, you're trained. Let's face it most people I know would run a mile if they came up close and personal with one of these things, never mind a gang of them.'

'Believe me, if I had a mile I would've run it,' Tannis said bluntly.

The haze began to shift, Fraser moved closer to Tannis, 'We've got a better chance of getting through this if we stick together.'

Tannis motioned for him to stand in front of the haze, 'Oh, I intend to get us through this, don't worry,' she seemed to scan the wall of haze looking for a weak spot. Satisfied, she had found one, she shoved the Captain through and followed him, her hand still on his shoulder.

'I'll take it from here,' Jack told her as he took the gun from her hand that now trembled from the pain of her wounds.

'Colonel Marsters?' Fraser gasped in shock, then seeing Ben leading his wife away he did a double take, 'Major Rhodes?' He couldn't believe his eyes, he was still in his desert camouflage uniform, but they were dressed in civilian clothing and were as calm as anything, and another woman was with them too.

'Good to see you alive Logan,' Jack grinned, but as Tannis had done he still trained the weapon on him as they climbed the stairs.

Once inside the room, Jack gave Tannis' side arm to Amanda indicating that she should watch Fraser. Ben led Tannis to sit on the dressing table chair, where she leant forward so he could look at her wounds.

'I know you're a medic sir, but I'm a doctor, and I really should look at that,' Fraser piped up.

'I got it covered, thanks Doc,' Ben said without turning.

Jack came out of the bathroom with a folded towel, which he gave to Tannis as Ben cut the back of her shirt and slid it over her shoulders, discarding the blood-stained item on the floor as she put the towel over her breasts. 'You're healing already,' he said softly as he cleaned the gouges on her back and dressed them.

Fraser just gaped open mouthed, 'How's that possible?' He looked at Jack.

'Look Doc, there's a lot of classified stuff going on around here, so just go with it ok,' was all Jack was prepared to say as he opened a drawer and took out some fresh clothes for Tannis. He passed them to Ben who then took her into the bathroom to get changed.

He closed the door, and she was in his arms trembling like a child waking from a nightmare. He tilted her chin up, and he could taste the salt of her tears as he kissed her gently. They stood holding each other for a moment, then he helped her to dress, neither spoke, but as she put her hand on the doorknob to open it, he took her face in his hands, 'Stay close, ok?' He whispered, then kissed her once more.

'You alright love?' Jack gave Tannis a concerned look as the two of them came out of the bathroom.

'I'll be all right Jack,' she half smiled, 'but we still have to find Amy.'

'I just checked downstairs, can't find her,' he shook his head. 'She could've walked into a haze.'

'What about him?' She was still speaking to Jack as she looked at Dr Fraser.

'Yeah, what about me, and how come she gets to call you Jack?' The doctor folded his arms defiantly.

Jack gave Fraser one of his how dare you looks, 'You are a security risk, we don't know where you've been since you left Iraq, and it's Colonel to you.'

'What do you mean since I left Iraq,' he looked at his watch 'I've only been gone five hours.'

'Over two years,' Jack gave it to him straight.

The Captain was struck dumb for a moment, but soon found his voice, 'Time travel, that's what that watch was on those remains we found.' He paced a little now trying to process the information he'd been given, 'So the remains of that guy we dug up, he was a time traveller?'

'Yeah, it's complicated, there was a time war, Cole was a casualty,' Jack gave up as much as he was prepared to.

'You know his name, how?' Fraser had so many questions.

'He was my brother,' Tannis spoke up again.

'He's still dead, why didn't you date the soil and go back to save him?' The doctor frowned.

'Leave it Captain,' Ben warned.

Tannis began to fidget with her dressings now, 'You want them off?' Ben touched her arms gently, she nodded, and he raised the back of her shirt and began to remove them, revealing nothing but some fading scars. Fraser tactfully kept quiet, but they all knew what he was thinking.

Tannis nodded to Amanda who handed her back her weapon and then took out her own.

A scream from downstairs hurried them out of the room, 'Hey, how about me, don't I get a weapon?' Fraser complained but was ignored.

Out on the landing, they saw Amy moving as fast as she could up the stairs toward them, she was gasping for breath when she reached the top, 'It was the same man from breakfast,' she puffed, her hand on her chest. 'Amy, this is Doctor Fraser,' Jack introduced. 'He's going to take you into the village, it'll be safer there.'

'But…' the breathless woman began.

'Amy, please,' Tannis took her by the hand.

'Oh, alright my dear,' she reluctantly agreed. 'I'll get my coat,' she walked toward her room. But a short distance from them, standing outside her door, she stopped and looked to the far end of the landing, 'Hello, who's there?' She called. Silhouetted against the huge window was the figure of a German soldier, this one had human form, however.

Everything seemed to happen in slow motion, Jack and Ben raised their weapons as they saw the soldier take aim at the woman, both sides opened fire, the soldier fell dead; but as Tannis ran to Amy, she too had collapsed, her chest covered in blood.

'Watch him,' Jack ordered Amanda to stay with Fraser as he and Ben both went over to where Tannis now sat cradling the dying woman in her arms, 'I'm sorry, you weren't meant to die,' Tannis choked.

'Don't be sad my dear, I'll be with my husband again,' Amy gave a small cough, and a trickle of blood ran from the corner of her mouth. Jack gave Ben a questioning look, how could she know her husband was dead. Then she started to slip away, but as she did so she grabbed Tannis' top tightly, 'Will needs your help Tannis,' that was when Amy's voice changed; it was no longer her own. Tannis recognised it as her brother's. 'Tannis, you've got to find them, help them, keep them safe, my diary is on The Eldridge. It's all in there, help them, little sister, I can't find the way back.' Amy's voice returned. 'He's not dead Tannis, Will is not on the other side, he's lost.' Amy exhaled her last breath and was gone, her grip released on Tannis as her life slipped away. Tannis gently lay the dead woman on the floor and stared at her, the three of them had heard the same thing, but no one could speak.

Once again, duty called them out of their thoughts as from outside they could hear shouting, the three of them went over to the window near where Amanda was keeping an eye on Fraser. Looking out onto the rear courtyard they could see Nazi soldiers dragging out what would've been their own kind but were now half turned *Nightwalkers* chained to one another. They lined them up against the wall and opened fire.

'Looks like we're well and truly in 1944,' Ben whispered.

'Right then, let's get down to the cellar and neutralise that power source,' Jack signalled for them to move out, as they turned and looked back along the landing, Amy's body still lay there, but all around now hung pictures of Adolf Hitler and flags bearing the swastika. 'Stay sharp people,' Jack whispered as he drew his weapon. With the execution squad busy outside, their path to the cellar was undisturbed. Jack, taking point, cautiously opened the door and they made their way slowly and silently down the stone steps. From their vantage point above they could see two guards standing opposite to where in the future the impassable wall would be. Jack motioned for Ben and Tannis to take them out, they both nodded their understanding and silently climbed over the stair rail, dropping simultaneously onto the unsuspecting guards, a quick twist of the neck for each of them, and it was all over. Meanwhile, Jack had reached the bottom of the stairs with the others so that he and Amanda could give cover, should there be any more, but the only other person in the room was the Phoenix agent that they had seen earlier. This time he wasn't strapped to the table, he was locked in one of the cages, and it was evident he had been bitten and was in the early stages of becoming a *Nightwalker*.

'Tannis,' he mumbled, he was finding it difficult to speak as his teeth were outgrowing his mouth.

'Bryce,' she whispered as she stood in front of the cage, 'tried to make a deal with the devil, did you?'

'Something like that, they have my timepiece over there,' he tried to point with his half-deformed hand.

Amanda moved over to it and shut it down, it was damaged, and apparently, someone had been tampering with it, she gave it to Jack, and he slipped it into his pocket.

'We've no love lost between us, you and I,' Bryce mumbled again, 'but if you have any compassion at all, end this for me now,' he begged.

'It all ends here,' Jack spoke as he pulled the trigger and Bryce fell dead, 'we can't leave time like this, there are *Nightwalkers* all over the place. Doctor Kelsey has stopped the power source, so time should be okay everywhere else,' he turned to Amanda now, 'Doctor, your job's done here, take Captain Fraser back to base and let the Admiral know what's going on.'

'Yes sir,' she nodded, she walked toward the stairs when from behind her in the shadows a man in an SS uniform grabbed her, he must've crept down the staircase while they were busy. Holding a gun to her head, he ordered the others to disarm and raise their hands. Amanda pretended to swoon, he loosened his grip on her a little, as he did so she threw her head back, and head butted him, as his hands went to his face she turned and kicked him in the groyne. He dropped to his knees, temporarily disabled, she grabbed his head with both hands and twisted as hard as she could, breaking his neck.

'You weren't kidding about the ass-kicking lessons,' Jack gave Ben a sideways look.

Amanda just winked at Tannis as she set her timepiece, grabbed Captain Fraser and vanished.

The room was in silence as Alpha team picked up the discarded weapons from the men that had been killed. 'Be handy if we knew where the armoury was, but I suppose as usual we'll have to make do,' Jack led the way to the stairs, then turned to his teammates, 'the *Nightwalkers* cannot be allowed to survive.' Tannis and Ben both nodded and followed their CO.

They searched the castle first, it was easier with most of the garrison, or what was left of it outside. The castle was clear and as they made their way down the back stairs to the courtyard, Ben looked out of one of the narrow windows, 'Looks like they're cleaning house themselves.' Outside now the soldiers were dragging out their officers and the scientists and lining them up to be shot too.

'Professor Colson said the whole garrison vanished,' Tannis frowned, 'but some of the men are still human, what happened to them?'

Ben took a closer look; the firing squad had fresh bite marks, 'Not human for long,' he motioned toward the infected group.

They made their way silently into the courtyard and with a quick head count, it seemed to Jack there was about thirty, ten to one he thought to himself, but then again, they had the element of surprise.

But that didn't last long; a *Nightwalker* had been stalking them ever since they had stepped outside; it let out its scream and charged toward them. 'The hard way then,' Jack took aim and fired, the *Nightwalker* fell dead, but now their element of surprise was blown. A full-on firefight ensued, with the added distraction of the *Nightwalkers* also wading into the fray.

Alpha team fought well, but the attack was hard and fast, their bullets were all used up on the advancing troops, which now left the *Nightwalkers*, their backs to the wall armed with only their pistols now. Alpha team looked for a way out that wasn't forthcoming, and it soon came down to hand-to-hand combat.

Then from the opposite side of the courtyard came the relief they needed, Charlie and Delta team had arrived fully armed and attacking straight away. 'Oh, you gotta admit, the Admiral's got timing!' Jack cheered as he kicked another half-transformed soldier in the face. Tannis too was down to beating her attacker with a shovel that she had found, hitting him in syllables 'Fuck,' whack, 'off,' whack, Ben finished him for her with his knife as another was about to bite his throat, she swung the shovel violently and took the beast's head clean off.

There was small arms fire now that soon died down, Major Charles made his way over to them, 'Sir, Dr Kelsey filled the Admiral in on the whole thing, so he thought you might need some backup.'

'Much appreciated Major,' Jack motioned toward the castle, 'we'll need a full clean up.'

A few hours later, the area was secure, and the bodies destroyed, nothing remained of the garrison, nor the lab of horrors. The last corpse to be brought out of the castle was in a black body bag, the small plump shape gave away the identity of the person inside.

Tannis hurried over and stopped the two men from Delta team, she unzipped the bag and looked down at the now peaceful face. Her team joined her, and Ben rested a hand on his wife's shoulder and led her away; Jack closed the zip, 'This one's coming back with us for burial,' he told the men who carried her, then walked on to catch up with his team. 'Thanks, Jack,' Tannis whispered, they both knew she was upset, it always got to her when an innocent was killed.

They walked on into the walled garden and turned back to look at the castle and watched the other teams make their leaps out of there. When they were alone, Tannis looked at the two men, 'When Amy was dying, did you hear what she said to me?'

Both men seemed uncomfortable as they nodded. 'So, I'm not going crazy, it was Will's voice I heard?' Her voice shook as she looked from one man to the other.

'Well if you are going mad, then so am I' Jack sighed.

'Me too, I heard it clear as day,' Ben agreed.

The last little blue flash as Major Charles made his leap gave Tannis a start. Ben looked at her concerned, 'You, ok?'

Her eyes were open, but nothing was registering, she was lost in a memory, she was back reliving the final battle with Phoenix. Her teammates took a hand each and were swept away with her too; it was just before Will's death, as they faced Tannis' attacker a small blue flash caught the corner of their eyes, then they turned to see Will killed. Tannis gasped and fell to her knees; they were back at the castle now.

'Why were you reliving that memory?' Jack asked as he and Ben helped her to her feet.

'I never lived that memory,' she said softly, 'it's new to me, the blue flash, did you see it in the corner of your eye?'

Both men nodded slowly.

Tannis stepped in front of them both, 'the past has been changed, we need to get back to The Eldridge,' and with that, they were gone.

Chapter Nine

Ned sat open mouthed at the debrief, as Alpha team now covered the part where Will had spoken through Amy.

'You're sure it's not just Phoenix messing with us?' He asked when he finally found his voice.

'I'm positive,' Tannis confirmed, 'besides you know they can't mess with my head like that.'

'Don't you have all of your sibling's effects in safe keeping at your place Ned?' Hennessey was clearly referring to the part of Will's alleged dialogue where he told them his diary was still on The Eldridge. Ned nodded, 'You're right Admiral, that's why I'm finding this all a little hard to accept.'

Tannis banged her fist on the table, 'It happened Ned, don't you think I can't recognise our brother's voice,' she looked at her teammates, 'they heard him too!'

Jack broke the awkward silence that followed Tannis' outburst. 'You know I used to be a sceptic, but didn't we recently travel back fifty thousand years to a spirit world.'

Ned still didn't seem convinced which was beginning to rile Tannis; Ben could see this, so put the obvious solution into words 'Why don't you just look for the diary, then when you read it, the mystery will be solved?'

'Excellent idea Major,' Hennessey could see a world class Tannis and Ned argument brewing, and this was to be avoided at all costs, they could turn ugly and usually resulted in Ned being blasted somewhere unpleasant.

'It's not that easy Admiral, I know what's in Will's stuff in my barn, and there is no diary,' Ned seemed to fire this back at his sister more than to the Admiral.

'And you're supposed to be the smart one?' Tannis rolled her eyes, 'Will said it was still on The Eldridge.'

'His quarters were cleared out along with the rest of them, you know that' he hissed at her.

'Like he'd leave something so personal laying around, he would've hidden it,' she snapped, 'like you used to hide yours behind the bath panel in your quarters along with your Belgian chocolates.'

'You cow… that, was you?' Her brother was gob smacked.

'Don't worry, I only pinched your chocolates, I never read your diary,' Tannis grinned at the fact she could still surprise him, then she turned to the Admiral, 'Major Harmon has Will's old quarters, do you think he'd mind letting me in?'

'You're not going in there without backup,' Jack blurted out before he realised what he was saying, 'I mean, someone should go with you, protocol you know.'

Ben hid a grin, he'd had the same thought too, but Jack's big brother protectiveness and the comfort of rank had made him jump in first.

'Bravo team returned from their latest mission this morning; I will arrange for access to the Major's quarters,' Hennessey stood now, the debrief was over.

'I thought it was rats,' Ned narrowed his eyes at his sister 'There are no rats on my boat,' Tannis replied haughtily.

'Ship,' he corrected her.

'Don't even go there,' she replied.

A few hours later the four of them received permission to check Major Harmon's quarters. As they were cramped for space and Ned and Tannis would have the best idea where to look, Jack and Ben waited outside in the passageway.

'You know, when the Admiral asked if I'd mind showing you my quarters, I didn't realise we were going to have a chaperone,' Harmon pretended to sound put out.

'Now Major, you wouldn't want to break all those hearts in town if they'd found out you had a woman alone in your quarters,' Tannis said as she ran her hands along the wall panels.

'To be alone with you, I would forsake all others,' he smiled at her.

'I'm a very happily married woman Major,' she reminded him 'Yeah, to the guy standing right outside the door,' Ben poked his head in now, glaring at Harmon.

'Nothing,' Ned reported as he came out of the bathroom.

'It's got to be here somewhere,' Tannis muttered as she looked around the room. The only piece of furniture left in there that had been Will's was a large brass circular ships barometer, she walked over and pulled at it.

'It's stuck fast,' Harmon stood next to her, 'I've tried a few times to get it down, but didn't want to risk breaking it.'

'Can I try?' She looked at him for permission.

'It belongs to you more than me,' he replied genuinely.

Her teammates stepped in the room as Tannis took a firm grip on the instrument and pulled hard, but it wouldn't budge. Moving closer, Ben looked at the stubborn object then sighed and gave his wife and Major Harmon a chastising look as he gripped it but turned it instead of pulling and unscrewed it from its mount. Once removed he handed it to Tannis and smiled, as there inside was an old leather-bound diary. She took it out and opened it, 'It's Will's handwriting,' she confirmed then handed it to her brother.

'He really spoke to you,' he gasped.

Tears welled in Tannis' eyes as Ben led her out of the room and Jack helped a stunned Ned from the chair he had occupied and led him along the passageway.

Once inside his office, Ned sat at his desk and began to flick through the pages, 'Give me an hour,' he looked at the three of them, 'I need to be thorough.'

Reluctantly, they left him to it.

It was less than an hour though when Alpha team were called into the briefing room and Ned hurried in, looking a little nervous. He took his seat not really knowing what he was going to say, so he laid his brother's diary down on the table and just blurted it out, 'Will, fell in love, got married and had a son.'

Tannis almost fell off her chair, 'What, who, when and why the hell didn't he tell us?' she demanded.

Ned looked even more uncomfortable as he continued, 'Seems they met on a mission back in the fifteenth century.'

'So, he couldn't take her out of her own timeline, would it have affected history?' Ben puzzled.

'Not quite,' Ned fidgeted, 'you see, she was on the run, she wasn't in her own timeline.'

A look of shock washed over Tannis, 'No,' she shook her head.

'Yes,' Ned replied bluntly, 'Will fell in love with a Phoenix agent on the run.'

You could've heard the proverbial pin drop.

'She was using him, mind control,' Tannis tried to find a reason.

'No, Tannis, you know their mind powers are only temporary, and Will was married to her for three years,' Ned admonished.

'Then why couldn't he tell us?' She choked.

'We were at war with Phoenix, he was worried we wouldn't accept her, and besides with her Phoenix DNA, he couldn't bring her to Atlantis,' Ned said, his tone a little softer. 'He had to keep his wife and child in hiding to protect them,' he then went on to explain that her name was Tara and that she had taken the same stance as Tannis' mother, grabbed a timepiece and ran. But Phoenix were wise to turncoats, so had installed tracking devices into the new recruit's timepieces. When Will met her, she threw herself on his mercy, he took pity on her and helped her, and after a short time, they fell in love. He would move them from time to time using his timepiece, but Tara kept hers for emergencies, knowing that if Will didn't make their pre-arranged meeting one time, she would leap to the next herself and ditch the timepiece and try to live her life the best she could with their son.

'So, it's to be assumed that Will didn't make their last meeting point and Tara made the leap herself, but to where?' Hennessey looked to Ned for an answer.

'Now that, I do need time to work on,' Ned admitted. 'Will's coded it, I'm sure I can crack it, but it'll take a while.'

'Very well, we shall reconvene when Ned has the relevant information,' Hennessey addressed them all.

'You'll let us go after them?' Tannis was surprised.

'Your brother's wife and child are at the mercy of Phoenix, it is our duty to protect them,' the Admiral sighed. 'Also, the child must not be allowed to fall into Phoenix hands,' he looked directly at Tannis now. 'So far, you were the only child born with such powers, but if your brother has inherited the same altered DNA from his father, his son could inherit some powers too, and if the child has just half of what you have and falls into the wrong hands, it would be disastrous,' with that he left the room.

'What about the coalition?' Ned voiced his concern. 'I don't mean the Admiral or the Joint Chiefs, but have you forgotten the attempt that was made on Tannis, they even dragged Ben into it.'

'My brother's son will be no one's lab rat, nor be forced into the life I was made to live; he will be a child for as long as possible.' Tannis was adamant.

'He might not have any powers Babe,' Ben tried to help.

'I hope for his sake he doesn't carry this curse,' she sighed.

'Ned, get on to the time and place for Tara's final leap, one way or another, we're going after them,' Jack ordered.

'What did they call him?' Tannis asked.

Ned smiled at his sister, 'Apparently; he already has an untameable mop of blond curls, so his name fits him well, they called him Will.'

Tannis grinned, then bit her lip, 'What powers does Tara have?' 'The usual mind control, but not very strong, it seems her specialty is moving things with her mind.'

Tannis said nothing more, just nodded and Ned left them to it.

'You were young Will's age when your powers started to come through,' Ben looked at his wife.

Jack nodded, 'Time's running out literally.'

A day passed and still nothing from Ned, he hadn't been himself since they found the diary and Tannis had begun to worry about him. She and Ben called by his office earlier to see if they could walk home together, but he had dismissed them, saying he was too busy and needed to concentrate.

That night in their apartment, Ben couldn't help but notice his wife's thoughts were elsewhere, 'Penny for them?' He wrapped his arms around her as they stood in the kitchen pondering dinner, 'cos I know it ain't food.'

'Oh Ben, I'm worried about the mission,' she leaned into him. 'Little Will can't be allowed to fall into Phoenix's hands, we're all agreed on that, but like Ned said, what about the coalition, can they guarantee his safety too?'

Ben put his hands on her shoulders and looked at her; he didn't say anything, he didn't have to, she knew what was on his mind just as he had known what she was thinking.

'Ben, I promised you I would never do anything like *The Wind Dancer* again without telling you, but it has to be considered.'

'Not without me,' he said softly.

'It would be the end of us with the coalition.'

'Some things are more important,' he kissed her now.

'I couldn't ask you to do that for me,' she returned his kisses.

'You wouldn't have to ask,' their kisses grew stronger and more passionate now as he walked her back towards the wall; she felt the cold tiles on her back, his lips were still on hers as he ran his hand up her skirt, Tannis undid his belt as she felt him pulling at her panties, then his hands were on her hips, and he was inside her, she gasped at the sensation. He began to move slowly the way he knew they both liked, then he took her face in his hands and kissed her again, they were both trembling, 'We travel the road to come what may together, remember?' He whispered, then his mouth was on hers as their passion increased.

Later that evening, Jack called round to their apartment, he knew what would be on his teammates' minds and needed to speak with them. 'I know you're both thinking about taking things into your own hands to protect the child,' he began.

'Sir, we would go through the proper channels, hand in our resignations,' Ben cut in.

'If we're going to resign over this, we need a safe place to take Tara and young Will,' Jack pressed.

Ben made to speak, but Jack raised his hand, 'Of course I'm going with you, we're a team, so don't even bother to protest,' he looked directly at Tannis now, 'you took care of my family when I couldn't, so now we'll take care of Will's family when he can't.'

Tannis smiled at her CO 'Avalon.'

Jack nodded his approval. 'Only you can take them there, and no one else can get there without you.'

'Better still, if young Will does have any powers, he won't be able to accidentally leap off the island,' Ben added.

'You know, we should put this to the Admiral in the morning, there's a good chance that the Joint Chiefs will go for it, after all, in the real world it's the acronym boys that cause all the trouble,' Jack put it to them.

So, it was agreed, first thing in the morning they would talk with the Admiral.

As requested, Hennessey met with Alpha team the next day, they sat in silence in the briefing room while they waited for Ned to join them. The Admiral had already surmised what the meeting was going to be about and was keen to get on with it, so he leaned forward and pressed the intercom in front of him, 'Barbara, ask Ned to report to the briefing room please.'

Tannis almost knocked her chair flying backwards as she ran out of the room when they heard Barbara's raspy voice reply, 'Sir, Ned didn't report for work today.'

She was already standing in her brother's office when the others caught up with her, holding a handwritten note addressed to her. She didn't speak, just stared straight ahead as Jack gently took it from her and read it aloud.

'Well little sister,

It's my turn to put things right for a change, I know you'll be mad at me for going it alone. But I can't ask you to choose because I know in a heartbeat you would go with me, and Ben and Jack would be at your side. But your jobs as Alpha team would be finished, and with Phoenix and God knows who else still out there, the world really does need you. God willing, I will see you again soon, don't worry about me, one way or another I'll do the right thing, no one lives forever. Take care of Elea and the children for me; this is one mission she does know about. You always were the best of us Tannis, stay safe and be happy. Oh, and I've destroyed my notes and taken Will's diary with me, so you won't be able to follow,

Ned.'

When he had finished reading the note, Jack handed it to Hennessey who told them, 'Last night I put it to the Joint Chiefs that

Alpha team undertake the rescue mission and subsequent safe placing of Tara and young Will.'

All three of them looked at him as he continued, 'It was unanimously approved.'

Tannis walked around her brother's desk, true to his word he had left nothing behind. She looked down at a framed picture; it was of the two of them on her wedding day. Picking it up she looked at her brother smiling back at her, that was when she lost her temper and dropped it face up on the desktop, bringing her fist crashing down on it and shattering the glass. She didn't even realise that she was bleeding until Ben walked over to her and looked at the wound 'C'mon, I'll take you to the Doc, get this cleaned up.'

Still angry and frightened for her brother, Tannis didn't even flinch when Dr O'Brian picked out the few remaining shards of glass in her hand.

Ben had filled the doctor in on what had happened; he had listened quietly as he had gone about cleaning and dressing Tannis' wound. When Ben had finished the doctor just sighed, 'He's not lost, you just don't know where to look.'

Tannis sighed too, 'Over his shoulder at his notes would help.'

Dr O'Brian smiled as he saw the look of realisation dawn on her face.

'Oh, my God, do you just hang around here like a fountain of knowledge?' She leaned forward and hugged him, then kissed him on the cheek before she hurried out of the room, dragging Ben with her.

'No one must see you,' the doctor called after them.

Halfway down the passageway, Ben pulled her to a halt, 'Babe, what the hell is going on?'

'I'll explain when we get back to Ned's office,' she grinned as they hurried on.

Once inside, Tannis opened the top drawer of Ned's desk and took out a small brass key; Ben looked at the wardrobe-sized cabinet that stood behind the desk, 'You're gonna leap back, and read his notes,' he smiled.

'God, I can be so thick sometimes,' Tannis grumbled.

'Doc O'Brian should be a General,' Ben agreed.

Back in the briefing room now, Ben and Tannis explained the plan to Jack and the Admiral.

'Good old Doc O'Brian always comes through when you need him,' Jack said proudly.

'Very well Tannis,' Hennessey gave his permission, 'CCTV has him still on board at 17.30 hrs, we know that you and Major Rhodes had left by then, so I suggest you aim for around that time.'

Tannis nodded 'I can only do this for a short time, or I risk a paradox, being so close to myself on the island.'

'Then, be quick,' Jack added unhelpfully.

From her position opposite him, Tannis smiled at her husband and was gone.

It was cramped and stuffy inside the cupboard, Tannis managed to open the door a crack and peeped out. Ned was at his desk, writing the letter she would find the next day. Slightly above it and to the left, she saw Will's diary and more importantly, Ned's notes.

Gotcha, she thought to herself as she saw everything she needed to see. Her cover was almost blown when the cupboard door began to swing open, quickly she made the leap, leaving a confused Ned wondering how the door had come open when he was sure he had locked it.

Tannis reappeared in the briefing room seconds after she'd left, but this time wearing a big grin, 'Fourteenth century anyone, well 1st November 1313, Alnwick Castle, Northumberland, England to be exact.' She could see that she had their attention, so continued to explain that in 1309 Henry de Percy bought Alnwick castle from the Bishop of Durham, but not long after, the Sheriff of Yorkshire had Henry imprisoned on trumped up charges against the crown. All of this had been helped along by Phoenix, who were hoping to wipe the Percy name off the map for their own gains. Will had secured Henry's safe release, and all charges were dropped, so it would be a safe bet that Henry owed him.

'A good choice,' Hennessey seemed to approve of her brother's actions, 'his wife and child would be afforded all of the comforts and protection of the castle, and should Phoenix track them down, Tara would be able to sense them and take action.'

'Oh, there's no doubt Phoenix will track her as soon as they hear the signal,' Tannis said bitterly.

So, it was agreed that Alpha team would make the leap back to 1313, their priority being to find Ned and work with him, as he must already have a plan to make contact and get Tara and young Will out. They met in the hold after changing into appropriate clothing and arming themselves accordingly, the three of them were dressed as travellers with wool shirts and trousers, long boots and long wool cloaks. Even Tannis was dressed as a man, although she would also carry women's clothing, should the need arise, and along with their long swords, Tannis also chose to take a crossbow.

'Alpha team, good luck,' Hennessey gave the order to leap.

They arrived in 1313 in a densely wooded area close to the castle, but far enough away so as not to be seen; they knew the date and place roughly that Ned was leaping into, so had aimed as close as possible.

'I'll kill him when I get my hands on him,' Tannis muttered as they took in their surroundings.

'Mission first,' Jack said casually as he checked his compass, 'you can kill your brother later.' Satisfied that their arrival had remained undetected, he led the way toward the castle.

It was a beautiful crisp, cold sunny morning; deep untouched snow lay all around them as they crunched their way through it. They had only been walking for a few minutes when the silence was shattered by a scream that echoed throughout the wood. It was difficult to get a fix on the position, so the three of them stopped and listened again, this time the sound of metal on metal reverberated through the trees. Tannis closed her eyes, turned to her left and slowly removed the crossbow from her back, then pointed, 'Over there.'

Jack nodded for them to move out, they ran as fast as the deep snow would allow and it wasn't long before they came across a caravan under attack from bandits. Two men lay dead in the snow, their blood still seeping into the brilliant white. It seemed that the woman who had screamed was trying to hide her children inside the wagon, while another man fought off the other four attackers.

'Ned,' Tannis didn't realise she had spoken aloud, her team hadn't noticed it was her brother fighting for his and the other people's lives as he was still cloaked and hooded. It was his fighting style that she had recognised straight away. She raced forward, although her brother was under attack from four men, only one was armed with a sword. As Tannis ran to her brother's aid, Ben made to follow after her, but Jack put a hand on his arm; Tannis had already discharged her crossbow bolt into the bandit that carried the sword, and now she was fighting her way through the other three. 'I think we should let her work off a bit of that anger, do her good.'

'You ok there, Babe?' Ben asked nonchalantly as he and their CO stood, arms folded watching her make short work of the bandits.

'Fine thanks,' she called back as she shoved her hand, palm up into the last but one man's jaw, sending him dead at her feet.

'Oh, she's pissed,' her husband sighed.

'Yep, wouldn't like to be in Ned's shoes later,' Jack concurred, then noticing Tannis had killed the fourth and final man and was marching straight for Ned, he nodded to Ben and the two men rushed after her.

Ned was breathlessly leaning against a tree for support; he lowered his hood now as his sister drew near. As she did so, she dropped her sword to the ground, and that was when he saw her expression, but it was too late she had him by the throat.

'Tannis, enough!' Jack ordered.

She released him instantly, but her glare was enough to tell him that it wasn't over.

'Go with Ben, see if there's anything you can do for the survivors,' he added.

She did as she was told and joined her husband who was checking one of the men who had been lying by the wagon. The occupants of which, a woman and three frightened children had climbed down now and were sobbing, trying to wake him. Ben knelt by the man's side and checked for a pulse, he was still alive, Tannis helped him to turn the unconscious man over, the wound to his shoulder was superficial, but he had sustained a lump on the back of his head as he had stumbled and fallen when struck by the blade. They patched him up as best they could and helped the family on their way, as it turned out there was a fever in Alnwick, so they were heading out to the country to stay with family until the danger was over when they were attacked.

Jack and Ned heard all of what the travellers told Ben and Tannis; this could prove a problem; the castle would be sealed if there was a fever in the town.

Once the travellers were a safe distance away Jack turned to Ned, he pointed at Tannis who now stood next to Ben, 'She's under orders to behave, but I'm not. What the bloody hell were you playing at, fair enough you had doubts about the coalition, but us?'

'You must've read my letter; you know why,' Ned defended his actions, then frowned, 'anyway, how the hell did you find me?'

'Doc O'Brian gave us a little help,' Ben too was a little frosty with his brother-in-law, 'Tannis leaped back and read your notes over your shoulder.'

Ned looked at his sister now for absolution, but she wouldn't give it, she totally ignored him as she walked off to pick up her discarded crossbow.

'She's really mad, isn't she?' Ned sighed.

'Oh yeah,' Ben muttered as he followed her.

'So, what was that little scuffle about?' Jack asked as the two of them followed on.

'Oh, wrong place, wrong time, couldn't really just stand and watch, could I?' Ned picked up and sheathed his sword as he passed by where it lay.

The four of them now walked on in silence to the castle, no one knew what awaited them there, but whatever it was, they would have to think of a way around it.

The streets of the town were still busy with traders and travellers for all the threat of fever. The snow hadn't long settled, but the carts and wagons had soon churned it to mud. They made their way along the track road to an inn, the closest they could find to the castle and took lodgings there for the night. It was probably going to take the rest of the day to recon the area and find out the situation inside the castle, let alone try and make contact with Tara.

Once in their rooms, Tannis changed into her dress so that they could play the part of a family of travelling merchants, if they looked wealthy enough, it may gain them access to the castle.

They went out in two's, Jack went with Ned, knowing it was better to keep him as far away from his sister as possible at the moment, sure he knew Tannis would behave, she always followed her orders, but what was the point in antagonising her. So, she and Ben went to check out the part of the town near to the main keep of the castle, they strolled arm in arm, looking at the wares in the market. But all the time their eyes were elsewhere, checking out what they needed to know, how many guards, what were their positions, ease of access, possible threats and escape routes in an emergency. All this they noted as they went about a seemingly pleasant shopping spree.

The night was drawing in when they all met back at the lodgings, they took their meals in their room and made plans for the following day.

From the intel they had gathered, it seemed that the fever was already in the castle, and tomorrow a small caravan carrying the wives and children of anyone of importance would be leaving for a nearby abbey. It would be a day and a night's travel, perfect for them to follow and make contact with Tara, but also ideal for a Phoenix attack too.

Tannis had remained unusually quiet throughout the whole time they drew up their plan, and it had not gone unnoticed, her constant glances toward the window, her thoughts seemingly elsewhere.

'Tannis,' Jack frowned, 'anything you'd like to add, you usually do?' He said a little sarcastically to get her to bite.

She stood up and walked over to the window, looking out toward the castle, 'It's not a fever in there.'

Ben stood and joined her.

'Phoenix?' Ned had a sinking feeling in his stomach.

'Not Phoenix,' Ben corrected, he knew his wife well, 'a Feeder.'

'Christ, we never thought of that,' Jack jumped out of his seat too.

'If Louis knew about you, the Feeders could've found young Will, if he has powers like yours,' he looked at Tannis.

'If the Purity's knew you had been born and sent Louis to watch over you, they must know about young Will too,' Ned looked across at his sister. 'Can you sense one of them?'

Tannis shook her head, 'No, I just had a feeling for a moment, like when I was with them back at the house with Louis,' she too frowned, 'it's gone now.'

Jack looked at his timepiece, it was past midnight, 'Let's get some rest, Tannis you and Ned get the bed, Ben and I will take first watch. If there is a Feeder out there, chances are it'll pay us a visit too.'

Against all odds, the night passed without event, Jack and Ben sat in the fireside chairs and took their watch, when it was time for Tannis and Ned to take their shift, Jack got up and gently touched her shoulder. During the night, Ned had spooned in behind his sister and put a sleepy arm around her. As she opened her eyes slowly, she looked past Jack to where her husband sat and gave him a puzzled look 'Ned,' he mouthed as if reading her thoughts, then her expression changed to one of shock as she jumped out of bed. They had both remained clothed, and Tannis now stood glaring at her brother 'What?' he asked sleepily then rolled his eyes, 'oh, that,' he reached down and pulled his dagger from beneath the bedclothes, it had been sticking in her back when she woke. 'Ugh,' she shuddered as Jack gave a chuckle, which soon turned into a cough when she turned her glare on him. 'I'm flattered,' Ned grinned as he climbed out of bed.

Tannis was still pissed at him for his first misdemeanour; this was just adding to the list, 'Don't be, I didn't think it was you,' she snapped.

Both men now gave Ben a quizzical look as he returned theirs with a smug one.

It was dark when the four of them made their way to the castle gates; they could hear the commotion coming from inside as servants hurried around getting everything ready for the journey. Ned had procured four of the best horses money could buy for them. It had been decided that Tannis should dress as a man for this part of the mission, if there was a Feeder out there, they needed every advantage they could get, no matter how small. And Tannis could fight better without the restraints of skirts.

They watched from the shadows as the small but well-protected caravan made its way through the sleepy streets. It was a frosty morning, and Tannis wrapped her cloak tighter around her, but for once it wasn't the cold that made her shiver.

The caravan was protected by fifteen armed men; seven covered the rear, seven led and one apparently, the knight in charge, rode in front of them all.

'Interesting,' Ned looked across at his sister.

'Templars,' she concurred with his findings.

'Knights Templar?' Ben remembered conversations with his wife about Will's past missions involving them, 'you think Will had something to do with them being here?'

'It would be my guess if not, they're taking a significant risk, Templars have all but been branded heretics,' Ned mused.

'Could be a problem getting close to Tara,' Jack thought aloud 'your brother has protected his family well.'

The three wagons were covered, so it was impossible to know which one Tara and Will were inside. Jack led them at a safe distance as they wound their way along the rough track through the woods. The wagons struggled at times; the muddy ruts had frozen and made their passage very difficult as sometimes a wheel would get wedged and prove a major obstacle to overcome. Jack and the others noticed that at all times the Templar escort remained vigilant, almost as if they were waiting for an impending attack. Sure, there were bandits in the woods, Ned and Alpha team had already come across them, but these guys were on the look-out for something more, they were constantly on the alert.

When the sun reluctantly rose, it bought little or no warmth with it. The caravan continued on its way, not even stopping for breakfast or a midday meal, the occupants must've had provisions stored for them inside the wagons. As the night began to draw in, the travellers finally stopped and made camp, allowing the women and children to disembark and stretch their legs.

Ned and the others looked on hopefully from their position. They had no idea what Tara looked like, but as soon as she cautiously poked her head from the canvas flaps that covered the wagon, no one was in any doubt it was her. She looked to be in her late twenties, maybe early thirties, slim, about the same height as Tannis, but with jet black waist length hair and the most striking green eyes.

'Well, your brother certainly fell for a stunner,' Jack grinned as he watched the woman jump down from the wagon and hold up her arms, as she did so, a toddler came into view with a mop of blond curls and the cutest smile for his mother as he jumped down into her embrace. It was also noted that as soon as she and the boy were out in the open, the Templars were never very far away.

'Looks like a good time to introduce ourselves,' Jack led them on toward the camp where they were soon surrounded by the armed men, their weapons drawn, ordering the strangers to dismount. They did as they were bid, and before anything further could be said the leader of the Templars stood his men down, sending them back to cover the camp with the others. The striking young man made his way directly to Jack; he was tanned, probably recently returned from the holy lands with his men. His hair was dark and his eyes bright blue. 'Guy de la Boyer,' he spoke with an English accent, 'forgive my men, years of service, to then be outlawed by many as heretics has cost them some of their manners.'

'Not at all,' Jack replied, 'a well-trained body of men, you should be proud.'

Guy smiled and inclined his head, 'I am, but they are not really my men to lead, they have been loaned to me for a task I must undertake,' he turned his attention to Tannis, 'and you my lady, why do you disguise yourself as a man?'

'It's safer to travel that way,' Jack spoke for her, 'we are on our way to place my sister in the care of the Abbey, where we know she will be cared for, while we pledge ourselves to the King.'

'A noble quest I'm sure we all embark upon,' Guy nodded. 'You are most welcome to join our caravan, and we can share one another's protection.'

'That was easier than I thought,' Jack told them all later as they sat around their own fire and ate their meal. It was dark now, and they sat mostly in silence, keeping watch.

Little footsteps came tottering toward them, it was Little Will, he had slipped from his mother's arms and was heading straight for them, with her hot on his heels, 'Will, no!' she called after him in a hushed tone. But the toddler was on a mission, he did his best hurried waddle and burst into the circle of people that were Alpha team and Ned. The latter smiled at his sister as the young child wrapped his arms around her neck, she gave him a cuddle, then pulled him away to look at him as he babbled her name.

'It is you,' Tara gasped, 'he's been saying your name since yesterday,' her eyes welled with tears now as the fact hit her head on, her husband was dead. But she still didn't want to accept the fact 'Where's Will, where's my husband?' She choked.

'Dada' young Will called for his father.

Ned helped Tara to sit and as tactfully as he could, filled her in on the events of the past few years, right up to the Halloween mission.

'So, you're telling me Will was dead, and now he's not?' Tara struggled to take it all in.

'Dada, on wrong lantis,' Will babbled, then pointed to his mother's timepiece, 'Dada's bwoked.'

'He keeps saying that' Tara shook her head, 'he says Will is on the wrong Atlantis and his timepiece is broken.'

'It isn't broken,' realisation dawned on Tannis. 'Will's in another dimension, our timepieces don't work in them.'

'Whoa,' Ned slowed his sister, 'that's a bit of a stretch.'

'No,' Jack thought back to the Halloween mission 'you had a memory of the final battle with Phoenix and said someone had changed the past.'

'The blue flash in your peripheral vision,' Ben added, 'that wasn't there before.'

Tannis nodded, 'and Cousin left me a surprise, remember.'

'We buried him Tannis, that memory hasn't changed,' Ned whispered.

'A replacement from another dimension or even her own wouldn't be difficult,' Jack leaned closer, 'and Will would be the obvious choice, he was the furthest from the fight, he had gone after his target remember?'

'And his face was battered,' Tannis choked.

'Christ,' Ned sat back in a little bit of shock, 'we have to find him,' he looked at his sister.

'We will, but we have to concentrate on this mission first,' Jack brought them back to the present. 'Will is alive if his son can sense him, and he's a pretty handy chap, so I think we can assume he'll stay that way, but now, we have a different priority,' he looked at Tara. 'Young Will's powers are growing all the time I take it?'

Tara nodded helplessly, 'Phoenix will come for him, I'm so scared, and he tells me that he can see the doors in his head sometimes when he closes his eyes,' she shrugged, not sure of what her son meant.

'Oh, another leaper in the family,' Ned smiled, 'don't worry, there is a place Tannis can take you and young Will, it's a bit like Atlantis, but only Tannis can get you in and out, no one can touch you there.'

Tara sighed, 'I never understood all of the Phoenix power trips,' she rolled her eyes, 'why would anyone want all of the hassles of ruling the world?'

'Hey, I'm with you on that one,' Tannis tutted, 'but if you're so against it all, why did you volunteer?'

'Oh, I didn't, my brother abducted me and handed me over to a creepy Germanic scientist, they altered my DNA, but I escaped before they could try reprogramming me,' she shuddered, 'my brother is a perfectionist, said I would produce God's for children.'

Ben looked at Tara again now, but through new eyes, 'Your brother's name wouldn't be Rafe by any chance?'

'As a matter of fact, yes, have you met him?'

'Oh yeah,' her four companions chorused dully.

Little Will, bored with the conversation, stood in front of Ben with his arms open for a hug. Ben opened his arms and the toddler snuggled inside the warm cloak. His eyes soon began to droop, and before long he was fast asleep.

'We should find a safe place and make the leap out of here,' Jack looked around, but they had left it too late. Guy and three Templars had made their way over to them.

Guy bowed to Tara, 'My lady, a tent has been prepared for you, my men will escort you and stand guard,' he then turned to Jack, 'one has been prepared for you also, you may sleep soundly tonight, my men are vigilant.'

Jack reluctantly thanked him and watched as Guy led Tara whilst carrying the sleeping child away, 'Bugger, there's no way we'll get them out tonight,' he cursed under his breath.

So, Jack and Tannis took the first watch, they found a vantage point and sat, waited and watched, shivering in silence. Jack's thoughts turned to his partner for the watch, he knew Tannis hated being cold with a vengeance, yet here she sat right by his side and never complained once, and it was cold. He looked across at her, all that was visible of her as she huddled tight in her cloak were her eyes, and although she shivered, they never dulled nor stopped scouring the countryside.

'Jack?'

'Hmm?'

'Guy.'

'Hmm?'

'He doesn't eat or drink.'

Jack quickly turned his gaze from the camp back to her, 'You sure?'

'Well, he didn't eat all day, neither did his men though, but when we made camp, he made sure his men were all fed but didn't take anything for himself.'

'Maybe he ate in his tent, not all senior officers rough it with the lower ranks,' he gave her a friendly nudge.

'He's a Purity, I'm sure of it,' she continued.

'Surely, he would've introduced himself, Louis said they would if we met one of them again.'

'Maybe in his timeline we haven't met Louis yet,' she pondered. 'Hmm, gonna need more proof than that before we say anything.'

'Well, he can't be a Feeder, he would've attacked Little Will or me by now.'

'Hmm, well we'll just have to wait for him to make his play, unless you fancy going down to his tent and asking him if he fancies a snog?'

Tannis looked down her nose at him now, 'I don't find you funny,' she said a little tongue in cheek.

'You still intent on kicking Ned's arse when we get back?' He continued.

'I'm a woman of my word,' she replied dryly.

'Go easy on him, his hearts in the right place.'

'I make no promises.'

Finally, it was time for a change of watch, Ben and Ned had made their way to the tree line where Tannis and Jack had taken position. They were standing now, trying to get the circulation running through their cold and stiff joints. Ben stood in front of his wife rubbing her arms, trying to warm her, that was when he felt her go rigid.

'What is it?' He drew his sword as did she.

'I think it's a Feeder…' was all she managed to get out as swiftly and suddenly, she was grabbed and dragged into the woods. Her teammates and brother ran after her. 'There should only be one, Louis said the nest we found was rare,' Jack called to the two men who ran with him. They caught up with them deep in the woods. Fortunately, the moon was full, and the white snow helped light their way. Tannis was pinned against a tree, her feet kicking wildly as the Feeder lifted her over a foot from the ground by her throat. It was close to her now dislocating its jaw ready to take her life. But Tannis wasn't going down without a fight, she reached down into her belt and pulled out a dagger, the Feeder had knocked the sword from her hand when it took her. She shoved the small blade into its ribs, with an inhuman squeal it bashed her head against the tree, stunning her, and pulled the dagger from its side. That was when it realised, they were not alone; it turned to where the three men stood, revealing its true hideousness to them. It was male and hungry by the looks of it, as it darted towards them and knocked Ned clean off his feet, distending its jaw once more to feed. Jack raised his sword above the monster, but it was too quick for him, leaving Ned on the ground, it lashed out sending Jack through the air and crashing into a tree. Then it turned on Ben, he managed to stave off a few attempts with his sword, but again the Feeder's speed was too much of an advantage, it knocked his weapon from his grip and lunged for him. Ned rallied himself and picked up his sword; he brought it down right between the Feeder's shoulder blades. Ben pushed the beast off him, and it lay dead in the snow.

Tannis crawled over to where Jack lay half dazed, his ribs had taken a beating, but he would be ok.

'It would seem my thanks are in order,' a voice came from the shadows.

'Told you he was a Purity,' Tannis rubbed her bruised throat.

Guy moved over to the Feeder and closed its jaw properly, 'It wouldn't do to have it found like that.'

'Not being rude or anything, but where were you?' Ned looked at Guy as he offered Ben a hand up.

'I was forced to make the decision, between you or the child,' he walked into the moonlight now and inclined his head to Tannis, 'I knew that you would be well protected.'

'How come these things have only just shown up on our radar?' Ned had a head full of questions.

'It has only really been this once, and that was because it sensed the child's powers. Usually, our paths will never cross. The last time when you met Louis, that was because you went looking.'

Ben stood with Tannis and checked her neck, it was badly bruised and showed perfect finger marks where the Feeder had held her, he knew that they would soon fade, but still hated to see her hurt.

'Well, now that we're all introduced, can we take Tara and Little Will to safety, before Phoenix shows up and starts kicking off?' Jack winced as he held his ribs, Ben made to look at his injury, but Jack shook his head, 'be alright,' he told his friend.

'Perhaps tomorrow, the Templars I travel with are loyal to Tara's husband, they will not allow anyone near the wagon, we will have to try in daylight,' Guy shattered their hopes of an early leap.

Even though Guy had assured them, there was only the one Feeder, Ben and Ned still took their watch, while Tannis and Jack tried to get some sleep in the relative warmth of the tent. Although they were wrapped in furs, they still shivered, it would take a while to warm up. Tannis lay looking at her CO as they both huddled trying to get warm, then Jack opened his arms, and they cuddled together, shared bodily warmth soon sent them off to sleep. Daylight hadn't even broken when the camp began to stir, Jack woke first, Tannis was still sleeping, her head on his chest. With the arm he had around her, he rubbed her shoulder gently, 'Tannis love, come on wake up.'

She opened her eyes slowly and sat up, it was freezing inside the tent, even though they were both still fully clothed, she quickly lay back down and covered them up again.

The tent flap opened, letting if it was at all possible even more cold air inside as Ned and Ben hurried in, hastily closing it behind them. They had brought four bowls of pottage and some warm ale with them, they forced down the tasteless meal, it was better than nothing, and at least it was hot. Then they made their way outside.

The camp was already making ready for departure as Guy walked over to join them. 'I have arranged for Tara and Will to ride with you this morning, I will leave it to your discretion Colonel as to when you make your move.'

'Much appreciated,' Jack shook Guy's hand.

'Guy,' Tannis lowered her voice, 'there was no fever in the castle, was there?'

Guy looked sadly to the ground, then back at her 'No, it was the Feeder.'

It wasn't going to be as easy as they had hoped, getting away that morning, the Templar knights were not letting Tara and Will out of their sight, Guy too was trapped, he couldn't leave either until he knew that his wards were safe.

They had been riding for a couple of hours when Young Will who sat in front of his mother began to get agitated; he was getting more and more distressed until he turned and buried his head in his mother's cloak, 'Bad man mommy, bad people,' he cried. Tara gave her companions a terrified look, 'They've found us, Phoenix have found us, we have to leave now, there are too many innocent people here,' she made to pull on the reins, but the Templars turned and blocked their way into the trees.

'They're being controlled,' Ned drew his sword and moved his horse in front of Tara's. Phoenix showed themselves now, it was Rafe and Elsa, but they were not alone, as well as controlling the Templars, they had bought clones with them too.

Jack turned quickly to Tannis, 'Get them to the trees and make the leap,' he ordered.

Tannis gave him an angry look, she knew that she was the only one that could get them to Avalon, but that would mean leaving her brother and her team.

'That's an order Tannis,' Jack gave her a hard stare. She looked from her husband to her brother, both men nodded to her, their weapons drawn, so angrily she followed her orders as she had promised to do, and roughly grabbed Tara's reins as the attack began and hurried them to the safety of the trees. Guy followed her, protecting her as best he could, killing three of the clones that gave chase.

They dismounted, and Tannis looked back to see her team and her brother fighting for their lives. In what must've been a fit jealous rage, Rafe broke his concentration allowing the Templars to awaken from his control as he charged toward Ben, sword at the ready. Tannis could only watch as the two men fought hell for leather. Ben made ground on Rafe and wounded him with a side cut and thrust, the agent fell to his knees, but before Ben could finish him, he made the leap. Realising that she couldn't control all those that she needed, Elsa too vanished. The fight was over, all the clones lay dead, the Templars had survived, that was when they turned on Jack and his men, realising that they had failed in their duty and that Tara and Will were gone, they forced their prisoners to their knees.

'Go,' Guy quickly turned to Tannis, 'return after your safe twenty-four hours, meet me at the Abbey gates, I will see that they come to no harm until then.'

Tannis nodded, and after taking one last look, she took Little Will's hand and then Tara's and was gone.

'Hold!' Guy called out as one of his men raised a sword above Jack's head to bring down the fatal blow. 'These men will be taken to the Abbey and tried and executed for their crimes there,' he looked at the three men on their knees, now battered and bruised, but other than that unharmed. He also noticed that one of his men had removed their timepieces and shoved them under his tunic.

Their hands were bound, and they were dragged the rest of the way to the Abbey by mounted Templars. It was impossible for Guy to speak to them and vice versa.

'Tannis must've got them out,' Ned whispered what the others already thought, as they both just nodded, saving their energy for who knew what was to come, but Ned had more to say, 'you know, she'll be back when the window is up, we must be ready.'

When they reached the Abbey, there were no cells to hold them, so they were imprisoned in the stables, under close guard by the Templars. The nuns came and cleaned their wounds, giving them a little bread and ale, then as night came Guy entered their prison, 'You have been tried and found guilty of the abduction of the woman and child, your sentence is death, you will hang tomorrow after

Matins. May God have mercy on your soul's,' then he looked at them and raised an eyebrow and winked, 'I suggest you prepare yourselves for then,' and with that, he left.

As long nights go, and for saying they faced execution in the morning, this one really dragged, all three of them sat in silence. Ned and Jack were thinking of their wives and children, trying hard to swallow the lumps in their throats, but not Ben, sure he was thinking about Tannis, he knew she was alive and that she'd got Tara and Will out, he was more worried what she was going to do next.

Morning came as it inevitably would, the condemned men were given their final meal, and as they heard the bells ring out for Matins, Guy marched into the stables he only had a short time, his men weren't far behind him. 'When they kick the blocks away, it will be difficult, but do not struggle, the ropes are set to choke you to death, not break your necks quickly.' He could say no more, the guards came in and dragged the prisoners out into the courtyard, leading them to their hastily prepared gallows on the Abbey wall, there the three of them looked down and contemplated a jump to freedom, but the fall would be too great, they would never survive it.

A crowd gathered, and the nuns prayed for their souls.

They all three scoured the onlookers for any sign of rescue but saw none, along the front of the small crowd stood a line of Templars, cloaked and hooded, their swords drawn and pointed at the ground. The prisoners then had the nooses placed around their necks, and without warning, the blocks that they stood on were kicked away. They tried their best not to struggle, but it wasn't an easy task when having the life throttled out of you.

From a short distance away, Guy took a circular metal disc from under his tunic; it was only the size of his palm. But when he squeezed it, seven razor sharp blades protruded from the sides, he took aim and threw it, discus-style, at the dangling ropes on the gallows. It sliced through everyone, allowing the three choking men to fall to their feet, as it returned to him, the blades retracted, and he caught it and watched what unfolded next.

Ben's feet hit the ground; he was almost doubled over, still choking. But as he and his companions looked up, three of the Templars threw off their cloaks and ran towards them, was he imagining it all, was Tannis one of them, and Major Charles with his

Sgt were heading for Jack and Ned. He didn't get the chance to put his thoughts into order, whoever it was almost rugby tackled him at waist height, and now they were falling backwards over the wall. He braced himself for the pain that must surely come next, but instead of the thud, there was a splash, they were underwater now, that brought him to his senses as the two of them kicked for the surface, through the blur of the salt water, he saw it was her. It was Tannis, she had a hold of the front of his shirt, pulling him to the surface, which they broke and gasped for air. As they trod water, she pulled a dagger from her belt and cut his hands free, he coughed a little, then took her face in his hands and kissed her. Two more splashes either side of them indicated Jack and Ned's safe return, and the final splash a few moments later showed Captain Johnson had also returned safely after retrieving the stolen timepieces.

A small boat picked them up and returned them to the jetty by The Eldridge. The three men thanked Charlie team for their help as they headed for the locker room, Ben gave his wife a wink and squeezed her hand gently as he went to change, a little further along Tannis stopped as she heard someone hurrying behind her, it was Jack, he pulled her to him and kissed her on the cheek, then turned and carried on his way. Tannis smiled to herself and whispered, 'You're welcome,' then went to change.

Half an hour later in the briefing room, Hennessey congratulated them all on a mission well done, although it seemed Ned was not flavour of the month with the Admiral as he tore a strip off him. Debrief over, they were dismissed for a week's leave, everyone but Ned and Tannis stood, she just sat glaring at her brother. Hennessey knew what was coming, Tannis had followed her orders, but now the mission was over, 'Alright, let's get it over with,' he sighed.

Ned got up and raced for the door, but Tannis just made a small leap and stood in front of him, then she blasted him and vanished too, no doubt following him somewhere they wouldn't be disturbed. Seconds later they both returned and, Tannis holding him up by the wrist dropped her bruised and battered brother to the floor, she was not entirely unscathed either, but nowhere near as bad as him. Ned sat up, and spat out a tooth, 'She still loves me,' he grinned, then passed out.

'Family issues resolved; I take it?' Hennessey folded his arms across his chest.

'Not quite,' Tannis moved to stand with her team and looked the Admiral directly in the eye, 'Now we bring Will home!'